THE
CONSEQUENCES
OF FINDING
DANIEL MORGAN

THE CONSEQUENCES OF FINDING DANIEL MORGAN

PETER J
ROBINSON

Matador
9 Priory Business Park,
Wistow Road, Kibworth Beauchamp,
Leicestershire. LE8 0RX
Tel: 0116 279 2299
Email: books@troubador.co.uk
Web: www.troubador.co.uk/matador
Twitter: @matadorbooks

ISBN 978 1838590 536

British Library Cataloguing in Publication Data.
A catalogue record for this book is available from the British Library.

Printed and bound in Great Britain by 4edge Limited
Typeset in 11pt Sabon MT by Troubador Publishing Ltd, Leicester, UK

Matador is an imprint of Troubador Publishing Ltd

For Susan

INTRODUCTION

LIKE PHIL ROYLE IN THE FOLLOWING PAGES, I TOO HAD A WORK colleague killed by a tiger, though, unlike Daniel Morgan, Dave was birdwatching in India. Nevertheless, Royle and Charlie Lacey, together with Daniel Morgan, Doug Whitland and all others featured in the following pages, are entirely figments of my imagination; no individual living or dead influenced the creation of my characters. Similarly, all commercial organisations and government departments are fictitious, though I admit to drawing substantially upon my sixteen years' experience heading up the Criminal Investigations Section of the Royal Society for the Protection of Birds.

I set out writing a story around a single individual, professionally involved in combating international wildlife crime. What emerged, however, was something at least as much to do with human relationships, with all the complexities they involve. Certainly, few working partnerships could be more difficult, or more volatile, than that involving Royle and his unexpected, and initially unwelcome, partner Charlie Lacey.

It may also be noted that events portrayed in my story have no fixed position in time (though Royle's use of satellite tracking technology suggests the story is recent). In no small part this is because the main storyline, wildlife smuggling, is itself timeless; the problem has been around since before any of us were born and seems likely to continue long after we are gone. However, whilst we will be replaced by even more humans, numerous birds and other animals that we and our families currently know and enjoy will not survive to anywhere near the end of the 21st century. Most authorities now rate the international illegal wildlife trade as second only to the drugs trade in global importance.

Scarily, the African elephant currently occurs in thirty-seven African states, yet the forecast for its total wild-extinction is set at around the year 2050, primarily due to the continued (mainly Asian) demand for ivory. Similarly, the Asian tiger population declined from 40,000 to 2,000 animals in just one hundred years, in no small part due to the oriental medicine trade, though the tiger's occasional addiction to eating local people does little for its image! Of more relevance to the following story, however, is the fact that around one-third of the world's 390 parrot species are officially classified as threatened with extinction.

Part of what follows occurs in Mexico and Australia. In the first of these countries, recent figures suggest that 80,000 parrots are annually trapped, as part of this illegal trade in the world's wildlife, from amongst that country's twenty-two species, six of which are officially endangered. And whilst everyone knows where Australia is, comparatively few of us have been there, though all who have will have been surprised to find fifty-plus parrot species living throughout one of the most beautiful and still least populated countries on Earth – one species of which is already extinct.

Some countries perhaps claim to have no illegal wildlife-trade problem, but such a suggestion flies in the face of reality. Personally, I doubt there is a country anywhere that can justify such a statement. Added to which, we live in a rapidly changing world, where uncontrolled technological advancement assists us all, including those involved in criminal activities. Ranked highly amongst the latter are people seeking to exploit the world's wildlife for their own personal gain, some of whom you are about to meet. And in true crime-thriller tradition, people get shot or otherwise die in unpleasant circumstances, plus you never really know who you can trust.

ONE

IT DID NOT TAKE A BUSH-HARDENED BIG-GAME HUNTER TO SEE THAT some large and seriously dangerous creature had killed and partially eaten whoever this was, lying there under the burning Florida sun. Royle could see how the animal had scraped grass and leaves over the gruesome remains, the scattered smaller messy bits suggesting foxes or vultures had also taken their share.

Clutching his rifle, he wiped his sweaty forehead with his free hand, taking a moment to consider their situation. Admittedly, there was little here he had not seen before, in one form or another, though his companion was clearly having trouble. Seeing her disappear behind a bush he moved across, finding her throwing up.

"Bit dangerous wandering away in here," he suggested. "You've seen what these creatures can do if they put their minds to it."

In truth, several things were rattling around inside his head right now, in addition to the obvious danger these animals posed. The two big questions, though, were the same ones destined to occupy both their minds over the coming weeks, in the process dragging the pair halfway around the world. What the hell reason could Dan have for being in a place like this? And perhaps more importantly, what was so secret about it that he had felt unable to tell anyone else in the Department?

TWO

Most other passengers were already comfortably settled as Royle made his way along the aircraft, checking the seat numbers as he went. Experience had taught him to view this boarding part of any flight as a defining moment, like that point in a bullfight where the matador is about to deliver the fatal sword thrust, what Spaniards call *la hora de la verdad*: the moment of truth. You never knew who you were being forced to spend the next ten or so hours of your life sitting next to, and he had suffered some particularly memorable experiences. Like the Catholic nurse returning to an African war zone, who spent the whole eight-hour flight counting her beads and praying not so quietly to herself. Or the overweight Russian woman who spent the night from Singapore to London occupying her own seat plus half of his. True, there had been some equally pleasing encounters, but inevitably it was the bad ones that left a lasting impression.

Reaching his row, Royle saw he was about to be accompanied back across the Atlantic by a young man in a 'Save-the-Forests' tee-shirt. He nodded towards the window seat, at the same time squeezing his bag into the overhead locker. He'd had a hard day, so with more than a slight feeling of relief he buckled up, switched off his mobile and carried out a quick search for any overnight additions – blanket, pillow, whatever.

He also realised how tired he now was, having caught an early flight out of Veracruz, over on Mexico's east coast,

2

to meet up with a valued and long-time informant here in Mexico City. He had tried snatching some sleep whilst waiting to board this onward flight, but inevitably found his efforts frustrated by the roving mariachi bands. What was it about Mexican Sunday evenings that always made them take on such a festive atmosphere? Already he felt the aircraft lumbering its way across the tarmac, pausing only briefly before thundering down the runway and climbing steeply into the evening sky, turning slowly east in the direction of its Texas fuel stop. Surprisingly quickly the drinks trolley appeared and Royle opted for a cold beer, already wondering what problems awaited him back at his London desk. He had enjoyed the conference, but now it was a case of getting back to reality, though not before he had caught up with some sleep.

He awoke with a start, finding the tree-saver tugging his sleeve and pointing to the flight attendant, who leaned across and quietly explained there was a call for him up at the front of the aircraft.

What now? he wondered, struggling to get his brain working. He followed the attendant along the aircraft, through business class to the forward galley where she indicated a phone on the wall.

Hesitantly he lifted the handset, anticipating the worst.

"How you doing, buddy?"

He recognised the gravel voice of Doug Whitland, Federal Wildlife's Florida Head of Enforcement.

"I'm great, Doug, or I was until you woke me. Some kind of problem?"

Whitland sounded uncharacteristically stressed. "Damn right, young fella. We may have a situation here; your old partner Dan Morgan's not reported in for days now."

Royle waited as Whitland paused.

"I gather you're on your way home to London via Amsterdam, with a fuel stop at Houston. What's the chance of you breaking your journey in Texas and getting yourself over here sometime tomorrow?"

Clearly Royle's doubts had been justified. "I could probably do that, Doug, subject to any re-ticketing complications. I'm travelling light so there'll be no hold luggage to offload at Houston. But I'll need some sleep somewhere along the way, and I'm also using my British passport, with no current American visa."

"Knew we could rely on you. You're already booked on a flight out of Houston; it leaves an hour after the one you're on lands. No economy seats so you're booked business class; you'll have to handle the additional comfort best you can. You still getting me, Phillip?"

"Loud and clear."

"Good. Gets in around five in the morning, but Miami's not short of hotels. And don't worry about that visa business, I'll sort that for you. Be talking at you later."

The connection went dead, Royle realising he was not now going home to London but instead was off to Florida. For who knew how long.

The stewardess turned as he replaced the phone. "Sounds like you won't be going all the way with us tonight, Mr Royle?"

"That would have been nice, Julie," he responded, noticing her name badge. "But more importantly, any chance of a large whisky whenever you're ready?"

Royle dutifully handed over his passport at the Houston arrivals hall. The border officer scanned it, studied his computer screen, gave Royle an exploratory glance and then pressed a button or two on his keyboard. Then, stapling something into the passport, the officer handed it back, telling him:

"Have a nice day, Agent Royle."

Checking the passport, he saw that his temporary American address was shown as the US Federal Wildlife

Service. Evidently Whitland was on the ball still and he was officially back with the Department. Albeit temporarily.

Landing at Miami International there was the usual on-board riot to gain access to overhead lockers. Recovering his bag, Royle slotted into the impatient queue leaving the aircraft to the chorus of mobiles being switched on. The upside being that his exit from the airport was quick and hassle-free, both because there were no passport checks off internal flights, and because he did not have to wait for any hold luggage to be offloaded.

Crossing the arrivals hall, he became aware of a public announcement: "Mr Phillip Royle, arriving from Houston, please go to the information desk."

Putting down his bag, he thought this unexpected development through, aware that probably only Whitland knew of his presence in Miami airport at that moment, or of his route there via Houston. Certainly nothing in their mid-flight conversation had suggested otherwise. Besides which, Whitland already had Royle's mobile number should he feel the need to speak. Either way, Royle felt uneasy about this development so, picking up his bag, he headed for the taxi stand, casting an eye over the many Latino porters before selecting one about his own height and build.

"What do they call you, *amigo*?"

"Diego, *senor*."

It occurred to Royle that Diego's features perhaps might not stand critical examination as a white European. Nevertheless, it was not the reaction of the official behind the desk that interested him – what he wanted was a look at whoever was waiting to see who responded to the message. He needed to see who they were, and ideally find out what their interest in him might be.

"Like to earn a quick twenty dollars?"

Diego seemed attracted to the idea.

Royle held up a $10 bill. "This is yours now. Do as I ask, and you'll get the other ten. *Comprende?*"

Diego nodded enthusiastically.

"Go to the information desk and tell them you're Phillip Royle, alright?"

More nodding, "*Si, senor.*"

"Then come back and tell me what they said."

Looking more than a little confused, but eager to take advantage of the unexpected offer, Diego took Royle's money and turned to do as requested.

"Wait," Royle called, pointing to some stairs to the upper level. "Give me time to get up those then go to the desk."

Still more nodding.

Royle crossed to the stairs, climbing only enough to get a clear view of the information desk, his attention already directed at whoever might be taking an interest in his voluntary stand-in. Sure enough, thirty feet away was a male figure in a Miami Dolphins jacket, holding a camera – the only person taking any apparent interest in what was going on at the desk.

Extracting his phone, Royle took five or six photographs of the man. Then as Diego turned away from the desk, the mystery photographer also turned, hiding his face from the porter but providing Royle with even better pictures.

Arriving back, all Diego could say was that an unknown man asked them to relay the message, "But did not stay to see if Mr Royle he come."

With so little to report Diego seemed concerned the cash might be withheld, but then, discovering he was wrong, he agreed to call Royle a cab.

"Intercontinental," Royle instructed the driver, opening a door and throwing in his bag.

"In Miami long?"

"Just overnight."

Detecting Royle's English accent, the driver offered him some advice. "Saw you getting friendly with the porter there. Need to watch those guys, you never know what they're up to. Just so you know."

"Yeah, thanks for that." What was it about cab drivers, he wondered, that made them feel so protective towards their passengers? However, at that same moment his mobile burst into life with a message from his new service provider.

'Welcome to America', it read.

Yep, he thought, *welcome to America*.

Royle used the same hotel whenever he was in Miami, with outstanding service and equally outstanding views out across Biscayne Bay. Things were naturally quiet at that time of the morning, so while he was checking in he asked the desk clerk to order him a rental car. "One with some guts in it," to be delivered around midday. He then headed for his room, which at his own request was on the tenth floor – less chance of disturbing traffic noise up there.

Five hours later, refreshed by sleep, a shower, and coffee and doughnuts, he pulled on a clean shirt and began to feel something like his normal self. Checking with the desk, he discovered that the rental car was waiting in the basement parking lot. Ten minutes later he had signed the hire papers and was driving up the ramp and out into the bright sunlight of a late-spring day in downtown Miami. Easing the Chevy into the midday traffic he headed west a couple of blocks, along palm-lined streets busy with shoppers, before turning north on Interstate 95 and then hanging a right at the turnpike, in the direction of Fort Lauderdale. Calling the switchboard he asked for Whitland's office. Paula Howath answered.

"I'm about forty minutes away. Oh, and I've got some photos that need printing urgently. Fix that and you get a bunch of flowers."

He heard laughter at the other end. "Won't be a problem, honey, you know how we American girls can't resist that English accent."

"And get the kettle on."

"Whatever you say, lover. By the way, how did you like travelling in the expensive seats?" But the phone went dead before he could respond.

Briefly exiting the freeway he pulled off into a garage forecourt and purchased a bunch of red roses. He already knew that in everyday terms true power in the Florida office was equally divided between Department Head Doug Whitland, and the secretary Paula Howath.

It felt good being back, plus Whitland seemed genuinely pleased to see him. Royle had never been sure of his former boss's age, but seeing him now, sitting behind his big desk beneath the twin flags of the United States and Florida, he surely could not be far off retirement. Without doubt the man's face showed more lines than he remembered, plus the grey hairs had now taken over completely. He was also carrying extra pounds and seemed more than a little short of breath, perhaps already looking forward to chasing a golf ball around as his daily source of excitement. But then Whitland's next words made him feel guilty for entertaining such thoughts.

"Have to say you look in pretty good shape, Phillip, considering what you've been through overnight. I'll arrange us something to drink."

He disappeared into Paula's adjoining office and Royle used the time to reacquaint himself with his surroundings, though nothing appeared to have changed much. Whitland's huge polished leather-topped desk still dominated the room, its sole adornments being the computer screen and keyboard, plus two green wire-mesh filing trays marked 'In' and 'Out'. In addition to Whitland's own leather-seated swivel chair, two identical versions faced the front of the desk, one of which Royle now occupied. And as it always had done, a large upholstered leather couch occupied one entire wall.

The pictures, too, greeted him like old friends, particularly the enlarged colour photograph of Whitland singlehandedly sailing his yacht into Miami's Bayfront Marina, whilst on the opposite wall hung one of Whitland and Royle with the marlin they had managed to get on board during a fishing trip down the Keys one summer.

Whitland reappeared clutching a pile of papers Paula had asked him to sign.

"You been buying my secretary flowers again? Won't get you anywhere; she's still married to that man of hers. How was the conference?"

"The conference was good, but never mind me, what's Dan Morgan been up to?"

Whitland appeared uneasy. "To be honest we're not sure what he's working on. Couple of months back he mentioned people smuggling parrots in from Australia, but I heard nothing more. Right at this moment I've no idea what he's doing. Or where he is."

"That bad?"

"That bad," repeated Whitland, rising to open the door for Paula.

She placed the tray on the corner of the desk.

"No biscuits, I'm afraid, the doctor's put Doug on a diet so we all suffer." Then she reached back onto the tray, handing Royle a brown envelope.

He extracted his pictures of the airport photographer, checking them briefly before passing them to his temporary boss.

"Any idea who that is?"

"None whatsoever, though I'm guessing it's important?" Whitland suggested, dropping his gaze to sign one of Paula's letters.

"We perhaps need to find out, then," Royle confirmed. "I'm assuming only you, Paula and various airline and immigration staff knew I was arriving at Miami this morning, yet that person placed a public announcement for me. If you hear of a baggage porter named Diego found dead at the airport, then let me know. They took *his* picture not mine."

Whitland took a long thoughtful sip from his mug.

"We seriously need to get our backsides into gear on this one, Phillip. Start searching for Dan as a matter of priority, without getting sidetracked."

But then he paused, Royle guessing his former boss was considering whether or not to mention something.

"There's already one possible line of enquiry; Paula thinks Dan may have been getting information from out near your place. I took the liberty of telling them you're back. We could drive out there tomorrow, while you collect some clothes and things?"

Royle nodded his approval, realising something needed clarifying. He pointed a finger at his own chest.

"Am I right in thinking I'm back on the payroll? As a badge-carrying member of the Department?"

"You damned better believe it. We're counting on your experience to both help track down Dan and get to grips with whatever he's working on."

Royle watched Whitland add his signature to another of Paula's letters, before looking back up at him.

"I'm allocating you a partner on this job," Whitland said, picking up the phone and dialling a number.

"Have you got a minute?" Royle heard him ask, before seconds later in walked a young woman he had met briefly over breakfast at last week's conference. Perhaps in her mid-thirties, Charlie Lacey had that imperceptible something, hinting at what, back in the UK, might be referred to as a 'respectable middle-class upbringing'. A conclusion doubtless supported by the

Cartier watch she wore, though with a noticeable lack of any accompanying jewellery – including the absence of any rings.

"You never made it back to London, then, Phillip?"

Royle smiled. "I got hijacked, Charlie."

"Charlie's been partnering Dan since she joined us a few months back," explained Whitland.

Largely for the benefit of his new partner, Royle outlined how they needed to establish whether the mystery airport photographer was related to Dan's disappearance and, if so, how? But then something else occurred to Royle, something that needed addressing as a matter of urgency. He turned to Whitland.

"You've paired Charlie and me, but is either one of us taking the lead role? Or do we play this by ear?"

* * *

Whitland leaned forward in his chair, elbows on the leather-covered desk, hands together, fingers interlocked. Experience already told him that Royle was not going to be overly impressed with the partnership arrangement, but he was prepared to stand his ground. He prided himself on knowing pretty much all that went on amongst his staff, admittedly with the benefit of whatever Paula could add. Consequently, he was aware of Charlie's ambitions within the Department. It therefore followed that she had a personal interest in any answer he gave to Royle's question. But he also knew that in terms of overall experience Royle was on a different planet to her, so as tactfully as he felt able, and looking particularly in Charlie's direction, Whitland addressed the pair.

"I already considered that. I would prefer you to work side by side," he explained from his seat under the twin flags of authority. "However, given Phillip's experience in what Dan seems to have been working on, if there is any disagreement then I suggest he gets the casting vote."

From the expression on the young woman's face Whitland got the clear impression that this arrangement might not run as smoothly as he hoped. However, he also prided himself on knowing the weaknesses of his agents, in which case Royle was not without his faults – he and Dan Morgan both. Nevertheless, he realised the futility of pursuing the discussion for the time being.

However, Whitland also knew Royle's own investigative style involved him sometimes withholding important information, at least until he decided there was a need to make it public. He had spoken to Royle about this whilst he still worked for the Department, though it seemed unlikely that several subsequent years of operating independently for various governments around the world would have made him any more forthcoming. Whitland knew, too, that Royle's personal style of criminal investigation relied substantially upon his individual, but nonetheless proven, ability – to the point where he often appeared reluctant to spend long hours, as Royle described it, 'wasting time searching departmental or national databases'. According to him, people-based enquiries called for a people-based approach. Similarly, Whitland had more than once spoken to Royle about his unhealthy tendency to get himself, and others, involved in dangerous situations without first ensuring adequate backup.

All things considered, then, Whitland realised he needed to watch this new pairing closely – particularly as it seemed likely Charlie might be the main casualty. Though, knowing what he did about her background, he had every confidence in her ability to look after herself. For the time being, though, he could do little more than be aware of the potential for disunity within this new pairing. He just needed to sit back now and see who emerged as the winner of this little battle.

Whitland was also intrigued that Charlie had not asked him how come he was employing the temporary services of some special agent from England, deciding she had probably meant to but had perhaps overlooked the point in the general discussion. In which case she was doubtless still keen to know the answer. Though, interestingly, it now seemed likely that the task of offering an explanation fell to Royle himself.

Having advanced the partnership issue as far as possible, Whitland commenced clearing his desk, starting by tossing an envelope in Royle's direction.

"That's everything Paula pulled off Dan's workspace she thought might be relevant. Have a go through it, Phillip. We three will meet here around eight-thirty in the morning, before heading on out for the day. Phillip will fill you in on that, Charlie."

Royle turned to Paula as he opened the envelope. "I need you to extend the car rental for me until there's a spare departmental vehicle, while I get across to the bank."

"Which reminds me," interrupted Whitland, "you should also speak with those bureaucrats upstairs about money, and a contract."

"Will do, but one more question."

"If you must," the older man muttered, beginning to move papers in the direction of his 'Out' tray.

"When did anyone last see Dan?"

"Don't think I saw him the whole week before I went off to Mexico," Charlie responded.

Whitland's brow was badly furrowed. "Could have seen him early that same week, but I can't swear to it."

"Then at the risk of asking the obvious, have we searched his apartment?"

"Got our security people to break in last Friday. There's a new lock; Paula has the key."

Paula, meanwhile, was in the process of clearing away the mugs and heading for her office, before pausing at the doorway. "I'd just like to say how nice it is having Phil back with us again. I'll be in my office if anyone needs me."

★ ★ ★

Their meeting now over, Royle too headed for Paula's office, leaving Whitland to continue purging his desk of paperwork. Charlie, though, exited directly into the main corridor, leaving little room for doubt she was unhappy with the new arrangement. Plus of course it meant Royle was unable to do as Whitland instructed and update her on arrangements for the following day. Focusing upon more immediate matters for the moment, he handed Paula the rental agreement.

She stood looking at him. "You don't look a day older, damn it. How is it men can do that, whilst we poor women don't just get older, we also look older?"

Royle grinned. "I've heard that suggested, but I don't buy it. Or certainly not in your case – you're still just as stunning. Anyway, there are two attractive ladies in the office now, though I already appear to be out of favour with one of them."

The 'power behind the throne' placed a hand lightly on his arm. "Give her time. She's a great girl but she's ambitious. She also has this idea of higher enforcement standards here in America than in Europe. And as you're always telling me, understanding the problem is half the solution."

"In a short while I'll be out of here again, so it's in Charlie's interests to stick with it and hope any credit lands in her direction. Though I suspect she's not seeing it that way. What I'm not sure of, though, is does she know what to pack for tomorrow? Could be a long day."

Paula dialled a number on her desk phone before passing him the receiver.

"Special Agent Lacey."

"Charlie, it's Phillip. Regarding tomorrow, I suggest bringing something for overnight, just in case. See you in the morning." He replaced the handset, his expression somewhere between a smile and a grimace.

"She's upset, Phil. She'll come around."

He shrugged his shoulders. "What's the situation with Dan's wife, Sharon. She presumably knows he's missing?"

"Dan and Sharon separated months back; there's another man in her life now. Doug explained how Dan seems to have gone off the reservation, that we're trying to find out where he is and what he's up to. As for Charlie, give her time to see things Doug's way. She really doesn't have any choice."

"One more thing, then I really must get to the bank. Has Dan got a new woman?"

"What on earth made you think of that one?"

"Easy. Here we are trying to trace Dan's movements and all we're coming up with is what we *don't* know. If he *has* hooked up with someone new, then she could have some answers."

Paula made her way back around to her chair. "Nothing I've heard suggests Dan's involved with another woman. And if you believe what Sharon says about his mental condition then no woman would probably want him."

Royle looked puzzled.

"Talk to Sharon. He's not the Dan you remember."

THREE

Whitland was surprised to find Royle already in the building when he arrived next morning. Agreeing it looked like being a long day they decided to go with Royle's suggestion and take the rental Chevy, for no other reason than that it kept the mileage down on Department vehicles.

Royle raised the matter of Dan's now estranged wife, Sharon.

"I told her Dan's gone missing. Not that she seemed too concerned," Whitland responded.

Royle was about to mention his new partner when Whitland raised the subject himself.

"Charlie somehow gained the idea that enforcement standards are higher in America than in Europe. Hopefully you're going to enlighten her on that one."

Then he hesitated, obviously choosing his words carefully. "She's a likeable and intelligent young woman, Master's in Behavioural Psychology, but as a criminal investigator she's still a beginner. If necessary, she'll have to find out the hard way just how inexperienced she is."

Royle was surprised to hear Whitland had so much to say about a fellow staff member, deciding it must be down to the pressure the older man was under. Whatever the reason, the day ahead beckoned and the pair of them made their way down to the basement car park, collecting Charlie on the way.

Royle headed west out of Fort Lauderdale on Interstate 75, then north up Route 27 towards the west end of Lake Okeechobee, roughly two hours away. Traffic was light, the sun was bright, and the local radio station was predicting high temperatures.

As Royle had anticipated, the morning's drive was a rather tense affair, both men making a conscious effort to keep any conversation on neutral ground. He realised Charlie must be wondering what his previous connection with the Department might be, but given her unfavourable reaction to their enforced partnership he was unsure how to approach the subject.

★ ★ ★

Charlie also decided to play the whole thing down, realising that at some point soon all would hopefully be revealed. She had been through a tough few days. As at all such conferences she had experienced late nights and early lecture sessions, plus she had slept badly last night. For some inexplicable reason she could not get the events of the past few days out of her mind, plus she felt offended by Royle's unexplained appearance on the scene. Neither could she help noticing how relaxed he and Whitland appeared with each other.

She had met Royle by chance over breakfast the morning following his conference talk. He had introduced himself and asked the usual questions regarding where she was from and what her interests were. He had also explained how he worked mainly on freelance government contracts in matters of wildlife law enforcement.

"You must travel a lot, then?" she had suggested.

He had nodded in response. "Guess I do."

"And you work for yourself?"

"For whoever asks me, but mostly that's governments."

She had found Royle's conference paper particularly interesting. Briefly he had outlined the difficulties posed for international wildlife enforcement by so-called 'lookalike species' – relatively common birds and other animals that nevertheless resemble endangered ones. Persuasively he had argued against imposing an endangered status upon these lookalikes solely to prevent their use to cover illegal imports of rarer kinds, instead suggesting the employment of customs officers skilled in species identification.

"The UK's Environment Minister seemed quite upset by your talk," she had suggested, recalling how he had shrugged his shoulders dismissively.

"You don't get any prizes for upsetting Giles Bamfield. We've known each other for years; he always was an idiot."

"We could tell you're not on his Christmas list."

She remembered how carefully he had considered his response. "I naturally get suspicious when politicians urge me not to worry over their proposals to allow trade in wildlife they previously said was threatened by that same trade."

"Was that what Bamfield was getting his knickers in a twist over?"

Royle had leaned across, refilling both their coffee cups. "The UK government proposes removing endangered status from a small bird confined to an equally small Caribbean island. A UK protectorate." He had paused, apparently ensuring he had her attention. "The bird's entire world population amounts to a couple of hundred individuals, all on that one island. What do you think the UK government's up to?"

"You tell me."

"A big multinational company discovered important mineral deposits on the island. It wants to mine them, and the UK government's worried about possible objections over any threat to the bird, so they're proposing to downgrade its protection status."

"I guess that's governments for you," Charlie had joked, immediately realising he was not in the least amused.

"What if I tell you Bamfield's father is company chairman?"

"Obviously, that's very worrying," she had responded, deciding on a change of subject. "But I'm more interested in how you Brits don't go much on the use of guns in law enforcement." She had expected him to become defensive, but his mood seemed unchanged.

"I'm not suggesting firearms play no part in enforcement. Just that in Britain we keep them in the background. Not out there in your face, as seems the American way." But then he appeared to think for a moment before asking, "What is it you do, Charlie?"

She had laughed as she explained she worked for the government. "I'm one of those 'Rambo' American enforcement officers you told the audience worry you so much."

She sat quietly now, watching the scenery flash past as Royle pushed the Chevy along at a good speed, leaning forward occasionally and working his way through the radio channels.

"Anything interesting amongst Dan's things Paula collected?"

He reached forward again, turning down the radio. "Nothing suggestive of what he might be investigating. I also went through his filing cabinet and his phone messages."

She glanced across at him.

"What puzzles me is the absence of his diary and laptop, plus there's no notebook."

"You went through all that this morning?"

"Last night and this morning. I slept on Doug's office couch – can't afford to waste time on this one."

She glanced across at her new partner again, uncertain which made the greater impression. That he had stayed in the office overnight to check on Dan's recent movements? Or that he had omitted to mention it to either her or Whitland?

"Who's this Deming Akroyd over in Los Angeles? He left messages asking Dan to ring him?" Royle asked.

Charlie confirmed the name meant nothing to her.

"Then maybe we already have a few things to follow up back in the office."

"Such as?"

"Might be useful you calling Akroyd, seeing who he is and what he wants with Dan. We also need to speak with Sharon Morgan and get a look inside Dan's new apartment. Oh, and I got Paula to start someone tracing Dan's phone."

Ten minutes further on he made a call on his plug-in mobile, which was in speaker mode. "Mac, Phillip Royle. Been a long time, mate. Got something going on you may be able to help with."

"How are you, mate?" the speaker responded. "Paula mentioned you were back. What's yer problem?"

"I've got photos of a guy taking pictures of me off an early flight. Could be he's in your records somewhere?"

"I'll give it a shot, Phillip. Drop 'em over."

"It's pretty urgent; Dan Morgan seems to have gone missing. I'll get Paula to email them."

"Leave it with me, I'll get it sorted."

"One of your old contacts?" Charlie wondered as he disconnected the call.

"That was Lieutenant Steve McGill, Miami Homicide. He's Paula's brother-in-law."

★ ★ ★

Somewhere around mid-morning Charlie realised they had left the wetlands behind and were now driving through open grassland, with herds of cattle spaced out across obvious ranching country. At an intersection in the road stood a sign pointing to 'Aguila Rancho' and Royle headed the Chevy in that direction. Cattle quickly became even more evident, and from the amount of dust and the number of riders involved Charlie guessed some cattle-related activity was in progress.

She heard Whitland ask Royle, "Good to be back?" to which he responded in the affirmative.

At a bend where the dirt road passed through some tall scrub, Royle braked hard to avoid contact with a stationary horse and rider, the latter casually rolling a cigarette with one hand, gripping the reins with the other. Royle leaned out of the driver's window and called to the man, who seemed advanced in years for something as energetic as chasing cattle. He was also Native American, which in Florida had to mean Seminole.

"Still at it, then, Billy?"

The rider looked down over his shoulder. "Phil Royle, heard you might be around. Good to see you, man."

Royle indicated the distant riders. "What's going on?"

"Just branding a few calves."

"She with you?"

Billy inclined his head towards the distant dust cloud, obviously aware who 'she' was. "Middle of that lot, somewhere."

Charlie watched Royle open the door and walk over to the man sitting on his sweaty cow pony, seeing the rider lean down to grasp Royle's hand. Not some brief formal handshake, but one that spoke of a long and close relationship. She also realised that, like Paula Howath, Billy called him Phil.

"Fancy a comfortable lift back to the yard in a car?" Royle queried, sticking his head back in the window to check if Whitland objected to taking on board a dusty cowhand.

Charlie watched Royle slide his left foot into the stirrup and swing himself aboard, the lively animal spinning itself in a full circle before taking off at a gallop.

"Good to see he's not lost it," Whitland said, addressing the replacement driver. "Charlie here's one of our agents, Billy."

The aging cowboy extended a dusty hand. "Good to meet you, Charlie."

Billy eased the now dusty Chevy in between several even dustier pickups parked out front of a sprawling house at the far end of the stable yard. The screen door opened as they emerged from the vehicle, a second elderly Native American descending the steps to greet them. Unlike Billy, though, this man was dressed in shorts and a clean white shirt.

Whitland and the man exchanged a brief hug. "Good to see you, Wesley. I don't believe you've met Charlie."

She held out her hand. "You must be the boss man."

He laughed. "Supposed to be, though I sometimes wonder. Wesley Cyprus; good to meet you."

They were about to climb the steps up to the porch when they heard laughter and the clatter of horses' hooves. Turning, Charlie watched Royle enter the yard on Billy's mount, a riderless pony trotting behind on a short line. Up behind Royle she could just make out another person: a young woman, her arms around his waist.

The girl slipped to the ground as the horses came to rest, her covering of dust making clear she had been involved in activities out on the plain. Mid- to late-teens, medium height, skin a soft warm brown, with raven-black hair tied loosely in bunches. It was obvious she too had Seminole blood coursing through her veins. Charlie watched the girl throw her arms around Royle's neck as he too dismounted, before running to Whitland and greeting him excitedly. Catching up with her, Royle took the girl's hand.

"Charlie, this is my daughter, Sam. And this," he said, indicating Wesley, "is my father-in-law."

At this point Mama Cypress also appeared, inviting them all into her enormous kitchen, its surfaces laden with plates and bowls. Royle gave his mother-in-law a long squeeze, and in no time everyone, including Billy and several other cowhands, were seated around the table and the sound of conversation filled the air.

Charlie watched Royle deliberately seat himself between Whitland and Wesley, whom he said he had not seen for months.

"How's my little girl, then?" she heard him ask Wesley.

"You already know your daughter's a joy to have around, but what's the story with Dan?"

"We know next to nothing," Whitland admitted, picking up on the question. "We think he could be investigating illegal wildlife imports, perhaps getting information from out this way. Ring any bells?"

"Can't say it does. Billy there's the one knows all the local gossip."

Meanwhile, back across the table, Charlie had seated herself next to Sam.

"What are you hoping to do when you leave college?"

"I'd like to work with the environment, hopefully after getting through university." But then she surprised Charlie. "How long have you worked with my dad?"

"We only met properly yesterday, though we should get along fine with practice." But then it was Charlie's turn to raise a question. "Isn't your mother joining us?"

The girl hesitated. "Dad didn't tell you? She died when I was born; my grandparents brought me up. He doesn't talk about it, but I know he still misses her."

It crossed Charlie's mind that the girl's father did not seem particularly good at communicating important details. "He seems to know a lot of people," she suggested, "and I don't just mean in America, so does he travel much?"

23

"He spends lots of time in Asia and in Africa, plus he has a house near London and an apartment in Australia. He has a sister out there."

★ ★ ★

Back across the table Royle turned to Whitland. "I suspect it'll take us time establishing what Dan was doing out here. What do you think to us stopping over and getting back in the office tomorrow?"

"Not a problem for me, though I'll need to ring Paula first. Plus, you'll need to check with Charlie, assuming she's speaking to you."

Royle frowned. "Been thinking about that. It's time she and I straightened out a few things, once we get back to the office."

Later, then, lunch over and having checked with Charlie and Mama Cyprus about an overnight stay, Royle grabbed two cold beers and steered Billy toward the quiet of the stables, leaving the rest of the hands to mount up and head back on out to catch up with the cattle.

He handed Billy a beer. "I need to know what Dan was doing out here."

Twenty minutes later Royle tracked his partner down to the rear decking, in deep discussion with his daughter. Lightly grasping her arm, he waited for Charlie to acknowledge him.

"Just to prove how little we know about each other, do you ride?"

She seemed surprised he felt the need to ask. "Come on, Phillip, this is America and we are in Florida, of course I can ride."

"Then I suggest you get changed. The three of us are going with Billy; he's saddling up some horses as we speak."

"Do I get to know where we're going?"

"To see an old Seminole who Billy thinks Dan visited."

The four of them rode for about an hour, eventually swapping the grasslands for flooded woodland, the horses now splashing through shallow water much of the time. Royle explained they were going to see an old American Indian still living the traditional life out there in the swamplands, surviving mostly by catching fish and trapping and shooting birds and other animals. Assuming of course he was at home and not off hunting somewhere.

Billy mostly led the way, with Royle taking over occasionally. Mostly they headed east, presumably back in the direction of Lake Okeechobee, the water often up around the horses' bellies now.

★ ★ ★

Whilst they were mounting up back in the yard Charlie had noted that Royle was now wearing a hat; the kind of hat that around those parts made him disappear into the crowd. His daughter too had changed, swapping her dust-covered denim jacket for a colourful Seminole top. Ten minutes into their ride she also noticed Royle had a rifle tucked down in front of his saddle.

"I thought you Brits didn't carry firearms?"

He turned in his saddle. "Different situation out here; you never know when it might come in useful."

As a federal firearms officer Charlie had the weapon down as a lever-action Winchester. Not at all the kind of weapon she expected to see in the hands of some Englishman. She recalled, too, the ease with which he had earlier taken over Billy's spritely cow pony and could not help noticing how at home he seemed on a horse out here. Right at that moment no one could possibly take him for anything other than a working cowhand. He even had on a pair of light leather gloves to shield his hands from the constant friction of the reins; gloves that had obviously already spent many hours in the saddle.

Nor could she help noticing how easily he appeared to switch between American English and his own native version – to the extent that he often seemed unsure which was appropriate: was it parking lot or car park, rental or hire car, restroom or toilet?

Lost in such thoughts, she was only half aware of a deer getting up off to their left, and by the time she did see it the animal was up to speed and almost into cover. She jumped at the explosion of a weapon close behind her, watching the animal somersault into a motionless heap. Turning in her saddle she saw Royle lever a fresh shell into the Winchester, before applying the safety catch and returning it to its holster. Without a word Billy manoeuvred his horse to where the deer lay, dismounting and securing it up behind his saddle. Charlie realised Royle had killed the deer at full speed with a single shot from the Winchester and, equally interesting, neither Billy nor Sam appeared to treat it as unusual.

★ ★ ★

They eventually began seeing signs of human activity. Not 'civilised' activity, just the odd stump or two where trees had been cut down. Royle drew their attention to faint trails through the wet sawgrass, made either by man or alligator, and once they came across an American Indian burial site on a slight mound.

Emerging eventually from some tall reeds, they found themselves confronted by a rough log cabin resting on low support poles on a small island. Immediately, the source of the wood smoke they had been detecting became clear; a single metal pipe emerged from the cabin's roof, the smoke suggesting someone was at home.

As the four of them sat taking in the scene, the horses impatiently tossing their heads, a male figure in Seminole dress emerged from the low doorway. He descended to the ground and exchanged words with Billy across the dividing water.

"Billy's saying we've come to see if there's anything we can help with," Royle explained to Charlie.

The man had been followed out by what they assumed was his wife. More conversation followed and it was obvious from the beckoning signs that they were welcome. The horses emerged from the water, up past a dugout canoe carved from a single cypress tree, before coming to a halt again.

"What's going on now?" Charlie asked.

"Billy's going through the customary greeting; this guy speaks a little English, but not her."

The cabin's owner shook hands all round and Billy handed over the deer. Sam made to disappear inside and help, but Royle grabbed her, giving her a tin of coffee and two tins of peaches from his saddlebag.

"Some things I pinched from the kitchen," he explained.

The formalities over, Charlie and Royle spread themselves over a couple of rustic benches, leaving Billy to get on with the business side of things. He and the other American Indian talked at some length, though even from a distance it was obvious the old hunter was having trouble remembering answers to the questions he was being asked. But they seemed to be making progress, and at one stage Billy showed the old Seminole a piece of paper – Dan's photograph. The man disappeared into the cabin, before reappearing, shaking his head.

Royle, meanwhile, had been noting various traps hanging from the cabin's outer walls, most designed for catching four-legged animals, though a few seemed more suited to taking birds. Indeed, piles of feathers at the water's edge testified to the frequent plucking of ducks, whereas a heap of dried white bones clearly had an alligator origin.

Billy eventually broke away from the conversation and turned to the two government agents.

"Right, Dan was here, couple of weeks ago or more – this feller has no idea of dates. Dan was asking if anyone had been offering money for live birds. Apparently, a man did come, three or four 'moons' ago, wanting eggs for hatching. Our man remembers eagle, and the 'hawk that eats snails'."

Royle was nodding his head. "The hawk will be snail kite, and the eagle must be bald eagle. Is that it?"

"Not entirely. He says the man gave him a paper; turns out he means a business card. Thinks he gave it to Dan."

"Was the man coming back?"

"Seems not. He was offering money, so not much use to this fella. Plus, he didn't want people wandering around in his hunting area."

Royle considered this for a few moments before indicating the sky. "We can do little more here and it's already getting dark. I suggest we head back and talk things through over supper."

Somewhere on their return journey the four of them stopped to water the horses, Charlie easing her mount in beside Royle's in the moonlight, both leaning back in their saddles as the horses stretched their necks to drink. He momentarily struggled with his animal, easing the reins as it shook its head, already keen to be moving again. A horned owl advertised his threatening presence from the nearby trees, whilst somewhere way out on the prairie a lone coyote howled at the moon.

Feeling a slight breeze, Royle pulled his collar up around his neck. "You ride like someone used to being in the saddle," he observed quietly.

"Strangely enough I was thinking pretty much the same about you," Charlie responded, her slight smile escaping his attention in the darkness.

FOUR

A COUPLE OF HOURS AFTER THEY ALL SAT DOWN TO SUPPER ROYLE watched Whitland push back his chair and yawn before announcing he was off to bed. Whereupon Sam suggested it was her bedtime too. Only then did he realise that Wesley and Mama Cypress had already disappeared and that for the first time since last week's conference he was alone with Charlie. Seizing the opportunity, he too left the table, crossing to a cabinet and removing two glasses before extracting a bottle of wine from the refrigerator.

Addressing his partner, he pointed out through the doorway towards the darkness and the rear decking. "This seems like an opportunity for a glass of wine. Maybe clear the air a little?"

He headed for the door, relieved to hear Charlie's chair being pushed back as she followed. Reaching the decking he offered her a seat, positioning himself opposite. He held up the bottle in the moonlight.

"White okay, or should I find a red?"

"White's good for me and you'd better make it a large one."

He did as she instructed, making them both large ones.

Charlie took an exploratory sip, gently swirling the glass in her hand. "Seems I underestimated you. This is really quite good."

"You interested in wines?"

"I'm no expert but I think I know a good wine when I taste it."

He reached out in the darkness, turning the bottle's label towards him. "We could argue about what makes a good wine, but what does this one say?"

"I thought perhaps it was a Sauvignon Blanc, but it's actually a rather light Chardonnay. Very pleasant and, knowing you, I'm guessing it's French."

He smiled to himself. "Do you?"

"Do I what?"

"Know me? You said, 'knowing you'." He watched her hesitate.

"I obviously don't. Is that what we're doing out here, then, under the stars?"

Ignoring her question, he pointed to the bottle. "It's Australian. Anyway, what did you make of today?"

He realised she must still be feeling annoyed. Not only did she seem to be questioning Whitland pairing them together, she now knew he had neglected to tell her about his connections with the ranch, and the existence of his daughter.

"To be honest I'm still considering it," she admitted, sipping her wine before placing the glass gently back down on the table. "And still being honest I admit I needed to make some adjustments. The big surprise, though, was Sam. By what strange circumstances does someone living on the other side of the Atlantic come to have such a charming daughter? And a Seminole daughter at that."

"It's a long story."

She made an exaggerated show of glancing all around them in the darkness. "Seems to me we've plenty of time. Everyone else has gone to bed so why don't we start from the beginning?"

He commenced by topping up their glasses. "Well, for starters I'm not entirely English; my mother was from California. I met Sam's mother while I was still in the British

Army. She was Seminole and, as you have already demonstrated, most Americans think I'm a full-blooded Brit."

"What happened?"

"Sukie was a lawyer working in Native American affairs. Surprisingly, her parents, Wesley and his wife, were extremely supportive. The answer to our problem proved easier than we imagined; I simply transferred to the US Marine Corps. Sukie gave birth to Sam while I was away… You know the rest."

"That was a long time ago, so do you still miss her?"

He stared into his glass, taking time responding. "Don't we all miss someone special?"

"So where does your previous connection with the Department come in?"

"I was looking for a job when the Marines and I parted company, and Whitland took a chance on me."

"I noticed you two get along well together, almost a father and son relationship."

Although this sounded like a statement, he assumed it to be a question. Either way he decided not to get involved, if only because the thought had never occurred to him until she just mentioned it.

"Where did this interest in wildlife come from?"

Again, he needed a moment to consider. "It always seems to have been that way, though I have to work at it. Conferences, museums, that kind of stuff. Anyway, enough about me, what dark secrets are you hiding from the world, Agent Lacey?"

She took a lingering sip from her glass and again he leaned across to refill it.

"Mine's definitely not a long story. I was born in Tallahassee and got a Master's in Psychology at Florida State. I joined the Department three years back, working in Licensing, before switching to Enforcement when I transferred down here six months ago."

"Psychology's a big subject, so did you specialise?"

"My thesis was on Sexual Tension in the Working Environment."

Great, thought Royle, *just what I need. A bloody psychologist.* Was she going to be quietly analysing his actions throughout this enquiry? Or was she perhaps already doing so? And what was this Sexual Tension bit?

"What about your parents?" he enquired, getting the clear impression she hesitated before answering.

"Both still up in Tallahassee. We talk on the phone a lot."

"So, what kind of thing presses your button?"

"Can't say I have any specific interests. I like reading and music, I have a wide taste in music, and I appreciate nice clothes. You'll probably laugh but I'm also interested in firearms. You're not bad with a gun yourself, by the way."

He guessed she was referring to the afternoon's deer incident. "I've been around firearms a while. Deer or sniper, neither gives you much time to get your shot off. What about boyfriends?"

"I've had my moments but there's no one obvious at present."

Royle nodded his acknowledgement, though this time it was him doing the hesitating. "There's something else you should know. I'm joint owner of this outfit, together with Wesley." He thought he caught the flicker of an eyelid in response.

★ ★ ★

The truth was, Charlie had trouble concealing her surprise at Royle's latest revelation. It had taken her a full day to find out he had previously worked in the Department alongside Dan Morgan, was half American, and eighteen years ago had married a Native American girl, with whom he had a daughter.

And now he casually lets slip he owns the land they had been riding around on all afternoon. Admittedly, Whitland had warned her that Royle's methods were sometimes unorthodox, but from what she had seen so far that did not begin to cover it.

She took a long sip from her glass, idly fiddling with it, her eyes briefly meeting his. True, she had been upset at Whitland's decision they should work together. With Dan missing she was surely the obvious choice to take charge of the section, though she knew nothing then of Royle's previous time with the Department. She had also noticed how Whitland appeared to leave much of the decision-making to her new partner.

On the other hand, he was beginning to grow on her. There was something about his calm, objective approach to life that she found both reassuring and perhaps strangely alluring. She was also aware how much she had enjoyed their ride back across the ranch in the dark this evening, recalling the unexpected feeling earlier, here on the decking, as he held her arm waiting for her to finish her conversation with Sam.

"I should probably have guessed that," she finally admitted in response to his latest revelation. "Though I'm still confused over which name you answer to. You say it's Phillip, but Paula and Billy both call you Phil?"

"Only special people call me Phil."

It occurred to her to ask precisely who qualified as 'special' but then she changed her mind, on the grounds that it could get complicated. "You've not said how you came to be working for yourself and travelling all over?"

"That just kind of happened. I'm not sure what Whitland thought, though he can't be too concerned if he keeps asking me back."

Leaning across again to refill her glass, Royle found himself surprisingly disturbed by the scent of her hair in the warm night air.

"I should have explained to you about Sam and my life out here, plus my time with the Department. You probably wish I'd stayed on the plane back to London."

She too leaned forward. "Only when you make me mad."

He pretended to consider for a moment. "Do I do that?"

"Not so much since lunchtime."

★ ★ ★

Royle and his daughter were out early for a ride next morning, and by the time they entered the kitchen for breakfast Charlie, Whitland and Wesley were already seated at the table, immersed in the aroma of bacon and eggs.

Royle was surprised to see his partner in a dress rather than yesterday's shirt and jeans. *Bet she has a job hiding her gun in that outfit*, he thought. "Any idea what time we're leaving?"

"As soon as we've had breakfast and got our things together," responded Whitland.

Consequently, somewhere around nine o'clock, they were all three down by the Chevy. Royle sprung the boot so they could load their bags, including a gun case he had produced from inside the house.

"Still packing the hardware, Phil?" Charlie joked.

He rested the case on the steps before opening it and removing two long-barrelled weapons: a fancy-looking Beretta over-and-under shotgun and yesterday's lever-action Winchester.

He handed her the shotgun. "What does that do for you?"

She checked it wasn't loaded before pressing it against her cheek and taking aim along the upper barrel.

"Okay, we can see you like it," he said, reaching out and recovering the weapon.

"We must give that a try sometime, if you're up for it?" she suggested, sounding as if she really meant it.

Meanwhile, though, on the other side of the Chevy, Sam Royle was in the process of giving Whitland a goodbye squeeze.

"Did she just call him Phil?" the girl asked, wide-eyed.

Clearly the point had not escaped Whitland's attention either. "She most certainly did, my beautiful."

Their agreed aim was to be back in the office by lunchtime and, as before, Royle drove, immediately calling Paula.

"What's on your mind, Phil?"

"Be a good girl and email Mac a couple of my pictures of that mystery airport photographer. And did they get anywhere with the phone tracking?"

"I'll send the pictures, and they're still trying to find Dan's phone," the secretary confirmed. "See you all shortly."

That little matter dealt with, Royle settled back with his thoughts. Glancing in the mirror he could easily have formed the impression Whitland was asleep, but he knew impressions could be misleading. Whitland had been around the enforcement side of the Department a long time, and in Royle's experience there was little his former boss did not know about what went on there. Even if, to those not knowing him, he sometime gave the impression of being unaware of what was occurring around him. Too willing perhaps to let others take on work he should be doing. Or make decisions he should be making. But Royle knew that would be misleading. What could sometimes look like indifference was actually the old department head's well-proven method of encouraging responsibility in those who worked beneath him.

Such an example was Royle himself, who after leaving the Marines had entertained thoughts of joining a police special weapons team. However, he was eternally grateful to Whitland for recognising his potential and offering him a place in the Department. Only later did he discover that it had then been Department policy to appoint from an academic background, and Whitland had been seriously criticised for not following procedure.

★ ★ ★

The Florida Federal Department Head was feeling good after all the uncertainties of the past week or so, despite the fact he still could not account for one of his agents. He had, though, obtained the services of a proven temporary replacement, with the singular objective of finding Morgan. Added to which, a potentially serious staffing incompatibility issue appeared to have been resolved, judging from what he had overheard last night on the decking below his bedroom window. True, he still needed to keep an eye on the situation, though hopefully Royle and Lacey were both professional enough to not let any disagreement interfere with their search for his missing agent.

In fact, he could not help but be struck already by the obvious strength of the relationship developing between the pair, though he was less clear on whether they themselves realised it. It was also apparent that any fears he'd entertained about Charlie being overshadowed by the strength of Royle's personality were unfounded. On the minus side it was true he had a little, well, actually a rather large, health issue hanging over him, but that was his business and right now life was looking up. In which case, he settled back in his seat, making a mental note to get the pair together in his office in a day or two to find out how they were doing in their search for his missing agent.

★ ★ ★

"There's a place just up the road if anyone fancies a coffee," Royle volunteered. "Bit rough, but I'm up for it and I'm sure Doug is, even if he has been doing some snoring in the back."

Sure enough, three miles farther on a sign 'Bar' pointed to a roadside gap in the trees. The building was single-storey timber with more than its share of advertising signs. Of particular interest was the large flashing, red-and-white sign above the barroom door announcing, 'Weddings Arranged While You Wait – Bring Your Own Gal', followed a close second by a multicoloured handwritten board promising a 'Hog Roast Bar-BQ' for the coming weekend, whilst amongst the proliferation of smaller signs was one proclaiming this the headquarters of the local gun and hunting club.

Equally interesting was the array of mud-splattered four-by-fours parked out front, most containing pairs of hunting dogs, some of which in Royle's view qualified more as dangerous wild animals.

It was obvious Royle's earlier observation about this place being a 'bit rough' was not without merit. It always reminded him of an Australian roadhouse he knew for which the guidebooks warned: 'Do not go inside unless you're an experienced barroom brawler.' Ideally, he needed a *quiet* coffee, but as neither of the other two shared his view he too headed for the door, though not before going to the rear of his vehicle and rummaging around in the trunk.

Inside, the place pretty much lived up to expectation. Decorating the walls were numerous mounted animal heads; mostly deer but also a couple of mountain lions. Most customers were engrossed in noisy conversations and few heads turned as they entered. Whitland went to order the coffees, leaving Royle to rearrange a table and chairs in a quiet corner while Charlie headed for the restroom. He could see Whitland up at the bar waiting to be served so, already feeling the lack of air conditioning, he removed his jacket before checking his phone messages.

Meanwhile, close by where Royle sat, a dispute arose over the time the pool table had been occupied, involving two Seminole youths and what could justifiably be described as a couple of young 'rednecks'. Quickly the matter came to a head, a punch was thrown and one of the Seminoles went skidding towards the restroom door, just as Charlie emerged. Realising what was happening she forced herself between the remaining upright American Indian and the other two, advising that they back off, whereupon one of the rednecks produced a hunting knife, waving it in her face.

Normally Charlie wore her handgun at her waist, and Royle watched her instinctively reach for the weapon. But as he had already observed, the dress was not designed with that purpose in mind; the gun was in her bag on the table in front of him. Seeing her apparently reaching for a gun, the owner of the knife became more agitated, pressing the blade against the side of her neck, though even as the cold metal touched her skin her partner was rising from his chair.

The first the young man could have known about Royle's presence was the noisy end of a firearm pressing against the back of his skull.

"It's just a suggestion, sunshine," Royle whispered in the man's ear, "but you might want to take that knife away from my partner's throat and drop it on the floor." Then, detecting no response, he tapped the Browning's muzzle against the man's head a couple of times. "Now."

The whole room heard something heavy hit the floor, Royle moving around to the man's front and kicking the knife towards the advancing Whitland.

"Our boss here is about to show you his badge, after which I suggest you and your young friend go somewhere else and learn to play nicely."

Royle noted his partner heading for the table. But then, catching sight of the barman, he went across and apologised for what had occurred, suggesting the man rustle up three coffees as a matter of urgency. He also ordered an immediate large whisky, leaving Whitland to bring the hot drinks whilst he took the glass back to the table.

"I know exactly what you're thinking so don't go there," he advised, handing her the glass.

She was clearly unhappy. "You realise I was about to take the little shit?"

"I have to say it didn't seem that way."

"I would have had him if you hadn't butted in," she repeated, making clear she was annoyed.

Royle guessed there might be more to this than the obvious. Two days back she had been questioning the need for his involvement, and here she now was having to acknowledge he perhaps had a role to play. He could see how that might annoy her.

"Like I said, let it go; it happened and it's over. The important thing is we learn from it."

"Couldn't put it better myself," contributed Whitland, finally arriving with the coffees.

Royle watched the colour return to Charlie's cheeks as she first emptied the glass and then reached for the coffee, nevertheless clearly unhappy.

"You have to admit it shouldn't have happened," she muttered.

"You're both missing the point," interrupted Whitland. He aimed a stubby finger at Charlie. "You got into a bit of trouble," the finger now pointed in Royle's direction, "so he came to your assistance. That's how partnerships work."

Royle could see Charlie was not about to let the matter rest. Or not just yet.

"You do surprisingly well for someone who doesn't believe in guns," she exclaimed, continuing to direct her frustration at him. "Where the hell did that cannon of yours appear from?"

"I can answer that," Whitland interrupted. "He keeps his favourite toys out at the ranch while he's away."

Royle's personal weapon of choice was a nine-millimetre Browning Hi-Power single-action semi-automatic. Seeing her outstretched hand he passed her the gun, watching with interest, beginning to appreciate just how comfortable she was with firearms. Apart from its weight, one of the HP's few faults was that the magazine safety was released by a plunger pressing down on the magazine, somehow adding unwanted tension to the trigger pull. Like many former service colleagues, he had resolved the problem by fitting a modified trigger spring, and he had just watched Charlie checking for this. His growing respect for his new federal partner just went up a couple more notches.

"Okay," she grinned, handing back the weapon, "you've got a big one, but you still have to show me what you can do with it."

A short time later they all three pushed back their chairs and headed for the exit, Royle's partner still muttering about the dress she was wearing.

Back at the office Whitland and Charlie exited the Chevy beside the main entrance, leaving Royle to return the vehicle to the basement parking area. He then checked in with Paula, who had already attended to Whitland and was seated in front of her computer.

"Doug says it was an interesting trip," the secretary observed, apparently inviting comment.

"We didn't get far with finding Dan, but we got a few other things done," he responded, ignoring her invitation.

"I heard."

He studied Paula from behind her computer screen. "If you're referring to the little problem Charlie had then it's not worth discussing."

"Word is, you two are quite good friends now, which you must admit is a change from a couple of days ago."

"I wouldn't read too much into that. We had to resolve the situation somehow and we seem to have done that."

"It's the *somehow* bit that interests me."

"Don't read anything into that either. We just had a long talk."

"Doug says you weren't only talking." But then Paula changed tack, "What happens now?"

"Well, for starters I need a desk I can call my own. Seems sensible I take over Dan's workspace until he's back."

"Are you sure he'll be back?" the secretary wondered, ceasing typing and pushing her glasses up onto her forehead.

"I'd be lying if I said yes, though it's a big leap thinking otherwise."

"The person dealing with phone tracking is upstairs; I've scribbled his number for you. Have I forgotten anything?"

"Anything from Steve McGill?"

"Nothing yet. I'll leave you to find Charlie; our boss seems to have spent most of his time away thinking of urgent things I should do."

Royle tucked the Dan Morgan folder under one arm, pouring two coffees at the corridor drinks dispenser, before entering his old office. Charlie was seated at her desk, his old desk in fact. He was surprised to see two other people had moved in since he had last worked there, otherwise things seemed much as he remembered.

"Paula agreed I use Dan's workspace," he explained, pulling out Dan's chair and sitting down opposite her. "The desk you have used to be mine, though I prefer the view from this one."

He cast an eye over Dan's desk and its surrounds, noticing the half-used cigarette packet. He held it up. "He's still not kicked the habit, then?"

"Keeps threatening to."

Leaning back and sipping his drink, Royle reflected on how little there was to go on in their joint search for their missing colleague.

★ ★ ★

Charlie watched him sitting there, his eyes busily exploring Dan's workspace. There seemed no denying she had changed her opinion of him. Even if their working relationship progressed no further, this was still preferable to Morgan. She was also beginning to realise her earlier impressions of him may have been mistaken. In fact, much of what she had seen and heard since Monday morning's initial meeting in Whitland's office had proved her wrong.

She was surprised, too, at how easily she accepted him sitting opposite her, almost as if he belonged in the chair.

"You and Dan obviously worked together a long time, but how close are you really?"

"You can't call us close, not by any stretch of the imagination. He gets upset too easily, likes to throw his toys out of the pram, as you probably discovered."

Charlie shook her head. "Things may have moved on some. In my opinion he's losing it, goes into black moods and won't talk to anyone for days."

"Hasn't he told you anything of what he's working on?"

"Doesn't talk much at all and he certainly never mentions his private life." She considered adding that this seemed to be a common fault amongst the men in this office, but then thought better of it.

★ ★ ★

Royle dialled the upstairs number Paula had given him, and from somewhere on the fourth floor a male voice responded.

"Communications. Daren speaking."

"We were wondering if you've had any success yet with locating our missing man's cell phone?"

Daren sounded deeply apologetic. "I'm afraid not, but I promise we're working on it."

Royle made a note on his pad before turning to Charlie. "They're still working on tracking Dan's phone," he explained, before lowering his voice and inclining his head in the direction of the office's two other occupants. "Who are these people?"

"There's a shortage of space in Licensing; they're the overflow."

He was obviously unhappy. "It's not good practice mixing enforcement staff with others. We should be careful what we discuss and make sure we remove or lock up all documents."

That little mystery solved, Royle suggested they firm up on their priorities in the search for Dan. "Say if you disagree, but I think we should concentrate on finding what he's working on. Knowing that might help us find where he is."

"Sounds logical. Perhaps we should list what we know already."

Just one of several challenges currently facing Royle was that whilst Charlie was as far as he knew reliable, he needed to keep in mind what Whitland had said about her inexperience. One of his priorities, therefore, was to establish exactly what she was capable of. And under what conditions. And he now saw an opportunity to start obtaining answers.

"What *do* we know, then?"

She considered his question. "Thinking about it, perhaps we should start by listing what we don't know."

"Which is?"

"Well, at the risk of stating the obvious, we don't know where he is or what he's driving. His department vehicle's parked in the basement covered in our Crime Lab's 'Do Not Touch' stickers. Neither do we know what he's working on, except that it might involve wildlife smuggling. Plus, we don't have his diary, notebook or computer."

Royle was nodding his agreement. "He probably has the last three with him. I'm still unclear when he was last seen, though; he could have been missing for more than two weeks now."

Charlie seemed to agree. "Our most obvious need is his phone, which we're working on tracing."

"We should check there's nothing in his apartment that we're still looking for," Royle concluded. "I'd also appreciate it if you could backtrack details of his personal vehicle, through the system, and come up with a description and registration number. I can't believe we don't know that... Oh, and don't forget that Akroyd character over in LA."

Later that same afternoon they went to have a look inside Dan's apartment, the same one Whitland had authorised emergency entry to the previous week. Although the inside did not seem unduly disturbed, in Royle's opinion someone had carried out a detailed search prior to Whitland's break-in.

"I understand how you know the apartment's been searched, but how can you tell when?"

"Easy. They can't have had a key to Whitland's new lock, so it had to be before then."

"Any idea who might want to get in here, or what they were after?"

"Who knows. But it may be useful at least knowing someone thought Dan's place important enough to search it."

"Where would they get a key?"

"That is a very good question."

"Does Dan keep any case files here?" Charlie wondered.

"I doubt it, he's never been big on taking work home. But you never know with Dan, he's pretty unpredictable."

Fifteen minutes later they were outside Sharon Morgan's new address, a flashy third-floor apartment on an exclusive gated development in the Deerfield Beach area, north of the city out towards the coast. They took the elevator and Sharon opened the apartment door; for a second he hardly recognised her. She appeared years younger than he remembered, so obviously something was doing her good.

She led them through into the living area, which by most people's standards was large, Royle noting that her lifestyle had clearly turned a corner since she used to spend time complaining about how difficult it was surviving on Dan's government salary. Dominating the room was a huge polished hardwood table and chairs, plus leather sofa and twin reclining chairs. Of note too were the various supporting features, including a pair of silver candelabra, a well-stocked wine rack and a six-foot wall-mounted television screen.

Sharon was the first to raise the matter of her missing husband. "What's Dan been up to that's got him into trouble this time?"

To Royle this was bad news. "You really have no idea what he's been investigating?"

"None whatsoever. I only see him now when he's feeling down and needs to offload."

Royle had known Sharon for years; he could not put his finger on it but something was not quite right with the way she was responding. "Are you sure there's nothing else going on in Dan's life?"

The woman looked troubled. "The Dan I last saw, four or so weeks ago, was not the man you knew. Kept banging on about how unfair it is the bad guys getting all the rewards, while the good guys just go to work every day."

"Same thought's crossed my mind often enough."

"But you only say it for a laugh," Sharon responded. "You don't mean it."

Charlie too had an interest in where this conversation might be heading. "What are you saying, Sharon? It's important we know exactly what we're dealing with here."

The woman hesitated. "If I knew more then I'd say. All I know is he's not in a fit state to be making important decisions."

The pair exchanged glances. There was no need saying anything; if Sharon was right then Dan was in no state to be performing his role as a federal agent. It might also go some way towards explaining why they were now having to search for him.

"Is he seeing anyone new?"

Sharon screwed up her face at his question. "My guess is women are the last thing on his mind."

As a long-time friend of both parties Royle was about to respond with something suitably neutral, when his mobile rang. He stepped out into the hallway, leaving his partner to come up with a response.

It was Paula. "Guys upstairs think they know where Dan is, or where his phone is. You might want to talk with them?"

Slipping back into the lounge he apologised to Sharon and informed Charlie they were needed back at the office. Then, literally as they were leaving, he turned to Sharon again.

"Rude of me not to ask about your new partner. I'm guessing he's at work?"

"His name's Greg Saunders and he works for United. He would have liked to have met you."

"He's aircrew?"

"Works in the ticketing department. He's on days now, though sometimes he works through the night."

Back in the car Royle briefly explained Paula's call, though Charlie could see he was frowning.

"We've just had good news so what's bugging you?"

He screwed up his face. "One possible explanation for the mystery airport photographer is that information on my movements came from the airline. Then lo and behold Sharon's new man works in United's ticketing office. You must admit it's a coincidence."

He got the impression Charlie still needed convincing.

"On top of which she's not telling us the whole story," he continued. "There's more to this than she's saying."

The drive back to the office took ten minutes, Royle making several calls on his mobile which as usual was in speaker mode. He also received a call.

"Phil. Todd Shepherd. You good to talk, mate?"

Briefly glancing across at Charlie, Royle declined Shepherd's request on the grounds that he was driving and was due back in the office on urgent business.

"I'll get back to you, Todd. Good to hear from you, though."

Back at the office, Communications Head Daren was feeling pleased with himself. Dan's phone was now known to have been static at a location a couple of weeks or so ago but had not been traceable since.

"Where are we talking about?" Charlie queried, and their attention was drawn to a pin in a wall map, way up in the north of Florida.

"It's one of those yuppie hunting ranches," Daren explained in a voice suggesting he disapproved. "Sad people pay serious money to shoot some poor unsuspecting creature imported from Africa or somewhere. But it can still be dangerous so there are bound to be permits involved. State Wildlife should know more."

Royle looked from his watch to Charlie. "How about you give your Tallahassee contacts a call, see who owns this place. And more importantly, what the access is."

FIVE

Royle listened to Charlie taking a return call from her State Wildlife contact over coffee and a roll in their motel next morning. They had checked out and were loading their bags by the time a big green State Wildlife truck pulled into the parking lot.

Ed Kimberley seemed a likeable guy and was probably not far off the end of his time with the state. It seemed the ranch was owned by an outfit going by the name of Big Experience USA, with addresses elsewhere, including California. Kimberley confirmed it was a dangerous place to go wandering around in, for the simple reason that there were all manner of large animals living under what passed for natural conditions. He enquired as to whereabouts they thought Dan's phone might be and Charlie indicated an area on his official site map. All three took note of the word 'CATS', printed large and in red over what looked like an extensive paddock area.

Royle was getting a bad feeling. He had worked with a range of wild creatures, none of which troubled him unduly, though there were exceptions. He always had confidence issues around snakes, and had learned the hard way to distrust large cats. He had worked in areas where lions habitually removed locals from their huts after dark, and he knew how much that focused the mind.

"Does that mean big cats?"

"Sure does," Kimberley responded.

"Lions or tigers?"

"Both."

"They get shut away at night?"

"Nope. Going in any time is like doing it for real; enter there and you put your life at risk."

Royle suggested Kimberley might be exaggerating and the man seemed genuinely hurt.

"What if I told you the tigers were removed from the wild because they're man-eaters?" Then he took a deep breath. "What on earth was your man doing going into somewhere like that?"

"All we know is that Dan's phone was in there at some point. We're just assuming he may have been with it."

The hunting ranch turned out to be larger than anticipated. It took several minutes' driving from the entrance gate to the headquarters buildings, through open grassland grazed by small herds of antelope, zebra and African buffalo.

It took the three officers a while convincing ranch staff they were serious about someone possibly being lost in their lion or tiger paddocks. Added to which the staff seemed unhappy with any suggestions that the three accompany them on a search, only eventually giving way to the considerable pressure of a federal demand.

There was a brief discussion on the need for weaponry, purely as a precaution, staff explained.

Royle promptly held up the Winchester and in response Ed Kimberley extracted his state-issue rifle, checking to see it was loaded.

Royle then surprised his partner by handing her his fancy shotgun, the same one she had handled back out at the ranch.

"It won't kill a big cat, but it should slow it down while either Ed or I get a shot at him. Probably best you stay close though."

Following which they all piled into the back of a pickup and headed for the big cat compounds.

There were two high wire-fenced enclosures, both extensive and well vegetated, reportedly holding five African lions and four Indian tigers respectively. Although no one said as much it seemed generally accepted that they were probably searching for a body. Cautiously working their way first through the tiger pen, it was Ed Kimberley who came across the partly covered remains. Attracted by the flies and the unmistakeable smell of death, enough of the body remained to make clear it was human.

Obviously, they had found the missing Daniel Morgan, all the signs pointing to a tragic accident, which would not have occurred had Dan remained outside the enclosure – in which case, for all they knew, the compound's rightful occupants were at this very moment considering reducing them all to the same messy condition. Royle also recalled what Ed Kimberley had said about these creatures being addicted man-eaters.

"I'm going to take some quick photographs then we'll see what Dan has on him," Royle explained to his partner.

The pickup had been called forward and one of the ranch staff produced a shovel before setting about recovering the body. Carefully, Royle went through each item of torn clothing as it was revealed, some of it no longer attached to Dan's remains. He also noticed that the number of people prepared to help recover the body had shrunk – to just himself and the man with the shovel. He decided that that suited his immediate needs. Someone next produced a large plastic sheet, which they spread on the ground before laying the various body parts onto it. The driver, meanwhile, had positioned himself on the vehicle, rifle at the ready lest any of the inmates decided to take advantage of the situation.

First Royle found Dan's phone, followed by his Department badge and what looked like a vehicle key. He took care to slip the badge into his pocket without the other man seeing. Marks on the ground suggested Dan had been attacked farther away before being dragged here, eaten and partly buried. Making a beckoning motion to Charlie, cautiously they followed the trail forty feet back through bushes, to what appeared to be the place of death. There on the ground lay Dan's handgun, and finding that it had not been fired he placed it in his inside pocket.

Back at the bodily remains they found everyone helping load what was left of Dan Morgan onto the pickup, all agreeing they get themselves out of the paddock as quickly as possible.

Space to temporarily accommodate Dan was found in one of their large freezers back at the ranch buildings. At Royle's suggestion Charlie then went to summon the local sheriff while he slipped out to give Whitland the bad news. Ed Kimberley, too, had come outside, and after a brief discussion the three of them agreed to let the sheriff's office think they were dealing with any follow-up issues arising from Dan's death, without revealing who Dan was.

Back inside someone had produced a welcome bottle of Jack Daniel's. Nevertheless, one thing still troubled Royle; well, two things actually. What the hell was Dan trying to prove by being in a place like that? And where was the vehicle that fitted the key in his pocket? He also took advantage of the opportunity to ask a few questions, quickly establishing that Big Experience's replacement animals originated from a variety of sources worldwide. Obviously zoos and wildlife parks, but also creatures removed from the wild where their presence was considered undesirable, as with Ed Kimberley's man-eaters. He also learned that all replacement animals entered Florida at Miami, from where they went into quarantine at a separate location.

The two new federal partners parted company with Ed at the main gate, agreeing to keep each other informed. Because it was still early afternoon Royle suggested they drive back to Fort Lauderdale, though he also suggested going via last night's motel. Once there he asked to look through the reception's registration book, the same one they had both signed when they checked in last evening. Ignoring Charlie's questioning expression, he commenced flicking back through the pages, before she realised what he was doing.

"What makes you think Dan might have stayed here?"

"It makes sense. If Dan needed a room, then this was the nearest place. But there's nothing here supporting that theory."

Charlie had earlier taken possession of the vehicle key found on Dan's body. Royle watched her searching her bag before pointing outside, "Where's the best place to look for a car?"

He returned the registration book and followed his colleague, watching her point the key at the nearest vehicles in the parking lot, and unexpectedly seeing the lights flash on a white Ford out in the adjacent street.

A quick search of the Ford revealed Dan's overnight bag in the trunk, amongst the contents of which was his diary and computer. Royle then surprised his partner by searching beneath the vehicle's carpets, before coming up with Dan's notebook.

"How did you know where to look for that?"

"Dan and I always hide our notebooks; the information in them is too valuable to lose."

He then did another quick check of the vehicle while Charlie briefly popped back inside. Just as he was finishing, a large white Lincoln sedan with red and blue roof lights and the word 'Sheriff' pulled up alongside.

"Agent Charlie Lacey?" the deputy enquired, winding down his window.

Royle indicated his partner who was just then re-emerging from reception.

"You folks got a problem with a body over at the hunting ranch?"

Royle's drive back down through Florida in Dan's vehicle went smoothly enough, and after a good night's sleep he was in the office before eight next morning, trying to make sense of Dan's death before he and Charlie met with Whitland. The work of locating Dan's body had taken precious time and now they were faced with the task of establishing what he had been doing in the tiger compound. And more importantly, why. To Royle's mind that was not going to be either simple or quick.

He commenced with Dan's notebook and diary, followed by a check for any calls and text messages on the recovered phone, which he managed to recharge overnight. He then went through the laptop's emails, relieved to discover Dan still using his old password. Surprisingly, by the end of all that he still had only a vague idea what had been occupying his former partner's mind. He was especially puzzled by the lack of calls to or from Dan's phone.

He fetched a coffee from the drinks machine, leaning back in Dan's chair and remembering how it had been whilst they still worked together. He cast an eye over the photographs, memos and scribbled notes pinned to the desk partitioning, including several business cards. Reaching out to examine one particular card, it slipped behind a photograph, and in his efforts to retrieve it he discovered two more 'lost' cards, including the one the old Seminole reportedly gave Dan out in the Everglades. Printed across the front were the upstate Florida contact details of Big Experience USA – where they had found Dan the previous day – plus the name Mark van Wynn and a mobile number.

* * *

Unlike her new partner, Charlie slept badly after her long drive back in Royle's rental Chevy, yesterday's gruesome events still vivid in her mind. She had not known Dan well, but she had worked with him, and finding any colleague dead in those circumstances was never going to be easy. She was feeling in need of female support and Paula Howath seemed the obvious choice. The secretary seemed keen to hear how they had found Dan, but then having listened to the younger woman's graphic account she seemed momentarily lost in thought.

"What about Phil, how did he take it?"

"Good question because I really don't know and I'm the one supposedly qualified in this stuff. Considering how far back he and Dan go I expected him to be at least a bit upset."

"But he wasn't?"

"Apparently not."

"He probably will have been but for reasons you don't know."

Charlie sat herself on the corner of the secretary's desk.

"Before they worked for the Department," Paula continued, "Phil and Dan were in the Marines together. They were sent on some special operation, rescuing soldiers down in Central America somewhere."

"Dan was in charge?"

"Lieutenant Royle was flying the helicopter, Sergeant Morgan was his number two. The helicopter ended up with more holes than a golf course, two of the rescued men were killed and Phil was badly wounded. But he got them out and they both received a medal."

"He didn't mention any of that the other evening."

"I heard about the other evening, honey. Considering the obviously stressful events of yesterday you seem far more at ease with yourself."

"There's something about the secure feeling I get just being around him. Though he's not one for showing his emotions."

"It's the quiet ones need watching," Paula responded as her colleague turned to leave.

But then Charlie paused. "Does Whitland have a son?"

"They *had* a son, but he died when he was young. Why?"

"I can't help noticing how easy he and Phil are with each other. I suggested it was a kind of father–son relationship."

"What did he say?"

"He didn't say anything. But he didn't deny it either."

★ ★ ★

Whitland kicked off Friday morning's meeting by confirming he'd visited Sharon Morgan to tell her they had found Dan. He also confirmed he was in the process of having Dan's body returned. As he did so Paula entered with the tray and there was a pause while she handed around the cups, Whitland taking advantage of the break to push his newspaper across the desk.

"Bottom of page three, 'Mystery Man Eaten by Tiger'. The press seem to have picked up on it. What the blazes was Dan doing in there?"

"Whatever it was he's been working on it for months," Royle confirmed. "According to his notebook he seemed convinced there was a serious import evasion, involving a large international company and some valuable birds."

"Commercially or environmentally valuable?" his partner enquired.

"It's one and the same, Charlie. If it's rare then it's valuable, and if the price is high then chances are it's rare."

"Nothing there we're not already aware of, in a general sense," Whitland suggested.

Royle was nodding his head. "Dan thought it also involved imports of larger animals. Mexico and Australia get several mentions."

Whitland seemed interested. "Go on."

"If Dan was right and it proves links from points of capture worldwide to the point of sale here in America, then it may be what we've been seeking for years. Oh, and we're also talking about smuggling eggs for hatching, mostly parrot eggs."

Whitland sat back in his chair. "That it?"

"Not at all. None of that explains what Dan was doing playing with the tigers, or why his gun had not been fired. Whatever else he was, he wasn't stupid. If he knew he was in a pen full of tigers then I'd bet on him getting a couple of shots off before they got to him."

Whitland had known Royle a long time. "Something else troubling you?"

"He seemed to think someone in import licensing was cooperating with this. Charlie managed to contact this California state man, Akroyd, who's been calling Dan. Says it's to do with Dan's interest in the Big Experience people."

"Any progress on the airport photographer?"

"Still nothing."

Whitland's response seemed particularly unenthusiastic. "Hmm."

"But I did find the missing business card the American Indian gave Dan out in the swamp. It's from a Mark van Wynn of Big Experience, where we were yesterday. Charlie's checking him out."

"You seem quiet, Charlie," Whitland said.

"I'll go with what Phil says. He's had a chance to see Dan's stuff. I suggest we use this weekend to work out where we go from here."

Turning to Royle, Whitland enquired whether he was still staying in a hotel, or had he sorted out an alternative?

"I'm still paying for the hotel room, though I don't seem to be using it over much. I was about to suggest I use Dan's apartment."

"Agreed," confirmed Whitland.

"And if I happened to be going back out to the ranch in the morning, perhaps Charlie might be interested?"

Charlie agreed she was interested – though she wondered what kind of person might consider sleeping alone in the apartment of a colleague he'd found dead in such unpleasant circumstances only the previous day. But then, remembering how close Paula suggested the two men once were, perhaps that had something to do with it.

They were in the process of collecting their papers together when Royle raised an additional matter.

"We've not discussed finances, Doug. Looks like there may be some travel involved so what's the budget for this job?"

Clearly Whitland did not need time to consider his response. "We do whatever it takes, Phillip, and that's official. Cost is not an issue, or at least not until I say differently."

★ ★ ★

Having read Dan's notes, and having thought things through overnight, Royle could not dismiss the possibility of someone in the Department being involved in whatever Dan had been investigating. Which, if true, might go some way towards explaining Dan's reluctance to share information. Added to which, Royle knew next to nothing about Charlie, except that she had recently worked in Licensing. He caught up with her as they left the meeting, recalling what he had said to Whitland about sorting a few things out with his new partner. She appeared surprisingly keen on his suggestion of dinner, even offering to book a table at a restaurant she knew and call by Dan's place to collect him.

Looking forward to dinner with his new partner, Royle stopped off briefly at Sharon's on his way to Dan's apartment. As soon as he entered he spotted the whisky bottle, a full glass next to it. Without asking, she produced a second glass, filling it and pushing it in his direction.

"Join me," she almost demanded.

He picked up the glass. "Who'd have guessed Dan would end his days that way?"

Sharon was slow responding. "I wasn't entirely honest with you. Dan was involved in something dangerous; he was obviously worried for his safety."

"How much did he say?"

"Not a lot. He did say to let you know if something happened to him." Then she lifted her glass again, "Dan Morgan."

He raised his own glass and took a mouthful of the whisky, an expensive single malt. "Is that it? He didn't give you any idea what might be worrying him?"

"Kept on about not knowing who he could trust. Said for you to watch out for…" but then she paused, scouring her memory for a name, the whisky obviously not helping that process.

He touched Sharon's arm. "It's important you remember."

She refilled their glasses, her hand obviously shaking. "Someone called Toombs, I think. Does that mean anything?"

Royle shook his head. "He didn't say anything else?"

"Like I said, he seemed to think he couldn't trust anyone."

"Was Greg present during this conversation?"

She seemed puzzled by the question. "Why?"

"Did you discuss any of Dan's conversations with Greg? Or anyone else?"

"I never mention Dan. It obviously annoys Greg, you know, makes him jealous. Goodness knows why."

He gave her arm a squeeze before lifting his glass and emptying it. "Probably best you don't mention this conversation."

The pair arrived by taxi just after eight outside one of the classier restaurants along the Fort Lauderdale seafront area. Having agreed they would dress up a little Charlie had put on something long and black, whereas he had added a tie to his suit.

"You come here often?" he enquired, seeing where she had brought them.

"I don't go anyplace much. Whitland brought us here for his birthday and I rather liked it."

The door was opened for them by a smartly dressed, jovial little man.

"Good evening, Mr Royle. It's always nice having you visit."

Royle shook hands with the man. "Good to be back, Roberto. This is my new working partner, Charlie Lacey."

Roberto indicated they follow him to their table. "I'll send someone to get your drinks," he promised, settling Charlie into her chair.

"How come you know this restaurant?"

"We all use it, Charlie. It's the office special-occasions venue, which was why Whitland brought you here."

Although no expert on women's fashion it was obvious to Royle her dress did not originate from some corner department store. Already aware she might be a woman of expensive tastes, it occurred to him he knew very little about her.

"Can I ask what your father does?" he asked, thinking she hesitated ever so slightly, as if trying to guess what motivated the question.

"He's a lawyer up in Tallahassee. Boring stuff."

To Royle's mind this perfectly fitted his expectations; he knew very few poor lawyers. "I guess I gave you a hard time this week."

Again, that slight hesitation. "You're a difficult person to read and I got it wrong," she admitted, pretending to study the menu, before looking up. Her eyes focused on his. "Paula told me about you and Dan in the Marines. You never mentioned that."

"Not much to say. We served together and both ended up working for Whitland."

Charlie studied Royle, deciding her new partner had no desire to discuss his life prior to joining the Department. But apart from the obvious, the past few days had produced something else for her to think about, namely his incoming phone call on their way back from Sharon Morgan's. It had not escaped her attention that, although Royle claimed he was driving, this had not stopped him earlier talking to various other people. The obvious conclusion being that he did not want her listening in on any conversation with the mysterious Todd Shepherd. She had thought about this, in the end deciding that simply asking who Shepherd was seemed unlikely to gain his cooperation.

"How much time do you spend in the UK?" she enquired, deciding to take the safer ground.

"I'm away about half the time, though with long periods when I need to stay put. Like when I'm studying."

She sat back in her chair, hands folded neatly in her lap. "You never mentioned any studies."

"I did Law, at Harvard."

She pretended to concentrate on rearranging the cutlery, before looking up at him, trying to conceal her frustration. "How is it you keep coming up with these surprises? Just when I think I'm getting to understand you?"

Now it was his turn to study the table. "If we start out underestimating people then we're perhaps in line for a whole string of surprises."

Charlie thought that one through, accepted his mild rebuke with a smile and their conversation continued. She tried hard steering it towards subjects unrelated to work, but as they commenced their dessert she finally put the question she had been wanting to ask since that evening out at the ranch.

"What's the most important feature in solving any case, like the one we seem to be involved in?"

He took a slow sip of his wine, watching her over the glass. "The secret is to work out beforehand what your opponent's options are. Then devise a plan for every possibility. Be as creative as you like."

"It's that simple?"

"It may sound simple, but it involves a lot of sleepless nights whilst your brain sorts through the possibilities."

"Are we at that stage yet?"

"We need a suspect first."

Charlie had seen her question as a way of exploring the deeper workings of his mind, but was it possible to plan ahead to the extent he suggested? She also noticed they were near the end of the wine. However, they'd had a challenging week and if there was to be an occasion for letting go then perhaps this was it. She ordered a second bottle.

"I stopped off at Sharon's again," he explained. "She threw in the name Toombs; claimed Dan said I was to look for that person in the event of his untimely death."

"Don't suppose he said why."

He shook his head. "Perhaps we should raise it with Whitland at Monday's meeting."

"What *are* our plans for next week?"

Royle was beginning to suspect the wine might be slowing his thinking, plus two large whiskies earlier at Sharon's. "We're off to California, then into Mexico. Mexico City to be precise, looking at a couple of places."

She wrinkled her forehead. "Another tiring week, then."

He leaned back, idly fiddling with his glass and, seeing how the conversation had slowed, Charlie decided to raise the other matter that had been occupying her mind all evening.

"Paula says you and Dan got medals for some rescue?" And she could see immediately that he was uncomfortable.

"Just occasionally Paula talks a bit too much. It was a routine mission, we just hit a problem."

"That's not how Paula tells it. She says you were badly wounded, plus some of your group were killed."

He seemed temporarily lost in thought, and when he did respond it was not what she was expecting. "Jobs like that have little to do with bravery. Someone's shooting at you and you have two options: sit there and die or get the hell out of it."

She watched him, saying nothing, realising he was becoming talkative.

"They were bad times. Dan and I, we spent a lot of time clearing away the bodies of colleagues. But I never expected to see Dan all chewed about like that."

Watching him she felt unexpectedly moved, so cursing herself for resurrecting some obviously dark moments she decided it was time to leave. Getting Roberto to call a cab, she gave the driver her own address.

"Change of plan. No Dan Morgan's apartment for you tonight. You're sleeping on my couch. In the morning I'll do us a real American breakfast before we drive out to see your daughter. And maybe find out how good you are with that shotgun."

SIX

ROYLE AWOKE ON SATURDAY MORNING IN BETTER SHAPE THAN HE perhaps deserved, surprised to discover he was alone in Charlie's apartment. More importantly, he was not on the couch, he was in bed. Her bed. Added to which, he could smell her – the whole bed smelled of her. He knew little enough about perfume, though logic suggested hers was an expensive brand. Certainly not the splash-it-all-over kind favoured by Paula Howath.

His mind seemed temporarily unwilling to cooperate, though he did have vague recollections of kissing her in the back of the cab. And even vaguer recollections of clothes being urgently removed.

Wrapping himself in a towel and going to make coffee, he discovered a note on the fridge door. 'Gone for a run. Don't start breakfast without me'. He showered while the kettle boiled, the bathroom's impressive array of mysterious creams and lotions emphasising how unaccustomed he had become to any female presence.

He decided he liked her apartment. The combined kitchen-cum-dining area had virginal-white walls and featured a polished redwood dining table, complete with jade-coloured Liberty lamp and potted orchid. Meanwhile a well-stocked china cabinet dominated one end wall, whilst opposite hung a Monet print. White also prevailed in the bedroom. White walls, white closet doors and white bed linen, all offset by beige carpeting and matching black art deco vases set into recesses either side of the bed.

Whilst it was an exaggeration to think Royle had remained celibate since his wife's death, few of those relationships could be described as enduring – or involving any bonding of personalities – having as much to do with sex as any permanent desire for female company. Nevertheless, he was beginning to feel that here might be someone different. Though the immediate difficulty, he realised, were the restrictions imposed by their newly enforced working partnership. Plus, of course, his suspicions that someone in the Department was involved in whatever had led to Dan's messy departure.

Royle was also aware of the opportunity he was being afforded here – with Charlie off on her run he had unlimited access. He could search where he wanted, look at whatever he wished. He was no stranger to searching people's homes, it was part of his job. Admittedly, it was a serious intrusion into their lives; nevertheless, it was a proven means of obtaining information. What it did best, however, was provide a reliable insight into the workings of people's minds.

This then was his opportunity to see whether Charlie had anything to do with bird smuggling. Or with Dan's death. But even as such thoughts crossed his mind, he realised he was having trouble with the idea of delving into her life in this way. Experience told him that the top bedroom drawers held underwear, in her case undoubtedly expensive underwear. And that the closet floor housed pairs of shoes – probably many pairs. There were no prizes for knowing this stuff. She also probably had a diary in the bedside drawer, but did he really want to know what she thought of him? Probably not.

Her shoulder bag was on the table where she had left it last night. However, he had learned the hard way that examining the contents of a woman's bag could be the near equivalent to an intimate body search. Apart from more general items, e.g. lipstick, deodorant, keys, he could expect to find far more personal items. Or at least a spare pair of pants. He knew male officers who leapt at the opportunity for such a search – but he was not one of them.

It also occurred to him that he was dealing with an intelligent young woman. If there *was* anything incriminating in the apartment, she knew it, the same as she knew she had left him alone here. So, ignoring any thoughts of a search, he instead did an inspection of the kitchen, making an acceptable job of laying the table for breakfast.

Not too much was said as they ate, though Royle did acknowledge feelings of guilt on hearing how far she'd been on her run, whilst he still slept. But it soon became obvious she had no intention of mentioning last night, though having thought the matter through in her absence he saw no way they could ignore it.

"I guess I had too much wine," he admitted, aware he was deep into hazardous territory.

"We both had too much, and now you're wondering how you ended up in my bed?"

He smiled nervously. "It crossed my mind."

"It was easier, letting you have my bed and me taking the couch."

From Royle's point of view this failed to assist; he was unclear still on the finer details. "It's probably a silly question but what was I doing in your bedroom?"

He watched her face turning pink. "We kind of headed straight there from the cab."

God, this is embarrassing, he thought, aware how much the idea of holding her naked body against his had occupied his mind over the past two weeks.

"Did we...?"

She gave him the faintest of smiles. "You fell asleep. That must have been some send-off you and Sharon gave Dan before we got to Roberto's."

"I undressed myself, then?"

Now her smile seemed aimed more at hiding her own embarrassment. "Not entirely, but I tried not to look."

He decided there seemed little point in persisting with this, concentrating instead on finishing his breakfast. He poured them both a second coffee, realising how quiet she had gone.

* * *

Charlie knew something else had happened last night, something she had not mentioned. Ordering the second bottle of wine at Roberto's, she had been aware of the possibilities that this raised, given the amount of whisky he appeared to have consumed earlier at Sharon's. But she had been interested in perhaps finding out what kind of person might be hidden behind that apparently calm exterior.

By the time they reached her bedroom they had already removed his shirt, though she knew this should not be happening. She was in the process of telling him as much when he collapsed onto the bed, clearly past the point of being dangerous. She really had tried not looking as she undressed him, but could not help noticing three round scars extending in a line across his back. Paula had not been exaggerating, he really had been badly wounded during that rescue mission all those years ago.

She wondered how it was possible to live with those kinds of memories. Whenever he undressed, there were the scars, constantly reminding him, impossible to forget. Admittedly, thousands of men probably had that same experience every day. However, she did not know these other men, but she did know Royle. And she was impressed by the way he appeared to not let it affect his life. Though last night at Roberto's showed just how close to the surface the scars remained.

* * *

66

After breakfast Royle inspected the many family photographs on display, while Charlie went to ready herself for the day. Several of the pictures involved women in lace headscarves outside churches, giving the clear impression she came from a Catholic background. He also noted several of Charlie in her teens, some involving horses. Particularly grabbing his attention, though, was a photograph of her in a gym somewhere, in a white judo jacket held closed by a black belt. He also remembered her federal firearms training. It seemed that one way or another Miss Lacey was more than able to look after herself. It also gave serious weight to her claim that she had been about to tackle the man with the knife on their way back from the ranch!

He next turned his attention to the bookcase, aware that, whatever anyone might say about themselves, their preferred reading provided a far more reliable character reference. Charlie's literary preferences ranged from some major classics, e.g. Jane Austen, and Tolstoy, to perhaps lesser contenders, such as Stephen King and Steinbeck.

Also present, however, were numerous classic medical references, including *Clinical Psychiatry*, *Man's Search for Meaning*, *A History of Psychiatry* and *A Critical Review of Contemporary Psychiatry*, though perhaps of more relevance to their present situation, or so Royle thought, was Bancroft's *Human Sexuality and its Problems*.

Royle suggested they take Charlie's car out to the ranch, this being his first opportunity to see what she drove. And he was surprised by her choice – a red Ford Mustang convertible.

"I didn't have you down as a Mustang woman, or not on a government salary."

"Daddy spoils me. Girls like being spoiled."

"He gives you whatever you ask?"

She laughed. "I wish. He lent me the money. Do you like her?"

"I'd be lying if I said no."

It occurred to Royle that Daddy must love her a great deal, though he remained less than convinced on how she might afford it. Nevertheless, he made a conscious effort to push such thoughts to the back of his mind, at least for the moment.

"I'm guessing you went to a convent school?"

"What makes you ask?"

"Your photographs suggest it."

"Mama's family came from Puerto Rico. She and Papa met at university. Spanish is my second language."

Royle processed this latest piece of information, especially in relation to their pending Mexican visit. It was always useful having someone along who spoke the language.

★ ★ ★

Out at the ranch Charlie decided on a walk around the nearby lake, leaving Sam time alone with her father. On the return route she came across Billy tending what was clearly a family grave.

"I was just tidying her up."

It was obvious who he must be referring to. "This is Sukie's grave, then?"

"Royle should be here soon; he always brings her flowers."

"What was Sukie like?" Charlie wondered, and was surprised by his response.

"She had your same calm approach to life; she made every day worthwhile."

Charlie struggled for a response, realising that somewhere in there she was being complimented. Leaving Billy to finish what he was doing she headed in the direction of the house, turning the Sukie situation over in her mind. She recalled what her friend had said back in the bar at the Mexican conference, as they discussed Royle over a drink. 'I heard he had a bad experience and went off women.' There seemed no doubting that Sukie's death had been that bad experience. But that was years ago, and he was surely too intelligent to go wasting his life in this way.

Back at the house she went in search of Sam and could see that the girl had been crying.

"Your dad told you about Dan?"

Sam switched her attention from what she was doing. "It must have been awful."

Charlie was cautious with her response, unsure how much detail Royle had given his daughter. "It's not something I want to repeat," she admitted, before changing the subject. "I found your mother's grave while I was walking."

"Were there fresh flowers?"

Charlie shook her head.

"Then that's probably what he's doing now; he always takes her flowers."

There was not a lot to say regarding the outcome of the shotgun competition. Royle believed he was the victim of some sort of feminine alliance, consequently he was not ready for several of the targets as Sam released them. Whereas Charlie merely pointed to the final score; though he did not deny it when she suggested he deliberately missed two crucial shots.

★ ★ ★

Monday morning back in the office for a case update meeting, Whitland commenced by casting a shadow over the occasion.

"The situation's changed. The lab says Dan was shot before the tiger got its claws into him – hollow-nosed thirty-eight through the back of the head."

There was silence while the pair took this on board, and Royle was the first to speak.

69

"On that basis, then, we can't be sure he was killed on the ranch."

"I already considered that, Phillip. In fact, the whole nature of this inquiry has changed; it's now a high-risk operation. Paula has new untraceable phones for both of you."

"And there's something else, something I already touched on," Royle interrupted, "that I need to raise again, now that things have taken this new direction."

Whitland made a beckoning motion.

"We may not like it, but it needs saying. The mystery airport photographer can only mean someone within the Department is involved."

"I know where he's going with this," his partner interrupted.

"Sure you do. We've got two Licensing staff in our office, so who do they report to?"

"I can answer that," Whitland responded. "They're from our upstairs Licensing office run by Licensing Head Gus Winnings, up in Tallahassee."

Royle was quiet for a moment. "We were at Roberto's Friday evening. While Charlie was powdering her nose, he told me that Sharon and her man Greg Saunders eat there and that Winnings is sometimes with them. I've never trusted the man."

Then, mainly for Whitland's sake, Royle briefly outlined how he had stopped off again at Sharon Morgan's apartment Friday evening, and how Dan had allegedly warned her about someone called Toombs.

"I've something on that," Charlie interrupted, "assuming I have the right Greg Saunders. He has convictions for drug dealing, plus he did three months for beating up his former wife."

The room went silent for a moment.

"What we seem to have, then," Whitland suggested, "is someone with a history of drugs and violence living with Dan's former wife. Plus, Dan had premonitions of his own death. Personally, I find that interesting."

"Greg Saunders could possibly be our murder suspect," Royle agreed. "But if there is a connection between Dan's death and the parrot smuggling he's been investigating, then we could blow the whole inquiry unless we're careful."

Judging by Whitland's facial reaction Royle's boss was with him on this point. "Agreed," he said. "And if I was trying to hide Dan's murder by feeding him to the tigers then I'd remove his phone and his gun, and more importantly his badge."

Then, taking advantage of a pause in the discussion, Charlie raised the name Mark van Wynn on the card Royle found by Dan's desk.

"I got nowhere looking for him in America, but eventually tracked him down via one of Phil's UK police contacts. Mark van Wynn's just a fancy name he uses; his real name's Mick White, from a place in England called Essex. Has convictions for the illegal transport of both birds and eggs."

★ ★ ★

Charlie grasped Royle's elbow as they exited Whitland's office, demanding to know what it was about Gus Winnings that worried him so. He steered her towards the lift before escorting her out into the ground floor parking lot, aware that, although she might not accept what he was about to say, it was nevertheless for her ears alone.

"You have to understand I don't trust Winnings farther than I could throw him."

She grinned. "I already got that bit."

"When I first came here Whitland was running the Department, until some months later when he got moved on and Winnings took over."

"Things changed?"

"Winnings had no idea about even the basics of criminal work, as a direct consequence of which the US Attorney threw out several of our cases. People who were undeniably guilty walked free, including a friend of Winnings'."

Charlie got the feeling there was no stopping Royle now.

"Dan and I were unimpressed, and we let it show. Winnings had us in his office, the one we've just been sitting in. Gave us a lecture on how we should follow his directions. Said we 'should not become emotionally involved in our work', whatever the hell that means."

Royle leaned his back against one of several trees shading the parking lot. "He even started instructing us on how we went about our investigations, bearing in mind he'd never been in a courtroom in his life. Even after all this time the best I can say for Gus Winnings is that he brings a lot of joy whenever he leaves the room."

Even as he said this Royle noticed Whitland watching them from his office window, realising the old warhorse would have guessed what the two of them were discussing so intently in broad daylight in the middle of the parking lot.

Charlie, though, appeared unconvinced. "Isn't that stretching our imagination, suggesting it proves a link with Dan's death?"

"Possibly," Royle conceded. "But I've known Winnings a long time, and there's always been a little voice warning me to be careful."

Sensing she was about to say something derogatory about his mental state, he stopped her. "I know what you're thinking. But there's one thing your psychology tutors must surely have taught you, up there in Tallahassee…"

"And what might that be?"

"Even the worst-case paranoids can be right on occasion. We absolutely need to keep Winnings in mind."

SEVEN

Later, after Monday's case update meeting, and four days now since the discovery of Dan's mutilated body, California State Officer Deming Akroyd met them at Los Angeles airport before whisking them down busy Interstate 5 to his office an hour south of the city.

"Booked you two a couple of rooms across from the office. Thought we'd meet up in an hour and get something to eat, so I can fill you in about your buddy, Dan Morgan."

True to his word Akroyd appeared at eight and they walked the couple of blocks to the restaurant. Then, having ordered meals and drinks, Royle waded in with the questions.

"How come you're involved in this?"

"Got a call from Dan months back, enquiring about a place dealing in exotic birds out in the desert east of here. He wanted to know where they got their stock from."

"So, where do they?"

"They breed 'em. Got rows and rows of breeding pens full of mostly parrots. Gets dammed noisy while I'm doing any visits."

"This place got a name?"

"Big Experience, run by people from Holland and England. Sells lots of baby parrots."

Royle let the waitress hand round the plates before responding. "What made you call Dan recently?"

"He wanted me to remind him when the birds were close to breeding."

"You know much about identifying parrots?" Royle queried, trying not to seem too interested.

"To be honest, no. People out at the farm have all that information, though."

Charlie took over, feeling her partner's questions were becoming a touch too focused. "These visits – what's involved?"

"Routine mostly. Checking on housing conditions, examining records, things like that. Nothing's scheduled; I just ring and tell 'em I'm coming."

"Any visits planned for the near future?"

"One pencilled in for this Thursday, as it happens. You two interested in getting a look around?"

Picking up on his partner's lead, Royle confirmed they would be interested in visiting the farm with Akroyd. "Oh, and since you and Charlie spoke on the phone, we discovered Dan had been shot. Does this place look like it could be involved in that sort of thing?"

Akroyd seemed shocked by the suggestion. "No way, they're just selling a few parrots." Then he reconsidered his response. "Well, actually, a whole lot of parrots."

"Tell you what," Royle suggested, "let's meet up in the morning and make sure we've not thought of anything else. Then Charlie and I need to leave for LA, though we could get back for Thursday."

Back in their motel Royle asked Charlie what she thought of their latest contact. In particular, could they trust him?

"There's always a problem with who we tell, and how much," she suggested. "But if we go around asking questions from professional people and not giving any answers, we'll likely run into a wall of silence at some point."

Their brief Tuesday morning meeting with Akroyd threw up no new leads, so they sorted out a one-way hire car and followed Interstate 5 back north into LA. By eleven o'clock they were in the California equivalent of their own Florida Federal Wildlife office.

"What's so secret, Phil, that you can't discuss it with me over the phone?"

The speaker was Mindy Goldsmith, an attractive middle-aged career woman who, like Whitland, had spent her whole working life with the Department.

"You presumably heard we found Dan Morgan dead," Royle explained in response. "Turns out he was shot in the back of the head before being eaten by a tiger, on one of those exotic hunting ranches. Dan never did anything the easy way."

Mindy leaned forward in her chair.

"Whatever Dan was working on he kept it to himself," Royle continued. "He seemed to think it was smuggling, involving the Big Experience bird outfit south of here. Know anything about them?"

Mindy now leaned back in her chair, crossing her arms. "We had something suggesting they were up to no good, so we recorded some telephone conversations and ended up even more confused. You may be just the person for that – the guys involved come from your part of the world. Where's Essex?"

Royle's and Charlie's eyes met briefly.

"It's that bit of England east of London and north of the River Thames," he responded.

Mindy picked up her phone and asked someone to join them. "And bring along those phone calls from the bird place."

The door soon opened to admit a young man and, at Mindy's instructions, he slipped a CD into the computer.

"We did a lot of recording," she explained. "It mostly seemed legitimate business, so let's get to the weird bits."

She nodded to her colleague, who skipped the CD forward. Royle recognised the voice as male, with an obvious London or Essex accent.

"Shaun, it's Mick. 'Ow you doing, mate?"

75

"I'm great, Mick. The weather's hot and the girls here are still as gorgeous." This was followed by laughter.

Mindy stopped the tape to explain. "This Mick character's in Essex, England. Shaun's at the Big Experience site here in California." She restarted the recording.

"Yeah, well, enough of that," Mick continued. "Listen, mate, word is you can't trust yer dog. Know what I mean?"

There was a brief silence. "Even as we speak?"

"You better Adam and Eve it. But you can talk about the weather and the girls as much as you like."

More laughter followed, and Mindy motioned to skip the recording forward to a point in the conversation concerning import permits for birds, referred to as the 'new arrivals'.

"Might be something I need to sort out with our friend up the apples. Leave it with me," Essex voice said. "By the way, 'ow are yer Farmer Giles?"

"What's going on there, then?" Mindy wanted to know.

"The Essex feller's using Cockney rhyming slang. Can't trust your dog means you can't trust your phone – 'dog and bone'. He's telling the man Shaun he had better believe it – 'Adam and Eve it'. The last bit refers to someone upstairs somewhere – 'up the apples and pears'."

"What's this farmer got to do with any of that?"

Royle grinned. "It seems Shaun here has haemorrhoids. Otherwise known as piles, or 'Farmer Giles."

Mindy motioned for the CD to be skipped forward again. "This one's even weirder."

Essex man was speaking again. "The clothes pegs will be ready soon, so you better get prepared for the garden gate."

"What's this about a garden gate, then?"

Royle considered Mindy's question for several seconds. "I'll tell you what I think. Essex man's telling Shaun there's a crate, 'garden gate', arriving at the desert site soon. He could mean mate but that doesn't make sense. But 'clothes pegs' translates into eggs, so there's a crate and some eggs involved."

"So, this Mick person presumably knew someone might be recording their conversations."

"Seems that way," Royle agreed. "More importantly, though, it suggests they wanted to discuss something they'd rather you didn't know about."

He poured himself another coffee. "The apples and pears bit could fit our current thinking. We, or to be more precise I," he corrected, exchanging glances with Charlie, "think there may be a connection with one of our Federal Licensing offices."

"Isn't it even more serious than that, though?" Mindy continued. "If they knew their phone was bugged then they must have been warned we were listening."

"Seems reasonable," Charlie agreed, easing herself into the conversation. "This Mick, you say he's in Essex. Wouldn't be Mick White, would it?"

Mindy's face was a picture. "Are you saying you're ahead of us on this?"

"Pure chance," Charlie admitted. "His name cropped up in connection with where Dan was found. He also uses the name Mark van Wynn, and he's listed as a director of Big Experience."

Royle was busily gathering his things together. "I'm all for grabbing lunch somewhere and quickly going over this again."

Fifteen minutes later the three of them were seated in a local diner, and Royle kicked things off again by addressing himself to Mindy.

"What do we think's going on out at this desert bird place? What are they trying to hide?"

Mindy took time pulling her thoughts together. "At a federal level we have little contact with a place like that, but they obviously have a guilty conscience about something. Your State Wildlife contact Akroyd is probably your best bet for getting in there."

Mindy paused while they placed their meal orders. "They do have a few birds of interest to us, mainly through endangered licensing."

"We're listening."

"Our informant suggested they were importing prohibited birds, which usually means endangered birds. We found no evidence of that in our files, neither was there anything on the recordings. Or not until today," she added, raising an eyebrow at Royle.

"Where do most of their declared bird imports come from? I'm guessing from across the border in Mexico?"

"How would you know that? You're right but we never discussed it."

"Just something I found amongst Dan's scribblings. I'm guessing Mexico City – it fits what one of my contacts mentioned recently."

"I'll dig out the Mexico City address and text it to you," she promised.

Royle scribbled on the back of one of his cards before passing it to Mindy. "They're our new office mobiles, plus I've added some other numbers."

Then at that point he headed for the restroom, leaving Mindy to add the phone details to her notebook.

"This Akroyd," Charlie asked, watching Royle leave, "can he be trusted?"

"None of us federal people know him well. Bit of a plodder, but I guess he's honest," Mindy responded, inclining her head after the departing Royle. "How you finding it working with him?"

Charlie hesitated. "We got off to a bad start, but he grows on you. And if it's reliability you're after then he's your man."

"Does he mention Sukie?"

"Not a word, and he's good at avoiding the subject. In fact, getting *any* information out of him is like pulling teeth."

"I noticed you call him Phil, so perhaps you get along better than you're saying."

Charlie's initial reaction was to not respond, before spotting the opportunity to obtain a more experienced opinion of the situation she found herself in. "I seem to swing between being attracted to him and wanting to smother him."

However, at this point the object of their discussion returned, to stand hovering over the table, keen to be moving on.

"We're down in Mexico tomorrow," he explained to Mindy. "We'll keep you in the loop on what comes of that."

Mindy and Charlie brushed cheeks. "Good luck with that other matter; give me a ring if I can help," Mindy offered.

Royle raised a questioning eyebrow.

"A girl thing, Phil," his partner responded as the two of them turned to leave.

Back at LA airport, mid-afternoon Tuesday, they prepared for their flight down to Mexico City. On their way out to the airport Royle had briefed his partner regarding his long-time friend and now main Mexican contact, Zip McGee. He also gave her brief details of the Mexican dealer he was hoping to get a look at, and who he believed gave Dan cause for concern. Interestingly, at the same address as the one Mindy had just texted him.

The boarding formalities completed, Royle leaned back, eyes closed, reflecting on what had occurred since chance first brought him and Charlie together in Whitland's office. Interestingly, he still saw her in much the same light: quietly spoken but not lacking in confidence; without doubt quick on the uptake; and well able to grasp the complexities of what they were investigating. There was no denying he now accepted her as his working partner, doubtless precisely as the scheming old Whitland had intended. But he still needed to find out more about her family background.

That same Tuesday afternoon, whilst Charlie and Royle were settling into their seats in preparation for the flight down to Mexico City, over in Fort Lauderdale Paula Howath's phone rang.

It was Mindy Goldsmith. "Hi, Paula, thought it was time I called. How are you?"

"I'm fine, Mindy, and I'm guessing there's a connection between this call and a visit you just had from our new special agent team?" She could hear her California colleague laughing.

"What's it like having Phil back?"

Paula tucked the receiver into her neck and continued typing. "Personally, I think it's a scream. Three weeks ago, Charlie was independent with not a care in the world, then he appears on the scene and she's all over the place. I bet they never mentioned their late night."

"Go on."

Paula stopped typing. "They stayed up late, talking and drinking; Doug overheard part of it but fell asleep."

"Does Royle know about her family?"

"Not yet and I'll not be the one telling him. If that's what Charlie wants then it's not my place to interfere. But is he in for a shock."

"Actually..." Mindy started, before pausing briefly, "I think Charlie's good for him. She's quite perceptive; I doubt he can keep her too much in the dark."

"You're not wrong. She asked if Whitland had a son, said she'd noticed how he and Royle got along so well. Suggested it was more of a father–son relationship."

★ ★ ★

Around ten o'clock Wednesday morning the pair arrived at Mexico City's North Bus Terminal, known locally as the

'*Terminal Central de Autobuses del Norte*', where Royle had arranged to meet his long-time friend and now Mexican contact, Zip McGee.

Over last night's hotel meal Royle had explained how she should not expect too much of Zip, who following a messy marriage breakup in Florida had abandoned any semblance of respectability, losing himself instead amongst Mexico City's back streets. Formerly he and Royle had been close, but as Zip's marriage slipped away so too did his hold on normality, to the point now where Royle had no real idea how Zip managed to survive, though survive he obviously did and by a variety of means, doubtless some legal, some not so legal.

"You name it, Zip seems to be into it," he told Charlie.

They stood watching Mexico City going about its morning business, until their attention was distracted by a battered pickup erratically weaving its way through the turmoil of buses, taxis and donkey carts. Piled high in the back, five or so slatted wooden crates full of live chickens shared the limited space with a large, and by all indications not too friendly, dog. The vehicle rattled into the kerbside and there was a loud explosion as the ignition was switched off.

"That's our man," announced Royle.

Zip wore a battered straw sombrero and over his shoulders a colourful but ragged poncho, both identifying him as part of the local populace and not some hippy gringo tourist. And as if that were not enough, it was immediately apparent he found difficulty making eye contact. But for all his appearance and obvious personality issues Zip still seemed genuinely pleased to see them. He was also attracted to Royle's suggestion that he take them to wherever they could buy him breakfast. Opening the passenger door, he swept a collection of newspapers and wine bottles off the seats and invited them to climb aboard.

The place he took them to appeared more suited to his own budget range, though the food proved to be above expectation and the service more than efficient. For Charlie's sake Royle explained how, among other things, Zip was involved in minor dealings in domestic birds, mostly ducks, chickens, turkeys and the like, but also captive wild birds. There was, it seemed, a lucrative local trade in pet birds, including small parrots, in the course of which Zip had built up local contacts. He pointed to Zip and nodded.

Zip hesitated, clearly summoning up the courage to continue, doubtless aware that some of the information he needed to disclose might not reflect him in the best of lights. Sensing this, Royle interrupted him before he could get started.

"Look, Zip, we realise life's different down here to back in the States. We're only interested in finding out who the big players are. We need the information you have, and we'll make sure you're reasonably compensated without anyone knowing where the information came from."

More than his assurance of anonymity, Royle guessed it was probably his suggestion of financial reward that tipped the balance. Whatever the reason, Zip took a deep breath as he pushed away his empty plate, wiping his greasy hands down the front of his poncho.

"The bird dealer you're interested in is the same I mentioned recently, Jose Antonio Cordero. Trades out of a former industrial site and claims he breeds the birds he sells, but that's total bollocks. Most were trapped from the wild, here in Mexico or various countries further south. Either that or they came into Mexico as eggs."

"Does he have any adults to explain away his possession of any young birds or eggs?"

"Almost none. That's what makes it so damned unbelievable he's got away with it all this time."

Clearly Zip was emotionally involved, and it seemed to Royle there were two likely explanations. Either he felt concerned at the damage being done to wild birds with already more than enough problems, or more probably he objected to the unfair competition from people like Cordero.

"Which birds are involved, or is it just parrots?"

"Mostly parrots. He sold upwards of three hundred birds last year, around one and a half million dollars, tax-free. And that's just what I know about."

"What I don't understand," Charlie interrupted, "is how he gets that number of birds into Mexico. Doesn't he have trouble with customs? Or the border agencies?"

Zip's laugh sounded more like a duck being strangled. "Perhaps that's how it works where you come from, lady, but down here money talks. Cordero can afford to make sure officials don't look too hard, or pay people to cross borders unnoticed. Anyhow, birds are not the only things crossing Mexico's borders illegally, so who cares about a few parrots?"

"We believe you, Zip," Royle interrupted. "You're probably also going to tell us someone is issuing papers stating Cordero's birds were bred in captivity. Either that or he sells them to people who don't care where they come from."

Watching Zip gulp down the last of his coffee, Royle caught the waitress's eye. "Of more immediate concern is how we get a look at Cordero's place. Any thoughts?"

The coffee arrived, and Zip was temporarily engaged in topping up his mug from a dented old flask he produced from beneath his poncho.

"I considered that," he mumbled, wiping his chin with his sleeve. "He gets lots of buyers from the States – tell him someone gave you his name. Just don't drop me in it; these guys are dangerous."

Royle studied his friend for a moment. "Seeing as you raised the subject, you should know Dan was shot."

EIGHT

MID-AFTERNOON THEY WAVED DOWN A CAB AND GAVE THE DRIVER
Cordero's address, which turned out to be quite a large piece
of land with a single entrance gate and high boundary wall.
In addition to the old hacienda-style residence there were a
couple of smaller brick buildings, retained from its former
industrial life. Most of the site, though, was taken up with
an assortment of wire-netted aviaries, some substantial in size
and holding many birds.

Royle had explained to Charlie why he needed to get a
look around Cordero's place – to both see what kinds of birds
he kept there and hopefully get a feel for what else might be
going on. He also explained that despite her Spanish it was
advisable in these situations to claim limited knowledge of the
language; it sometimes helped in the event of someone asking
difficult or potentially embarrassing questions.

"I can't apologise enough for our lack of Spanish, but your
English is perfect," Royle suggested.

Cordero nodded his acknowledgement. "Tell me what it is
you want, and I'll see if I can help."

"We're mainly interested in parrots, but you have so many
it's difficult deciding," Royle responded, hopefully sounding
overcome by the sheer number of birds available.

"Tell you what, why don't I leave you to look around.
You'll find me in the office when you're ready."

Royle could hardly believe their luck and was more than ready to take advantage of the offer. "That's very kind of you," he said, putting on his humble voice.

With that, Cordero crossed the gravelled driveway and disappeared into a low building marked 'Oficina'.

"Creepy sod," hissed Royle.

"I have to say it's arguable which of you two was the creepiest."

Charlie then followed as Royle moved from one aviary to another, drawing her attention to various parrots, and at times the noise was deafening. He also pointed out birds she was even less familiar with, including what he said was a falcon much in demand by bird-of-prey keepers worldwide. A single small building held nine or ten of these falcons, which he suggested sold for $10,000 each, though some buyers might pay twice that amount. There was between $100,000 and $200,000, quietly sitting there watching them.

Royle frequently paused, either to scribble in his notebook or cautiously take photographs. On several occasions she watched him produce a small canister and spray the feet and bellies of birds clinging to the wire. He also explained that most of the parrots climbing around on the wire netting were still too young to fly.

At one point they were standing by an aviary holding thirty smallish bright yellow parrots. All just a matter of days old, clinging to the wire.

"Exactly what I expected," he explained. "These are sun conures, probably from Brazil. The species is heading for extinction. There are too many for one pair of adults to produce, and anyway *there are no adults*."

"So, what do we make of all this?" she queried.

To Royle the answer was inescapable. The obvious explanation had to be that these sun conures, and any other young birds they were seeing, had arrived at Cordero's as eggs, had been incubated and were now being hand-reared ready for sale. It fitted what he knew went on worldwide. Eggs may be fragile, but they're far easier to transport illegally than noisy smelly live birds.

"Same again," he announced at the next pen. "Twenty endangered thick-billed parrots, all young and unable to fly. With no adults that we've seen."

Cordero reappeared soon after, enquiring how they were getting along.

"We're doing fine," Royle responded. "I'm particularly interested in the thick-billed parrots, though I'd still like to see what else you have."

However, even as he said this they were all three aware of a large black car crawling slowly up the driveway towards them. It came to rest just feet away, the two occupants wearing expensive dark suits, despite the heat. An immediate change came over their host, who now seemed extremely agitated. Ignoring the two agents, the newcomers addressed the dealer in Spanish, and even with his limited understanding Royle guessed this was not some friendly conversation.

Cordero responded by apologising to Royle and Charlie for his brothers-in-law arriving unexpectedly, conveniently suggesting they continue occupying themselves while he attended to a 'little family matter'.

"Come and find us when you're ready," Royle responded.

They watched the three men cross the driveway and disappear into the office.

"I'll tell you what," Charlie said, only half smiling, "when I get married I hope I get on with my in-laws better than Cordero. His so-called brothers-in-law just offered to shoot his kneecaps off if he doesn't pay up."

Royle grinned. "Are we suggesting they're not actually related?"

Charlie laughed quietly. "Could be a family matter that's gotten out of hand. But a pretty dysfunctional family, wouldn't you agree?"

"Do we know what it's about?"

"Something about Cordero not paying for birds."

"Well, then, that's his problem," Royle responded, a touch unsympathetically. "I suggest we continue while our dealer's mind's focused on retaining his mobility."

Twenty minutes later Charlie decided she'd had enough of this game. "The in-laws' car has gone. Perhaps we should go see what's left of Cordero."

Their host seemed in a surprisingly relaxed mood, presumably relieved to have resolved any financial misunderstandings.

"Did you find anything interesting?"

"Quite a lot," Royle responded in all honesty. "I'm still interested in the thick-billed parrots, though I'm unsure how I get them back into the States. Anyhow, we have a problem."

"What kind of problem?"

"My wife's just heard that her mother's been taken ill, so I guess we must forget the parrots for now. You'll have more next year, though?"

"Come about this time of year and we're certain to have those, plus most others you've seen. I get papers stating they were bred here in Mexico, and your government lets you take them into America."

Royle decided to play his naive card. "Don't the people who issue the permits come to see whether you bred them?"

Cordero smiled, a particularly arrogant smile. "Normally they never come."

Although unsurprised, they were both nevertheless taken aback by Cordero's willingness to as good as admit that the birds he sold were illegal. Nevertheless, to Royle's mind they had taken this as far as they could and asking further questions might be risky. He was also satisfied they had enough information to justify their little excursion down into Mexico on the Department's budget.

Charlie was still laughing as they searched for a cab out in the street.

"What's so funny?"

"You seem to enjoy those situations."

Her partner was obviously on a high. "It never ceases to amaze me how open these guys are about their dealings. He as good as admitted he's smuggling in eggs, and that if he asks for a permit he gets one."

"What's the spray stuff?"

"It glows under ultraviolet light, plus it contains a unique chemical marker. My notebook shows details of all birds marked, plus the date, place and identifying batch number. If we meet those birds again anywhere in the world, we will be able to prove it."

★ ★ ★

Charlie knew what Royle considered a major weakness in controlling international trade in endangered wildlife; he had outlined it to her in some detail during Thursday's early-morning flight from Mexico back to Los Angeles.

"A major failing is that birds legally bred in captivity are mostly exempt from international controls," he had explained, "providing they're accompanied by a certificate confirming they were captive-bred."

"What's wrong with that?" she had asked.

"A high percentage of these certificates originate in obscure countries around the world, which may not see things as we do. Plus, there's the considerable difficulty of knowing which birds go with which certificate."

She had agreed that this might lead to a breakdown in the system.

"The official view is that only so-called 'developing' countries are responsible for any certificate irregularities," he had continued, "whereas informed opinion suggests the problem is rife amongst countries that should know better, largely due to a mix of corrupt and incompetent officials."

"Which countries?"

"Well, you certainly can't exclude America or Britain, and Mexico's way up there."

"What's the answer, then?"

"Increased enforcement's certainly part of it. Though Bamfield's right, it would involve considerable extra cost."

It had all seemed perfectly understandable the way he explained it. But the bottom line, he had emphasised, was that the illegal trade went on whilst numerous kinds of birds and other animals, as he so eloquently put it, 'continued to go to hell in a handbag'. He seemed particularly concerned that around one-third of the world's parrot species were listed as in danger of extinction, suggesting it was debatable who was most to blame – the trappers, dealers, smugglers and bird collectors, or the politicians and government officials. Charlie decided he obviously had a thing about politicians. He had asked her what the difference was between a rat and a politician, and she had shaken her head.

"Easy – you can get to like rats, and there are some things they just won't do!"

★ ★ ★

Back in Los Angeles they drove a rental car back down busy Interstate 5, ready to accompany Deming Akroyd on his routine visit to the Big Experience desert site.

"Glad you could accommodate us," Royle said as they met up mid-morning. "Who do these people think we are?"

"Told 'em you were a couple of government pen-pushers needing to see how the real world revolves. Thought that might appeal to you."

However, at that same moment Royle's mobile rang, and Charlie heard him tell someone called Angie that he would get back to her.

"Your secretary in London?"

"Not even close. That was Angie Watts in Australia."

"Another of your informants?"

"Almost a relative," he responded, reaching back into his pocket as the phone rang again. Clutching it to his ear, he listened attentively for quite some minutes. "How sure are we, Mac, seeing as the body's been in the water a while?" Then he listened some more. "We'd appreciate it if you could leave any search of the apartment until we're available."

"What's happened in Miami?"

"Steve McGill's officers pulled a car out of the bay. The body looks like my airport photographer, in the driver's seat with both hands tied to the wheel. They've got an address but Mac's happy to wait for us before searching."

As Royle was explaining this they got their first glimpse of the bird farm, stuck out there in the desert like some military installation. It even had what appeared to be watchtowers at the four corners.

"Not an easy place to sneak up on. What do they need to guard so carefully?"

Akroyd was shaking his head. "It's not what it seems; it's an ex-government site. They've done a lot of grass laying, with one doozy of a water bill."

Royle heard what the man said but was less than convinced. For one thing, when they arrived at the gate Akroyd had to reach out, pick up a phone and announce not just who he was, but who was with him. Only then did someone remotely open the gates. They then drove through into the parking area, which as Akroyd had prophesised was surrounded by extensive lawns. The one word already going through Royle's mind was 'money' – someone here clearly had a lot of it.

An elegant, long-legged young woman appeared as they emerged from the vehicle, escorting them back into a smart reception area, where she picked up the telephone and reported their arrival.

"Mr O'Reilly will be with you in a moment," she announced. "Can I get you a drink?"

Akroyd suggested three coffees would be appreciated and these quickly materialised, before the girl settled herself back behind her telephone, the two agents using the opportunity to carry out a cursory inspection. A few coloured photographs of various parrot species hung on the walls, each of which Royle was able to identify, including a pair of Australian princess parrots. Through a small window facing onto an inner yard they could just make out rows of back-to-back aviaries.

Conveniently, just as they finished their coffees the door opened and a man in his early-thirties entered and exchanged pleasantries with Akroyd, who introduced his two visitors on day release from office tedium.

"I'm Shaun O'Reilly, Site Manager," he explained. "What is it this time, Deming?"

Royle and his partner exchanged glances, both recognising O'Reilly's voice from Mindy's recordings.

"More of the usual, I guess. Checking you're maintaining the hygiene standards and that there are no health and safety issues."

O'Reilly suggested they commence with a look at the birds. "Particularly as your colleagues haven't seen them before." Then he turned to the receptionist, "We'll be in the rearing rooms, Roxie."

O'Reilly first led them to the enclosed area they had glimpsed through the reception window, each aviary containing single pairs of parrots of various sizes and colours.

"We keep them in pairs for breeding. It takes time learning the different kinds, plus there's the difficulty of telling males from females, and adults from young birds."

"Must be a problem for people like Officer Akroyd here?" Royle suggested, noting Charlie's reproachful expression.

But O'Reilly seemed to agree. "It sure is, though the authorities have really tried getting their act together."

Royle waved a hand, indicating the aviaries generally. "What *are* most of these birds? They're all about the same size but some have longer tails."

"Mostly small South American parakeets, plus some from Asia."

Royle was aware that if you needed to know whether someone was lying, then you should already know the answer to at least some of your own questions. And one pair of birds had caught his attention.

"Those are nice," he exclaimed, indicating two Australian princess parrots.

There was no doubting O'Reilly hesitated. "They're Indian plum-heads; we sell lots."

Royle's mind, though, had already moved on. "There don't seem to be any young birds. Wrong time of year?"

Their guide explained how they routinely removed any eggs and hatched them artificially, before hand-rearing the young birds. "That way they grow up used to being handled."

By now they had reached the end of the aviaries and were standing in front of a windowless single-storey building. They watched O'Reilly key in an eight-digit code, and as the door opened they were hit by a blast of parrot noise. Inside, the experience was not at all what Royle had expected, being more like entering a hospital's intensive care unit. Regardless that the building contained upwards of perhaps five hundred live birds, it was nevertheless clinically clean. Most birds were housed in small wire-netted aviaries built against the outer walls, each holding around twenty-five individuals of a single parrot type. All were young birds, many still unable to fly.

"This is the sharp end of the operation," O'Reilly explained. "It's where we rear the young birds, and train those that have already been ordered."

No mention had yet been made of the hatching process. Royle was about to ask, when O'Reilly opened a door behind them, revealing what Royle recognised as an incubator room. They saw it contained twenty or so electrically powered industrial-sized incubators. As far as he could tell from looking through the plastic covers, all contained eggs, perhaps fifty or more per incubator.

O'Reilly was clearly proud of the set-up, explaining how they employed skilled staff to tend the incubators and care for the birds. Royle, though, was casually inspecting the contents of the incubators, which mostly fitted the impression being offered – that this was a legitimate business dealing in captive-bred, hand-reared parrots. But he had already identified some issues. Like the fact that although parrots lay white eggs, some in the incubators were the reddish-brown type laid by birds of prey. He also noted that a substantial number of eggs came from obviously larger parrots than any they had been shown so far.

"Do you only keep small parakeets, or do you have anything larger? What I call proper parrots."

O'Reilly indicated a door at the far end. "We need to go through to the other building for those."

The 'other building' turned out to be identical to the first, though with an even greater noise output, one of three such buildings joined in a line, and clearly this second building contained Royle's 'proper' parrots. The main difference here was that the small anteroom, the one that previously held incubators, now held numerous young birds, all still being hand-fed.

Again, they inspected the aviaries. "It's probably a silly question," Royle wondered, "but if birds die do you have them stuffed?"

O'Reilly turned, opening a freezer and searching around, before extracting a sack of dead parrots. "We sell them to a taxidermist."

Standing next to O'Reilly as he was, Royle found the freezer's remaining contents of even greater interest, particularly the frozen packs marked 'Day-old Chicks'. Just what, he wondered, did a place that supposedly kept only parrots want with commercial packs of frozen day-old poultry chicks? Of the kind used to feed birds of prey.

But O'Reilly interrupted his thoughts. "Well, that's about it. We need to get back to the office and let Deming check the paperwork."

O'Reilly and Akroyd then made their way back along the length of the building, discussing the next phase of the state man's inspection. Royle, though, took the farther walkway, passing several aviaries containing baby parrots, several coming to the wire netting in anticipation of food. Quickly he treated each to a spray, having first checked to ensure the other two men were not watching.

Ten minutes back up the road Akroyd pulled over in front of a diner and all three went inside.

"What did you make of that?" the state officer wanted to know.

"It was extremely useful," Royle responded. "We proved all sorts of things and raised several additional questions that need answering."

"What kind of things?"

Royle shrugged his shoulders. "This is where it gets serious. Anything we discuss here stays between us?"

"You got my word on it."

"Great. Then this is what we now know about Big Experience's California operation. Firstly, they keep large numbers of common parrots, probably legally.

"Secondly, a lot of the eggs and young parrots we saw do not have any corresponding adult birds out at that site. Or none we were shown.

"Thirdly, they're also hatching bird-of-prey eggs. Probably falcons.

"Fourthly, some of the young parrots without parents match hand-reared young birds we saw yesterday in Mexico.

"And lastly, many of the young birds are endangered species. Again, it's possible they have legal parents out there, though personally I doubt it."

"You can tell all that from just one visit?"

"All that and more. If they only keep parrots, which eat mainly seeds and fruit, why store bird-of-prey food in the freezer? And why did he give me the wrong name when I asked about the princess parrots?"

"Pretty sure I've never seen any birds of prey."

"Ever been in the third building?"

"Can't say I have. We will have asked where the livestock was kept, and they would have shown us on a site plan. Someone would then have drawn up an inspection schedule, and that's what I work from."

Royle was busy sugaring his coffee.

"What does all that boil down to, then?" Akroyd wanted to know.

"It means," Royle responded, lowering his voice, "that that place is about as believable as a nine-dollar bill. They truly are selling lots of apparently legal birds, and doubtless they make big money from that. But they make far more money selling rare birds they don't breed legally."

Akroyd sounded even more impressed. "I'm blown away by how you can go in there for an hour and then come away with all that information."

"There's no need to be," Charlie volunteered, glancing up from the menu. "That's what he does."

95

"I've been thinking," her partner then interrupted. "We need to see what Mac's found in Miami harbour. How about us catching a flight back this afternoon, have a lie-in tomorrow and then get a look at our dead photographer?"

Akroyd smiled. "You two certainly get around."

NINE

Lunchtime Friday saw Charlie and Royle in Steve McGill's Miami police office, a couple of blocks back from the Bayfront area. As a reminder, Mac first produced Royle's photographs of the mystery airport photographer, before making their way down to the police mortuary, where Royle confirmed the identification.

Mac nodded. "Then let me introduce you to the late Jimmy Quigly. We found something else – there's been blood in the vehicle's trunk." He handed Charlie a sheet of paper. "And this was also in the vehicle; our lab managed to make it readable again."

Royle watched her face as she studied the paper and realisation obviously dawned.

"You're going to love this," she suggested, handing it over for his inspection.

Confronting Royle was a clearly recognisable hand-drawn map of Big Experience's upstate Florida facility, complete with a cross marking the location of the tiger pen's locked access gate.

It was Charlie who broke the silence. "My bet's on the blood being Dan's. It's just too much of a coincidence."

"And if Charlie's right then it suggests Quigly was getting rid of Dan's body, presumably for someone else. You said you had an address?"

Mac held up a bunch of keys. "Down on South Beach. These were in his pocket and we got the address from the

Vehicle Registration Office. We'll take one of my uniformed guys."

Royle looked thoughtful. "Quigly would need at least one key to access the tiger pen. So, who gave him that, and what's their involvement?"

"Not only that," Charlie added. "Whoever killed this guy could just have hit him over the head and tipped him into the bay. Instead they tied him into the car – they wanted him to know he was going to die."

They both spotted the grin on Mac's face.

"Something else?" she asked.

"If the purpose of sending the car into the bay was to hide the body then the killer got it wrong. The aerial was poking above the surface at low tide; the call came from a passing boat."

"Talking of calls, I don't suppose there's any sign of Jimmy's cell phone?"

Mac shook his head. "Sorry, Charlie, we're guessing it's at the bottom of the bay still."

Inside Quigly's apartment it quickly became obvious he had lived the good life. Good enough to raise questions over where the money came from. Spotting a sagging bookcase Royle set about checking the dead man's literary interests, just as a scantily clad young woman emerged from the bedroom, demanding to know what was going on.

Having checked there were no other occupants Mac raised an eyebrow in Charlie's direction, pointing towards the girl and then the bedroom. Taking her cue, Charlie ushered the girl back into the bedroom, closing the door after them.

Royle continued with his book inspection. Amongst a surprisingly wide range of subjects, the undoubted revelation was the assortment of bird books. Or more precisely, books dealing with birds' nests and eggs, several hard-to-get volumes, testifying to Quigly's specialised interest. As he continued his exploration, the silence was interrupted by a muffled scream from the bedroom, and the three officers exchanged knowing glances. Obviously, Charlie had just given the bedroom's occupant the bad news regarding Quigly's unscheduled departure.

Mac knocked on the door and Charlie re-appeared, closing it quietly behind her.

"She's upset but she's dressed. Should I bring her out?"

Mac nodded and Charlie slipped back inside, re-emerging holding the still sobbing woman's arm and manoeuvring her towards a chair.

"This is Crystal Brown," she explained.

Mac also pulled up a chair. "Crystal, when did you last see Jimmy?"

The girl wiped the tears from her face. "A few days ago; he often disappears for days at a time. I thought it was him when I heard the door opening."

"What does he do when he's away?" Mac asked, but it seemed the woman had no knowledge of such things.

Royle, though, had ended his brief search of the apartment and had a question or two that needed answering. "Crystal, Charlie and I work for the government. It would help if you came through to what I'm guessing is Jimmy's office."

Once there, Royle indicated a large mahogany collecting cabinet, comprising two stacks each of twenty-five shallow drawers. He had seen numerous egg collections housed in similar cabinets around the world, plus he was acquainted with egg collectors and their bad ways. He also knew that in America, as in most countries, their interests involved activities prohibited not just by state or federal laws, but also international laws – the same laws controlling the parrot trade that Dan Morgan had apparently become entangled in.

Royle established that the cabinet contained eggs taken from countries around the world, as far away even as Australia. Most were marked with a combination of letters and numbers, indicating that somewhere there were corresponding record cards. Those cards would contain all the information needed to prove when and where these eggs had been collected, along with the names of any people involved. Given the serious criminal implications of those records being found, collectors were extremely careful about where they were kept. Usually they were hidden, often at a different address.

Two things therefore seemed obvious. Firstly, whatever else he might have been involved in, Quigly had been internationally trading in the eggs of some seriously endangered birds. What particularly grabbed Royle's attention, however, was the number of eggs that, in his expert opinion, originated from birds often found in captivity. Including many parrots. One question therefore demanding an answer was from precisely where had Jimmy obtained these parrot eggs? And Royle suspected he knew the answer. For one thing, there was an obvious relationship between eggs in Jimmy's collection and birds they had seen out in the California desert the previous day.

Royle directed the woman's attention to the cabinet. "What's this, Crystal?"

The girl looked at him from behind wet eyelashes. "It's Jimmy's. It's where he keeps his eggs."

He held up one of only four small data cards he had found in the cabinet. It read: '*Palm Cockatoo, L. Toombs, 4th October, Jardine River, C3.*'

"Who's this Toombs person?" he enquired, catching Charlie's eye.

Crystal's face was blank. "Jimmy doesn't let me near his eggs."

"I understand that, but do you know any friend of his called Toombs?"

Mac grasped Royle's arm, pulling him to one side as the girl shook her head, tears evident again.

"Do we take possession of all this stuff?"

Royle had already made up his mind on that point. "Afraid so. The eggs certainly, plus we need to go through the paperwork – this Toombs person probably gets a mention somewhere. Charlie and I will do that – you need to know what you're looking for."

Mac was agreeable, if only because of the work it saved him. "Who is this Toombs character?"

Royle briefly repeated what Sharon had told him. "Eggs in this cabinet originated from someone called Toombs," he emphasised. "We've no idea yet who that is, but I sure as hell intend finding out."

But then something dawned on him, so delving back into the cabinet he retrieved the four record cards.

"Palm cockatoo, Jardine River – fancy me missing that. The eggs on this card were taken from a nest in Australia's Cape York, up in Queensland. That's where the Jardine River is, and that's the only place in Australia where palm cockatoos breed. Our Toombs person's in Australia."

"What's the C3 bit mean?" Charlie wondered.

"It tells us there were three eggs in the nest. They were taken on 4th October, though no year is given."

Royle sat himself down beside Crystal. "Someone did something very bad to your Jimmy. We need to find out who that was, and who this Toombs person is. If you remember anything, it's important you let us know. I've scribbled some phone numbers for you."

★ ★ ★

At the end of a tiring week in California, Mexico and then Miami, Charlie had spent an hour talking to her parents on the phone the previous evening. She and Royle had agreed to meet up out at the ranch this morning, and on her way there she thought through the events of the past few days.

The undoubted main development had been their recovery of Dan's remains, though it seemed difficult believing they had made much subsequent progress. In fact, the follow-on part of their inquiry seemed particularly complex, though they should perhaps be encouraged by the Australian link Royle had uncovered at Quigly's apartment. They had agreed to spend this afternoon going through Quigly's paperwork, carrying that over to the Sunday if necessary, before Whitland's Monday case update.

Interestingly, Charlie felt she should probably admit to being happy now with their working relationship. Royle clearly was experienced, not just as an enforcement officer but more so in his specialist subject. She was less clear, though, on where they stood with their personal relationship. Mostly it seemed entirely professional, and certainly no one could accuse him of any sexual advances, with perhaps the one obvious exception! But even there she felt it unfair putting all the blame on him; hadn't she ordered the second bottle of wine? And hadn't she made the decision that they go back to her apartment? Neither could she deny all responsibility for what happened in the cab; indeed the jury was still out on what might have occurred had he not collapsed half in and half out of her bed.

When she did finally track Royle down, he was stretched out on the rear decking surrounded by his laptop and three boxes of Quigly's paperwork. Lying on an adjacent lounger was his daughter.

"I guess this is as close as it gets to a normal weekend in the Royle household," Charlie suggested, quietly creeping up behind them.

"He needs to relax more," Sam suggested, jumping to her feet and disappearing inside.

Charlie stared down at him. "I hope you appreciate how lucky you are having Sam for a daughter." She then followed the girl into the kitchen.

"I'm making us a sandwich; would you like one?" Sam asked.

"I would, please. Where is everyone?"

"Granddad and Grandma are off somewhere for the day, and the hands are out annoying the cows again."

Charlie volunteered her help, seizing the opportunity to speak to the girl without interruption. "Your dad and I had a long talk at Roberto's the other evening, but it didn't go quite as expected."

"He took you to Roberto's?"

"I tried discussing the medals he and Dan got, but he didn't want to know."

"I never heard them speak about it either. What else did you discuss?"

"He did what he always does, threw another surprise at me. In the form of his studies."

"What did he say?"

"That he has a law degree from Harvard. He never mentioned that the other night."

The girl was shaking her head. "He has a Harvard PhD in Environmental Law, plus a degree in Applied Ornithology from Cornell. Why would he tell you different?"

"Who knows. He's so difficult to read; unless you're working alongside him, then all the pieces fit together."

"I've heard Doug Whitland say as much to Granddad."

★ ★ ★

Whitland had been out all Monday morning, Royle and Charlie putting the time to use firming up on their understanding of where the investigation now stood, supported by a rash of coloured pins in their boss's wall map. Whitland's mail and the daily newspapers were still exactly where Paula had left them: in two orderly piles in the centre of the desk, mail on the left, newspapers on the right. During a short coffee break Royle snatched a brief look at the newspaper report of a man and a woman in separate cars, both dead from multiple gunshots somewhere nearby.

At Whitland's instruction Charlie kicked off the case update meeting by outlining their movements during the past week, suggesting that although they now seemed to be on top of the Mexican and Californian parts of their investigation, several loose ends remained still. She directed Whitland's attention to the map.

"Red pins show where birds are either being held or may be held, places we'll probably raid, including Big Experience sites in California and upstate Florida, plus Cordero's place in Mexico. I'm still tracking down a quarantine site near Miami, and I'll come back to the two pins in Europe in a moment."

She paused to ensure she had Whitland's attention.

"Green pins show people we're working with, including Steve McGill in Miami, Ed Kimberley in Tallahassee, Mindy Goldsmith and Deming Akroyd in California, plus of course Zip McGee in Mexico."

"How is Zip?" Whitland wondered. "Still away with the fairies?"

Charlie glanced across at Royle. "He seemed fine to me."

Whitland aimed a finger at his wall map. "What's the pin near here?"

"That's Sharon Morgan and her man Greg Saunders. We're not saying they are involved, but neither can we dismiss them."

Whitland was clearly taking all this in. "That still leaves the Miami pin."

"That's the dead Jimmy Quigly; Phil will get to him shortly. Before that, though, the two heavies at Cordero's are Columbian nationals, both known to our Drug Enforcement Agency."

"Something Charlie forgot to mention," Royle interrupted. "She obtained more info on our man Van Wynn, AKA Mick White. He's the Big Experience guy who went to see the old American Indian out in the swamp, and was also on Mindy's telephone recording. Apparently Big Experience is Belgian-based, dealing in wildlife from around the world, though any shipping seems to be done via a company in Germany. They're the two European pins."

Quickly, Royle then summarised Saturday's events in Miami, including their discovery of a map connecting Quigly with the site of Dan's death. "So, the questions arising from that are: who killed Quigly? Did they also kill Dan? And what exactly is behind all this?"

Aware they were taking up Whitland's valuable time, Charlie suggested Royle condense the details of Quigly's egg collection down to a few brief sentences. And they were surprised by their boss's reaction.

"Why are we bothering with birds' eggs?"

Royle smiled as he directed Whitland's attention to a lonely red pin, way over in the bottom right-hand corner of the wall map, near Australia's northern tip. "We're bothering with Quigly's egg collection because of that."

Now it was Whitland's turn to smile. "You did get somewhere with the Australian connection, then?"

"It's back to this Toombs person. Someone of that name took eggs Quigly had in his collection. I believe those eggs got to Quigly via the California Big Experience site."

"Bit of a long shot?"

"Not really. Dan went on about Australia in his notes, so I had a talk with my contact out there. Some Aussie bird dealer separated from his wife and now she's spilling the beans to customs."

"Angie Watts?" Whitland asked.

"Who the hell is this Angie Watts?" Charlie exploded.

"She's Controller of Customs in Sydney; and it gets better. The dealer's wife says he annually ships trapped parrots to Europe, along with eggs for hatching."

Whitland leaned forward in his chair. "Where's all this heading, then?"

"Charlie and I discussed that. Realistically we have two inquiries on the go, one into Dan's murder, the other involving wildlife smuggling, though they're probably the same investigation. The wildlife side is on a roll; we've proved connections with California, Mexico, UK, Belgium and Germany, and now Australia."

Whitland held his arms out wide, hands open, palms towards them. "And now we're planning to do what, exactly?"

"Easy," Charlie responded, aware things were getting a bit tense. "We're not just trying to find out who killed Dan, and now Quigly. We need to prove why they did that. And it increasingly looks as if the 'why' bit has something to do with parrot smuggling. So, in the absence of anything more to go on, our best chance of finding Dan's killer is to follow up the smuggling side."

★ ★ ★

Whitland leaned back in his chair. From Royle he was getting no more than he expected, given the man's experience level. What impressed him was Charlie, who in what seemed like no time appeared to have blossomed into a fully functioning criminal investigator.

From where Whitland was sitting, and from whichever way he looked at this, he was getting value for money. Not only did the pair seem well on their way towards catching the person, or persons, responsible for the death of his agent, they were also deeply involved in something showing all the hallmarks of a major international smuggling operation. And if he could trust Royle's judgment then they might be about to unearth a major weakness from within the belly of the Licensing Department.

Realising there were still a few details to discuss, Whitland called a break so he could respond to an urgent telephone message Paula had taken. "Back here in ten," he announced.

★ ★ ★

Whitland's break lasted twenty minutes, and when they did sit back down he obviously had bad news.

"Phillip, how did you return your rental car?"

Royle sensed there was more to Whitland's question than just the obvious. "The hire company collected it from outside Dan's apartment, sometime overnight. They drove someone over to collect it. I'm now officially using Dan's department vehicle."

"Local police have been in touch," their boss continued, opening his newspaper and hovering a finger over one of several pictures accompanying last night's shooting story. "Apparently that's your rental Chevy, with nice new ventilation holes."

Royle was trying not to arrive at the obvious conclusion. "Are we suggesting someone thought that was me they were shooting?"

"Difficult us thinking otherwise," Whitland finally responded. "It's the shot woman in the second vehicle who really interests me, the one who brought out the other rental driver." Whitland held up a family picture the press had obtained. "Looks a lot like Charlie here."

"Wow, this is getting creepy," she interrupted. "You're saying someone shot the rental driver, assuming it was Phil. And then shot the second driver, the girl, assuming she was me?"

"Where did this happen?" Royle asked.

"Traffic signals a mile or so from Dan's place."

There was silence for a moment before Royle responded. "This can only be related to Dan's death; there is no other sensible explanation. What I can't remember is whether I told Sharon I was staying at Dan's place."

Whitland was frowning. "Your point being?"

"Nothing solid. Just that Sharon's man Greg was in a position to know my flight details into Miami. Plus, she may be the only person outside this office who knew I was using Dan's place. Bit of a coincidence?"

"Greg works in a ticket office."

"That's just the point. Charlie did some research; Greg doesn't issue tickets, he's the IT manager, he has access to everything. On that basis alone he needs watching."

"You alright carrying on with this investigation?" Whitland enquired.

"I'm good, Doug, though we need to think about security."

"Charlie?"

"If Phil is then so am I. Seems to me the questions are the same as before. Who and why? Though whoever they are, they seem pretty determined."

"So, I repeat, are you two happy continuing with this?"

"Charlie and I can look after ourselves. There's only one thing concerns me and that's my daughter. Sam's safe out at the ranch, but I don't like the idea of her travelling to and from college on her own. Someone out there needs to drive her until this is over. Someone who can use a gun."

"Where exactly in Australia is this bird smuggling happening?" Whitland enquired once they were settled again.

"Around Cairns, up in the tropical northeast. The question is how do the birds and the eggs get out of that country."

"Do we know which airports are involved?"

"Aussie customs has an ongoing problem with literally hundreds of small airstrips, plus numerous places where you can get quite large boats into remote river mouths."

"Suppose you do track down these people, what then?"

Royle realised this was a crucial question. "We let them get on with moving the birds. Biologists, like those at the UK's British Trust for Ornithology, are fitting micro satellite technology to birds and all manner of other creatures worldwide, mostly aimed at proving where they go to, or come from – exactly what we need to know about smuggled wildlife."

"Have we looked at any of this?"

"We have, Doug. Some even call our mobiles."

Royle was beginning to sense they might just have their boss hooked. "Our main difficulty, though, will be getting access to the birds, or even the crates."

Whitland was quiet for some seconds. "Don't you lose the connection while they're on the plane?"

Royle seemed uncharacteristically smug. "That's the clever bit. Modern long-haul aircraft are fitted with loads of censors, constantly checking information – tyre pressures, fuel loads, all the stuff airlines need to know back on the ground."

"How does that help?"

Royle grinned. "On-board receivers pass on all these signals, without differentiating between airline transmissions and any others. Ours simply get piggy-backed out along with the rest."

Whitland continued tidying his desk. "What you two are after, then, is my approval to go wandering off around the world, in the hope you can catch these people red-handed."

Royle flashed a brief glance at Charlie. "I wouldn't put it quite like that. We're trying to prove that seriously organised gangs are plundering some of the world's rarest wildlife resources, so they can sell the birds involved for considerable financial reward. And let's not forget Dan's murder."

Whitland smiled. "Never doubted you, Phillip, but I had to ask. Let's do it."

"Charlie and I already talked it through. We think it might help, us stopping off in Washington and making sure the big guns are briefed."

"Washington's a sensible move. What's the timescale?"

"We need to finish off here. Perhaps fly to Washington in two or three days' time."

"Which way from there?"

"To Sydney, but via London. I need to catch up with what's going on in my own office."

A short while later, back in their own office, Royle noticed Charlie checking her voicemail and returning a call. She spent some minutes talking before replacing the receiver.

"Customs just came up with an address for Big Experience's quarantine site, out in the Everglades."

"Any recent arrivals?"

She read from a text message. "Last one two weeks ago. Five African buffalo, via a shipping company called Bundes Groß Animalisch International. In a place called Munster?"

Royle was accustomed to an ongoing level of American confusion regarding European geography. "Northern Germany, up near the Dutch border," he explained. "Probably why someone thought there was a Dutch connection."

Royle popped out to fetch two iced Cokes from the corridor machine, handing one to Charlie before sitting back at Dan's desk, thinking through their immediate plans. Top of the list was a visit to Ed Kimberley up in Tallahassee, to discuss the availability of keys for Big Experience's cat pens. Charlie then surprised him by suggesting they stop over in Tallahassee so he could meet her parents. However, before he could respond, the door opened to reveal Licensing Head Gus Winnings.

He advanced towards them. "Phillip Royle, and the lovely Charlie Lacey." He held out his hand, which was still as cold and unwelcoming as Royle remembered.

"So, this is where you came to rest after deserting us," Winnings exclaimed, addressing himself to Charlie.

Then, without waiting for a response, he turned his attention to Royle. "Heard about poor old Dan; be sure to catch the people responsible for his death. Been having a meeting with my Licensing staff. You take care now."

And with that Winnings was gone and the pair had the office to themselves again.

"Did he really just call you the lovely Charlie Lacey?" Royle queried, noting his partner's red face.

But he realised something far more significant may just have emerged from their brief unwelcome encounter with the Florida Licensing boss.

"Just how," he asked, "do you suppose Winnings knew someone might be responsible for Dan's death? And that it was not some awful accident?"

Then, leaving his partner to consider her response, he popped along the corridor for a word with Paula regarding the next day's visit to Ed Kimberley. He also mentioned they might stay overnight with Charlie's parents.

The secretary tugged his sleeve as he turned to leave. "Did she say anything about her family?"

"Only that her father runs some law company. Why?"

"I just wondered," the secretary responded as the door closed behind him.

TEN

Up in Tallahassee it was raining as the pair headed for the Capitol building. Ed Kimberley seemed pleased to see them, showing them around on their way up to his third-floor office. Once there he was keen to hear how their investigation into Dan's death was progressing, and Royle explained the police discovery of the hand-drawn map in Quigly's car.

"What's been puzzling us," Charlie explained, "is how Dan's body got past the various locked ranch gates, alive or dead. What's the situation with keys?"

"Various ranch staff have one, plus there's an emergency key at selected locations. Just in case."

"Such as where?"

"Sheriff's Office and I both have one, plus there's one downstairs here."

"You say one. It's the same key for all gates, then?"

Ed nodded. "Better than wasting time trying several keys, while someone's being attacked."

"Where exactly is the key downstairs?" Royle enquired.

Ed indicated they should follow as he headed back downstairs to the reception area, where he took them behind the glass security window. He indicated a keyboard on the wall inside reception, carefully positioned so whoever was on duty could both accept and hand out keys.

"Key at the top left's the one. Where it says Emergency Big Experience."

Charlie still had questions. "Who has access to that key, or even all those keys?"

"People come to the window and the duty officer either issues the keys or takes them back."

"Who has authority for the Big Experience key?"

Judging from Ed's face it seemed she had raised an interesting point.

"Not sure there is a set procedure. By the very nature of things, it's likely to involve an emergency."

"We're not sure who might get the key, then," Royle summarised, before going outside the reception window to where he could reach through and remove the Big Experience key. "Easy once you know where," he suggested. "You just need to make sure Security's not looking."

Ed took the key from him, examining it without saying anything. Next, he extracted a bunch of keys from his pocket, choosing one and holding it up for comparison with the key Royle had just removed. They could all see they were different.

"Do we take it that the one on your ring is a genuine Big Experience key, but you have no idea what that other key is hanging up there on the hook?" Charlie suggested.

"That about does it," the state man admitted.

She was searching her bag now, before holding up a bunch of keys and comparing one with Ed's known Big Experience key. This time the two were identical.

"These were on Quigly's body in Miami Bay last week."

The man seemed genuinely shocked. "Looks like some son of a bitch put one over on us. And we have no idea who or when."

"That's not entirely true, Ed. We can be pretty sure it was before Dan's death. Charlie and I also have an idea who, though this might not be the time to go into that."

Charlie then went to wash up before they left, and Ed turned to Royle.

"You two work well together. Is it just work, then, or does it go further?"

Royle's initial reaction was to suggest Ed mind his own damned business, but he'd quite taken to the older man. "It's work, Ed, we're not a couple," he responded, smiling politely and watching the older man process the information.

"It's just a thought, then, but women like that don't come along too often. Mind someone doesn't beat you to it."

★ ★ ★

Had he been asked, Royle might have suggested he knew his partner well enough by now to have formed a more than vague idea about her family background. Apart from the expensive education, there were the fashionable clothes, top-of-the-range car and Cartier wristwatch. Plus what he had managed to glean from the family photographs. Therefore, he was in little doubt she came from a comfortable background, where standards obviously mattered and where money, or the lack of it, was not a controlling factor.

Nevertheless, he was surprised by his initial view of the Lacey residence. Located in a quiet, tree-lined avenue in one of Tallahassee's more mature suburbs north of the city centre, it obviously dated from before the Civil War, or what was still sometimes referred to thereabouts as the 'War of Northern Aggression'. Back in the UK the property would have been described as an 'extremely desirable and spacious, character period residence'.

Classically constructed of white boarding, a porch, or portico, extended around the outside, overhanging a raised timber deck complete with swing-seat and rocking chairs, above all of which the Stars and Stripes fluttered at the head of a flagpole centrally positioned in a clinically manicured lawn.

It was difficult guessing how many rooms a family home of that size contained. He realised the ground floor would likely comprise the inevitable roomy entrance hall, a more than large kitchen and equally spacious living room. Plus no doubt a somewhat grand dining room and generous study. He also guessed that entry through the welcoming front door, with its ample porch and imposing ground-to-roof pillars, facilitated access to an attention-seeking staircase, which in turn provided access to six or so bedrooms.

As Charlie eased the rental into the driveway he saw that a sizeable annex had been added, attached to one end of the building within a large, well-maintained garden, or what his Americans friends were misleadingly inclined to call 'the yard'. The annex's ground floor comprised a triple garage and workshop, whereas the upper floor provided yet more accommodation.

What we have here, then, he decided, is a larger than normal, extremely comfortable family residence, situated in a mature respectable neighbourhood backing onto open land, and some twenty minutes' drive from the state capital. At a rough estimate he put the property's value at around $2 million.

He was brought back to reality by Charlie reaching into the rear seat for the flowers she had bought earlier. "Come and meet my folks. I suspect you and Papa will get along fine."

Even as she said this the large front door swung inwards and Ma and Pa Lacey emerged onto the porch. Charlie and her mother engaged in the anticipated long embrace, while her father extended a welcoming hand.

"I'm Vern. Good to meet you, Phillip."

Inside, things were much as he had imagined. Charlie steered him towards a comfortable leather sofa and Babs Lacey sat opposite, at which point Vern suggested they needed a drink after their long day. Watching him approach a well-stocked drinks cabinet, Royle got the feeling he had seen this man before. He nodded his head as Vern held up a whisky bottle, employing thumb and forefinger to indicate a small measure.

Charlie had warned him dinner would be in the formal dining room and that guests were expected, the two women soon excusing themselves to attend to the kitchen. And for a short while Vern found himself similarly occupied.

Seizing the opportunity, Royle snatched a quick look around the room. Much in evidence were the obligatory family photographs, including some he was already acquainted with. On the piano, though, were two he had not seen. A silver-framed one of Babs and Vern on their wedding day, plus one of the couple at some official function. Leaning forward to read the caption Royle quickly recoiled, a tingling feeling in the back of his neck. It read 'The Honourable Vernon and Mrs Lacey', followed by the date and location.

Now it all came flooding back. Eleventh Judicial Circuit Court, ten years ago in Miami. The case of Daggart v the People: a week-long appeal hearing following Daggart's earlier conviction for handling endangered species. Royle had been the lead federal witness, and the presiding judge had been none other than the Honourable Justice Lacey. Daggart, the cheeky sod, had appealed on the grounds that he had failed to receive a fair trial. The basis for this allegation being that the lead investigator, i.e. Royle, was not an American citizen and therefore was unfamiliar with both the legislation and criminal procedure.

The court heard not only that Royle was an experienced federal investigator but also a decorated war hero. Justice Lacey dismissed the appeal, commending the prosecution team for bringing the matter before the original court. Royle recalled how the judge had some particularly complimentary things to say about his own part in all of that.

They were both a little older now, but there was no doubting he had the right man. He smiled to himself. Charlie had been playing games with him all along.

However, at this point his thoughts were interrupted by a sudden exodus from the kitchen, Babs suggesting she show them up to their rooms.

Charlie, though, had other ideas. "First Phil must come and see the horses. We'll only be a minute."

With girlish enthusiasm she led him out through the patio doors, across a billiard-table lawn and around well-stocked flower beds in the direction of a row of stables. Royle allowed himself to be introduced to each of the four animals in turn, including an extremely capable looking black colt. He watched her pulling the horse's ears and stroking its velvet-soft nose, unexpectedly finding himself struggling for words. Part of him wanted to confront her regarding her failure to mention her father, aware now that she had deliberately engineered this whole situation. Clearly there was more to Miss Lacey than he yet appreciated. But he also recalled Ed Kimberley's earlier advice.

"You forgot to mention your dad's a federal judge," he heard himself saying.

Her reaction was interesting. "You mean like you forgot to mention you own the ranch, have American citizenship, an American daughter and used to work for the Department?" She did not raise her voice, but her dark eyes pierced him like lasers. "Anyway, why does it matter what my father does? You work with me, not him."

He moved closer, checking they were out of sight of the house. "You're even more beautiful when you're angry." Then, placing an arm around her shoulders, he kissed her, his other hand preventing any escape, not that she appeared at all interested in freeing herself. When their lips did finally separate her eyes momentarily remained closed, an expression of surprise on her normally controlled features.

"Are you trying to tell me something?"

He continued holding her close, enjoying the feel of her body against his. "It's time we faced up to it," he suggested.

"We both know what we want, and we're both adult enough to handle the situation."

She stared back at him, their faces inches apart. "But are we sure it's right?"

"If Whitland wants to terminate my contract, that's fine by me," Royle responded, his lips seeking hers again.

"Not now," she gasped, pulling herself free. "They'll come looking for us." She turned to him as they started back across the lawn. "You must speak to Papa; they've asked Gus Winnings and his wife to join us for dinner, as my former department head."

Grasping her shoulders, he turned her towards him, staring into her face disbelievingly.

"No kidding," she confirmed. "And you have lipstick on your face."

Babs showed her daughter up to the two annex guest rooms whilst the men went to fetch their bags from the car, Royle seizing the moment.

"Charlie thinks you and I should take a beer out onto the porch, Judge. There's something you need to know, before Gus Winnings arrives."

A broad smile lit up the older man's face. "You made the court connection, then."

A little later, out on the rear porch, Royle outlined to Judge Vernon Lacey the main features of their murder investigation, emphasising how and why he believed Gus Winnings might be involved, though he acknowledged there were obvious weaknesses in their case thus far.

The judge listened to what he said, realising, as he of all people should, that as things stood any court might be forgiven for believing that Gus's involvement in Dan Morgan's death was more imaginary than real. However, he also knew what his daughter had told him and his wife about the abilities of her new federal partner. He also recalled the impact Royle's past involvement in the Daggart case had had on the court, and of course on himself as the presiding judge.

"All we can do this evening," the judge suggested once Royle had finished, "is be aware of any potential risk to your investigation." But then he decided to do some exploring, knowing they had time to spare before the guests arrived. "Charlie says you have a doctorate – Harvard, I believe?"

Royle realised she had been discussing him in some detail.

"Plus an interest in comparing American enforcement methods with those in Europe – particularly the UK?"

He hesitated, unsure where this conversation might be heading. "That's certainly one of my interests."

"You must have much the same enforcement systems in the UK, surely?"

Royle realised the judge already knew the answer to his own question. "I guess the difference is in the level of public exposure American agencies get. Which in turn has a lot to do with firearms."

"Word is you're not bad with a gun yourself."

Yet more evidence of her confiding in her parents. "It's a long story—"

"And Charlie warned you might say that."

To Royle's mind there was an air of déjà vu about this conversation, his mind going back to his and Charlie's late-night discussion out at the ranch.

"The armed forces taught me how to handle weapons, and to not hold back if the situation demands it."

"Your being wounded on that mission with Morgan, did that bring you two closer?"

"It's not something I think about," he lied, but then the judge surprised him.

"And it wasn't any old medal they gave you, it was the Navy Cross. For 'An Act of Extraordinary Heroism in Combat'."

This was getting worse. "It's just a piece of metal," Royle suggested lamely.

"A former Marine lieutenant with the Navy Cross and a former federal agent, plus subsequent contracts with twelve world governments. Not to mention a PhD from Harvard and a master's from Cornell. Can't look too bad on your CV."

But then the judge paused. "Presumably you don't know that Doug Whitland and I did law together, here in Tallahassee, a long time ago now."

He was right, Royle did not know. So, Whitland knew of Charlie's background all along. It occurred to him this 'old-boy' connection might have a lot to do with Whitland taking her on, perhaps explaining why he had omitted to mention any past connection with her family.

However, the more he thought about it, the more Royle realised it was not that simple. For example, what might have been his own reaction to being told he was to partner some over-privileged rich girl, all as an apparent favour to her father the judge? Plus of course you could hardly accuse Charlie of being wildly keen on the partnership idea.

"Doug thinks very highly of you," the judge continued, bringing Royle back to the present. "Says you're highly motivated and for all the right reasons."

Not for the first time in this conversation Royle found himself struggling for a response. "I'd need to know in what context Doug said that."

But then the judge squeezed his arm as they both got to their feet. "You look after our daughter."

★ ★ ★

The guests were late, apparently owing to heavy traffic on the freeway, though from Royle's viewpoint this had the benefit of avoiding any pre-dinner small talk. There were four guests.

Gus Winnings and his wife Pat, plus Charlie's former Licensing colleague Abbie Wise and her partner. The maid served starters while the judge tended to the wine. On his side of the table Royle found himself seated next to Babs Lacey, with Abbie on his right and Gus Winnings on the far side of Babs – far enough away for Royle to discuss Gus with Abbie without him overhearing.

He soon realised Abbie liked her wine, and by the time the dessert arrived they were getting along like the proverbial house on fire. Apparently, she had recently been promoted as Gus's secretary and it seemed all was not well in the Licensing office. Nor, for that matter, in the Winnings' household. Gus was spending more and more time in Europe and Southeast Asia. Although not overly sure what he did there, Abbie thought it had something to do with work.

It occurred to Royle there could be very little in the job description of a Florida-based Federal Licensing Officer that required his presence in Southeast Asia. "Does Gus take his wife?" he enquired, and the girl seemed amused by the suggestion.

"Pat likes her home comforts too much, though she sometimes goes to Europe with him."

Not for the first time he refilled Abbie's glass. "Does he have any more visits arranged to Asia?"

"His annual holiday's coming up; he could be going then."

"What about Europe? What does he do over there?"

"I'm not sure, but he buys Pat some really nice jewellery."

He lowered his voice as he leaned towards Abbie, searching her face for the slightest sign of any reaction. "Does the name Toombs mean anything to you?"

"Should it?"

"Probably not. But if you do think of anything then give me a ring."

★ ★ ★

121

Babs Lacey's evening was equally interesting. The more wine Gus Winnings consumed, the more it became apparent he was disenchanted with his position in the Department, eventually revealing he was considering taking early retirement.

"What would you do then?"

He glanced across in the direction of his wife, sitting next to the judge. "I'm considering moving to Asia. I've always fancied living out there."

Babs was surprised to hear this, not so much by the suggestion as by his frankness. "And what does your wife think to that?"

Again, he glanced across the table. "I've not raised it yet, though I'm not expecting she'll be keen on the idea." Then he changed the subject. "Any idea how Royle and that daughter of yours are getting along with finding the people responsible for Dan Morgan's death?"

Babs immediately heard alarm bells ringing. "This is the first time I've met Phillip. Why do you ask about Dan?"

"No particular reason. If they do have any success, then we'll doubtless hear through the normal channels."

★ ★ ★

A far more amiable atmosphere prevailed on the far side of the table. Clearly Pat Winnings did not share her husband's enthusiasm for alcohol, getting as far as her dessert on a single glass of Chablis Grand Cru. Consequently, she and the judge enjoyed a pleasant evening discussing a wide range of subjects, including the apparent virtues of Charlie's new enforcement partner.

"I've not seen Royle for years," she explained. "Gus used to be their department head down in Fort Lauderdale. He and Dan Morgan."

"I didn't know that," the judge lied. "You must have met Dan, then?" He could not be sure, but he thought he detected some hesitation.

"I knew them both; where one went the other was sure to be nearby. Or at least in the early years. Did you know they were in the Marines together?"

The judge persevered with the casual approach. "I heard they got themselves a medal apiece."

There was that hesitation again. "I met Dan a few times after Royle returned to England. Gus and I keep a place down south, and we occasionally bumped into Dan and Sharon."

"I gather Dan and Sharon separated?"

"She found someone else; Dan was really upset."

He could not explain why, but her response left the judge in little doubt that Pat Winnings had seen Dan since he and Sharon separated. "The good news is that Phillip and Charlie are investigating Dan's suspicious death."

Instantly he realised what he had said, though this time there was no doubting it – Pat's reaction was not what he expected.

She put down her glass. "It wasn't an accident, then?"

Evidently Pat Winnings was unaware of something her husband clearly did know, namely that Dan's death was being treated as a possible murder.

"You didn't know that?"

"Gus said it was a hunting accident."

"Perhaps I misunderstood," the judge suggested, realising the damage had already been done. "Maybe it was a hunting accident," but he could see Pat was unconvinced.

Reaching across she took hold of the wine bottle, pouring herself a generous glass.

* * *

Dinner over, Royle helped the judge attend to drinks in the lounge while Babs had the maid serve coffee. As earlier, he made a conscious effort not to become engaged in conversation with Gus Winnings, who in any event appeared somewhat preoccupied. Royle attributed this in part to the amount of wine the Licensing boss had consumed.

Abbie too was quiet, though Royle thought she stood up to the occasion surprisingly well. Perhaps because all involved were working the next day, coffees and the brandy quickly disappeared, and in what seemed like no time Gus and Pat Winnings were preparing to leave. The usual pleasantries were exchanged, the judge and his wife seeing the couple to their car. Seizing the opportunity, Royle went to the lounge window, making a note of the vehicle's make and index number: a recently registered smart red Ferrari. Abbie and her partner stayed only a little longer.

With their guests gone, Charlie yawned and kissed her parents goodnight before heading for the annex stairs.

Royle also thanked his hosts. "I really enjoyed this evening. It was extremely useful; you'll be surprised what Abbie had to say. See you both at breakfast."

★ ★ ★

Up in the annex, four weeks of suppressed sexual anticipation were consummated in a mutual explosion of desire, precipitated by Royle steering Charlie into his bedroom and closing the door with his foot, already feeling her arms around his neck, her lips seeking his in the darkness. He heard the hiss of the zip as the dress slid down her now naked body, relishing the sensual smoothness of her skin, her fingers exploring his body. Grasping her arms he lowered her backwards onto the bed, her eager hands dragging him with her. Struggling for breath now, he felt her warm thighs encircle his body.

★ ★ ★

The judge descended the stairs next morning to find his wife laying the big kitchen table for breakfast.

"It occurred to me in the shower just now," he said, kissing her cheek, "perhaps we shouldn't disturb them yet?"

"Whatever makes you think that?"

"Just that they seem to get along extremely well, if you know what I mean."

She smiled. "If you're referring to the possibility of them sharing a room then that's none of our business."

But before they could develop the conversation, they heard footsteps, and the objects of their discussion entered the kitchen. The judge was the first to mention last night.

"Phillip seemed to get along well with Abbie."

"Yes, I noticed that," Charlie teased.

"Unfortunately, she likes her wine just a touch too much," Royle suggested, reaching for the toast.

Each in turn then outlined the more important elements of the evening's various conversations.

"What we appear to have gained, then," the judge summarised, "is that Gus Winnings is considering taking himself off to the Far East, we know not why, whilst his wife seems unlikely to go with him; in fact, the marriage is in serious trouble." He took a sip from his first coffee of the morning. "There's also a suggestion that Dan Morgan and Pat Winnings were emotionally involved. And unlike her husband, Pat did not know Dan appears to have been murdered."

"I don't suppose Dan was killed *because* he was seeing Pat," Charlie wondered.

The judge was shaking his head. "We're not sure. But that part of your investigation could perhaps prove more complex than you realise."

ELEVEN

AT THE DEPARTMENT'S WASHINGTON HEADQUARTERS THE PAIR TOOK THE lift to the third floor, where they were escorted to a large polished wooden door. It crossed Royle's mind that it was a long time since he had last stood here. He knocked and a male voice said, "Come." Pushing the door open he followed Charlie into the office of Warren Garcia, Federal Head of Enforcement, and sitting at an enormous desk overshadowed by the Union flag was the man himself. He rose and came towards them, the two men shaking hands as if remembering old times.

"Good to see you again, Phillip."

Royle introduced his partner to Garcia, noting that he seemed particularly pleased to meet her.

"I know your father, Charlie, heard a lot about you over the years. I'm pleased you and Phillip are working together on this Dan Morgan business."

Royle found himself beginning to wonder how many more people knew Charlie's father.

"We've fifteen minutes for you two to update me on your case," Garcia explained, "before I'm due over at the White House for the President's weekly briefing."

As requested, then, the two Florida-based special agents outlined the complexities surrounding Dan Morgan's recent mysterious death, including what had occurred since finding his gruesome remains. Whilst the amount of effort they were putting into the smuggling side of their inquiry obviously had Garcia's approval, they got the impression Dan's murder tipped the balance.

"I understand the complexity of the parrot smuggling, but where do we stand with catching those responsible for Dan's murder?"

Royle knew this was neither the time nor the place for avoiding the truth. "We've always been struggling with Dan's death, though we're certain now that it's connected with parrot smuggling. In which case, get inside the smuggling ring and we'll hopefully find our killer."

"That's pretty much how Doug Whitland explained it," Garcia admitted, having heard them through. "He also outlined what you said in support of the expenditure in cost and time. And I agree with you, no money can buy the government the kind of publicity a case like this generates. I also like your point about it all boiling down to the misuse of government permits around the world."

"You approve of our inquiry continuing, then?"

Garcia nodded, but then hesitated. "We're reviewing the Department's resource priorities. The kind of investigation you're into fits our revised thinking. In which case," he continued, addressing himself specifically to Royle, "might you be interested in heading up this new team, here in DC?"

Although surprised by this unexpected turn of events, Royle was aware of its significance. "Obviously I'll give it serious thought, Warren. How much time do I have?"

"It's still early planning, so consider at leisure. Though personally I can see it happening."

However, at this point they were interrupted by Garcia's secretary transferring a call from the White House Chief of Staff's office, in speaker-mode.

"Warren, the President's had to move things around some; any chance you can get across here for our meeting right away?"

"Sure thing. I've got Charlie Lacey and her partner, Phillip Royle, with me. They're just going."

"Great, Warren, see you in a minute. Oh, and tell Charlie be sure and give my regards to her father."

Garcia turned towards them, holding out his hand. "And remember me to your father too, Charlie. Now, if you two don't mind I have to go see the President."

They were the only people in the lift going down.

"I was taking my cue from you," Charlie explained. "Waiting to see if you mentioned Gus Winnings."

"I decided we had too little on him to start making allegations at Washington level."

She leaned across and touched his hand. "Question is, will you take this new job?"

"To be honest I'm not sure. I understand the compliment behind the offer, and I like the sound of it. But if it's primarily a desk job then I'm not interested."

Royle never felt good after long-haul flights and their early-morning exit from London Heathrow's Terminal 3 was no exception. He, though, was back on home ground, whereas Charlie was experiencing her first taste of the world outside of America. Inevitably it incurred a long wait, first at immigration and then for their luggage to be offloaded, enabling Charlie to point out the presence of armed police officers within the airport.

"I thought you Brits kept your firearms hidden away?"

"I promise you'll see no more weapons after we leave the airport."

Royle's so-called London property was situated in a quiet village deep in the Surrey countryside, overlooking the village pub, cricket pitch and Norman church, an hour's drive from central London on a good day. He left Charlie to carry out a brief inspection while he took their bags upstairs. Arriving later with the coffee percolator and cups, Royle suggested she might perhaps like to catch up with some sleep whilst he sorted out a few things in the office, further suggesting they later grab a meal over at the pub.

That evening Royle had a long phone conversation with his German contact, Dieter Schwartz. Like Royle, Dieter worked as a consultant in the wild animal trade, though mainly in Central Europe. He had been doing some checking regarding the Big Experience's Belgian operation.

"They deal in all manner of wildlife, from dangerous large animals down to birds and snakes. They pretty much sell anything that breathes," Dieter confirmed.

"Do they use their own vehicles to and from the airport?"

"My guess is yes. Probably Dusseldorf or Cologne, though Holland's Schiphol may actually be nearer."

Royle noted what Dieter said, aware that these, virtually uncontrolled cross-border movements between EU countries were just one of many issues helping drive the illegal wildlife trade.

Dieter called back later that evening. He had spoken with Dutch customs, who confirmed that livestock shipments from Big Experience Belgium regularly exited Europe via Schiphol Airport, including several bound for Miami.

"And it gets better," Dieter continued. "All Miami-bound consignments went to Big Experience USA, variously shown as deer, buffalo, leopard and, interestingly, tiger. Plus numerous crates listed as live birds."

They were booked to fly out to Australia late the next day but over breakfast Royle had a suggestion for Charlie.

"It occurred to me we're an hour away from a world-class bird-skin collection, including all the birds we expect to bump into during our Australian enquiries. You need to see this."

He made a few telephone calls and by mid-morning they were inside the British Museum's impressive Hertfordshire Bird Room. He first spent a while showing Charlie the range of bird species involved in the collection, before moving to the parrot section. And he was immediately impressed as she pointed out birds they had already encountered, both in Cordero's aviaries and out at the California desert site. Next, he showed her several skins of a stunningly beautiful parrot, small with an unmissable turquoise belly and startlingly crimson shoulders.

"These are paradise parrot skins. Collected where it then occurred in Australia. No one has seen it alive since 1927; it's now officially extinct."

She was silent for quite some time. "It's easy to talk about extinction. But to hold something this beautiful, and know it no longer occurs anywhere on earth... That almost defies understanding."

"There are still occasional claims of it being seen," he admitted. "And bearing in mind Australia's size, we perhaps shouldn't dismiss the possibility."

He worked his way through a further selection of birds but then, conscious that time was slipping by, he opened one final drawer. Roughly the size of the extinct paradise parrot, these had prominent gold-coloured markings.

"This one's important. It's a golden-shouldered parrot and it's endangered. All one thousand remaining wild birds are confined to Australia's Cape York Peninsula. Right where we're heading."

TWELVE

ROYLE HAD WARNED CHARLIE HOW LANDING AT SYDNEY WAS ONE THING, whereas getting out of the airport complex was entirely another matter, this having much to do with how vigilant Australia is when it comes to protecting its borders from unauthorised entry – not just by humans but also animals and plants, one inevitable consequence being long queues at both customs and immigration. Therefore, just as they were entering the crowded customs hall, they were both pleasantly surprised on being approached by a uniformed airport official.

"Phil Royle. Gidday, mate, fancy a cuppa along in the office?"

The source of this timely invitation was a middle-aged man whom Royle introduced as his brother-in-law, Erskine.

Erskine unlocked a door in the wall separating the public and restricted areas. "Come on through."

He led them along a corridor and through a door marked 'Customs Officers Only', where a somewhat imposing lady came forward and introduced herself to Charlie as Erskine's sister, Angie Watts.

"I thought we should have a quick word before letting you two loose in Australia," she explained, giving Royle a welcoming hug. "How long you here for, then?"

Charlie took an instant liking to Angie, a well-built woman who, although clearly used to exercising her authority, nevertheless retained an air of approachability.

"We'll presumably know more about that once we start work on this end of the inquiry," Charlie suggested.

Angie was obviously anxious to be somewhere else. "Anyway, can't stop now, Phil. How about a barbecue at my place this evening, to discuss what brings two US special agents halfway around the world?" And with that she was gone.

"Busy lady," explained Erskine. "Why don't we go and find your luggage, and get your passports stamped?"

Royle spent enough time in Australia to justify keeping an apartment in the fashionable Annandale suburb, overlooking Sydney's inner harbour and just ten minutes from the city centre. The property belonged to his sister Christine, who leased the upper floor to him, the ground floor being rented to a single lady by the name of Madge Broome – Royle's secretary-cum-assistant when he was in Australia, and his house minder when he was not.

Royle explained how it was not by chance he had teamed up with Madge. "She can fix a busted vehicle under true outback conditions, communicate with the most reclusive Aborigines, or find water where it's not rained for years."

They slept until midday before taking the train to the harbour's Circular Quay, where they dined in the shadow of two of Australia's major icons – the Harbour Bridge and the Opera House.

"When we're done here," Royle explained, "I want to show you just one of the many things that make this such an exciting country."

Later, then, in the city's Botanic Gardens, a stone's throw from the harbour, he steered Charlie to where several walkways met. There, in a tall metal cage, stood a tree. And as trees go it was full of interest, with strange feathery branches unlike anything she had seen before.

"It's one of the world's true modern wonders. A biologist recently visited a valley in the Blue Mountains, an hour from the city, where he found a handful of these trees. Until then it was only known from a 200 million-year-old fossil. Unbelievably, these seriously prehistoric trees were hiding themselves away just a hundred kilometres from Sydney."

Charlie said nothing as he paused.

"So, if they can lose a small forest almost within sight of the city's three and a half million inhabitants, how can we possibly be sure there are no paradise parrots left in the thousands of square kilometres of uninhabited outback?"

"Why's it in a cage?"

"Presumably so it can't be stolen. Though enough seedlings have now been cultivated for us all to afford a Wollemi pine for the price of a cheap phone."

Early evening the pair took the train across the Harbour Bridge, heading for Angie's house over on the north side. Royle was obviously familiar with the house's layout, quickly navigating them through to the rear garden, already full of people holding glasses and talking noisily.

He introduced Charlie to his sister Chris.

"What do you think of Australia, Charlie?"

"It's nowhere near as wild as I expected."

Chris laughed. "Drive west an hour or so from here and you're into some serious dry country."

At this point, though, their hostess Angie Watts appeared, dragging Charlie away to meet other guests. But then, catching sight of Royle over by the pool, phone clamped to his ear, she excused herself and went to join him.

"Finish sorting it out and call us back when you're ready," he was saying. "Great news, though."

"What news?"

"That was Mindy. The DEA just arrested Cordero's two

alleged Columbian relatives aboard a yacht entering America via San Diego. They seized a load of parrots and other birds, and guess who else was on board?"

"Cordero?"

"Absolutely. The DEA has already proved some of the birds glow under ultraviolet light."

"Are they searching Cordero's place?"

"Mexican-based US agents are at this very moment helping police turn over his house and all the aviaries, while another crew are at the Columbians' place. Nothing we can do now but wait."

Royle had just finished updating Charlie as Angie reappeared, glass in hand. She pointed them towards a stylish garden house, suggesting they wait inside whilst she fetched a fresh bottle and two more glasses.

The so-called garden house also served as additional guest accommodation, so in comfort the two agents updated Angie on the events of the past few weeks – from the recovery of Dan's remains to what they had subsequently discovered in Miami, California and Mexico. And more importantly, the developing connection with the Australian illegal bird trade.

"What you're suggesting, then," Angie summarised, "is that these people are receiving birds from Australia, but especially parrots. Probably from up north in Queensland. What you're not sure of is how they're doing it?"

Royle shook his head, casting a brief glance in his partner's direction.

"I can probably tell you exactly how they do it. Trapped birds get smuggled out to nearby Indonesia, where they get false captive-bred permits authorising shipment to anywhere in the world. Meanwhile, hatching eggs are somehow hidden in crates used to transport larger animals. What we don't know are the *who, where or when* bits."

Angie remained tight-lipped, except for the occasional sip from her glass.

Royle was aware there was no great revelation in what he was saying. Angie and he both knew that despite all the effort Australia put into safeguarding its wildlife, people still managed to beat the system.

"Most authorities seriously underestimate the extent of the wildlife trade problem," he suggested, "including some who should know better."

Angie still said nothing.

"The truth is, there are some extremely sophisticated scams operating, including the lot Charlie and I are investigating."

Their host leaned across and refilled their glasses. "I can't argue with that. But what makes you think these people are smuggling birds out of Australia?"

"Dan seemed to know a bit; I found a note of his concerning a dealer's wife giving information. He also seemed to think eggs were involved."

Angie paused before responding, long enough for them to wonder whether she still needed persuading. "Bugger it, Phil. If you're right, and I fail to cooperate, then that makes me partly responsible for whatever's going on."

They sensed Royle might have just won the day.

"I'll give you the information, but strictly on the understanding you keep me informed," Angie said, stamping her authority on the deal. "Plus, Australian customs get a share of any credit."

"We wouldn't want it any other way," Charlie confirmed. "We can't get anywhere without your support."

Angie reached behind a cushion and threw Royle an envelope. "Should find everything you need in there. It's for your eyes alone, though, and Charlie's of course."

He started to respond but Angie stopped him. "We both stand to gain. Besides, I'd hate to think I let these bastards get away with it. The dealer's name's Alynski. He's up in Queensland in a part of Australia heaving with birds found nowhere else on earth."

"What about the wife?"

"Still willing to help, last I heard, though she's worried about word getting back to Alynski. What are you aiming to do, catch these people red-handed? In case I have to arrange backup."

"Definitely not, Ang. We need to get at what they're smuggling – birds or eggs – and make them invisibly identifiable. Either that, or the crates they're travelling in."

He could see Angie waiting to respond.

"I know what you're thinking," he continued, "but we'll worry about how we get them marked as and when we have to. We have several interesting gadgets to help with that."

"I'll grant you it all sounds very high-tech, but it lacks any guarantee of success," Angie suggested. "You can't beat catching the bastards in the act."

Royle decided not to take the bait and instead changed subjects. "I'd value your advice on whether we let the local police in on this."

"I think you should, or at least let them know you're about. Now, if we don't quickly get ourselves outside all the food will be gone. Why don't you two use this place tonight?"

Royle was quick to accept the offer of overnight accommodation. "I'm thinking of getting out west into the dry country tomorrow. Something else I extracted from the muddle of Dan's notebook."

★ ★ ★

Royle was in the shower when his mobile rang next morning, so Charlie took Mindy Goldsmith's call and updated him over breakfast.

"They found over four million in US dollars at the Columbians' place."

"What happened at Cordero's aviaries?"

136

"There's only half the number of birds there now, but there's no list yet of what was on board the yacht."

"What about Cordero's breeding records?"

Charlie took time stirring her coffee. "Cordero wrote peoples' names against incubator details in his records. Mindy's matched these to names in his address book and on his phone."

However, what Charlie failed to mention was that she had seized the opportunity to have time alone with his phone, and searched for the mysterious Todd Shepherd, the same man who called him on their way back from Sharon Morgan's apartment. Shepherd was listed in the 'Contacts' folder and there were several recent calls to and from that number.

Royle glanced at his watch. "We need to get away from here and sort ourselves out back at my place."

"Remind me what we're doing today?"

"We're looking for a man Dan went on about in his notes. Trapping cockatoos in the outback before transporting them up north, probably to the dealer Angie just gave us details of."

"And you think we have a chance of finding him?"

"Dan's notes suggest he'll be out there now. If he is, we have every chance of tracking him down."

★ ★ ★

Mid-afternoon saw Royle's Land Cruiser far into outback New South Wales, driving west over the Blue Mountains as far as Broken Hill, close to the South Australia border, then north up the Silver City Highway – mostly just another dirt track – and through Sturt National Park, heading for the gate in the Dog Fence on the Queensland–South Australia border. Dropping down off the Blue Mountains, they had quickly left any so-called 'civilisation' behind, the scenery becoming much dryer, the main visible inhabitants now being kangaroos and numerous unfamiliar birds, including emus and parrots. Lots of parrots.

Unlike other countries Royle had worked in, out here there were no dangerous large animals. No lions or elephants, for example. Nevertheless, a whole new set of potentially serious dangers confronted the unwary traveller, in addition to the obvious ones like vehicle breakdowns or water shortage. Not least amongst these was an impressive collection of poisonous snakes, most of them worth staying well away from.

"Supposedly the world's ten most poisonous snakes occur right here in Australia," he explained. "The basic rule is the same as anywhere: watch where you put your feet."

Nothing in that appeared to worry Charlie – hadn't she grown up in a country where rattlesnakes proliferated? And she said as much.

"I guessed you might think that, but you're missing the point. Some of these snakes are poisonous to an additional degree, plus some are extremely aggressive compared to your average rattler. Get bitten out here and there's little possibility of urgent help, assuming you can actually contact anyone."

Charlie picked up on the communications issue. "Cell phones don't work well in the outback?"

He looked across at her as he drove. "If we relied on mobile phones then we'd be in trouble; we've been out of service most of the afternoon." He indicated the glove compartment. "My satellite phone's in there."

"Anything else I should know, if I hope to stay alive out here?" she responded, leaving him in no doubt she was getting bored with the conversation.

Suspecting he may perhaps have exaggerated the dangers, Royle tried making amends. "Anywhere as wild and remote as the outback has its hazards, the trick is to keep your mind focused. Not a lot different to downtown Miami on a Saturday night."

They were booked overnight in a remote area known as the Corner Country, where the borders of New South Wales, South Australia and Queensland all meet. Other than a small community a couple of hours back they had seen no other habitation for the last five hundred kilometres. All on dirt tracks. They were also the sole overnight customers at The Corner Roadhouse.

Royle crossed to the bar and shook hands with the owner.

"Ready for a cold beer?" the man queried.

Royle confirmed their need for cold drinks, then, formalities exhausted, he and Charlie unloaded their bags, ordered meals and occupied a table in the bar. Spreading his map, Royle ran his finger along what was shown as a driveable track, west from where they were, a hundred and fifty kilometres into South Australia, where it joined the main Strzelecki Track.

"Turn south there," he explained, indicating the Strzelecki junction, "and it's four hundred kilometres to the next occupied building. So, if you still haven't got the point, *this is a big country.*"

He drew a circle around a section of the Strzelecki Track some forty kilometres south of the junction. "We're looking for our man around there."

"How will we know him?"

"He's probably in a small truck with a big green water tank. Except the tank's been adapted to hold live birds."

"He got a name?"

"Mickey Bird, appropriately enough. Has convictions for bird trapping, plus a couple of serious firearms matters."

"Sounds like a bit of a headcase."

He nodded his agreement. "The standout parrot around here is the large pink cockatoo. I'm guessing that's what Mickey's after." He saw her studying the map.

"Okay, then, so here's my question. Won't we have our work cut out looking for one man in all this desert country?"

"It's nowhere near as bad as it seems," he rationalised. "Like us, this guy needs his vehicle, and that restricts him to the few drivable dead-end side tracks. There are a handful of abandoned buildings up those tracks and my money's on him using one of those."

Next morning involved an early departure from The Corner Roadhouse, though not before they had refuelled; Royle had an unwritten rule where the outback was concerned: if you see a petrol garage, you fill up.

They had a lot to accomplish and Royle was keen to get some kilometres behind them before the worst of the midday sun. He took the wheel, aware of the notoriously testing nature of the track up ahead: deep soft sand, dust-filled wombat holes and frequent rocks, plus numerous sand dunes to cross. Charlie entertained herself watching the scenery, beginning to appreciate what attracted Royle to the outback. After all, wasn't this a prime contender for the world's number one away-from-it-all experience? Almost no human habitation for thousands of square kilometres, and with some of the most exhilarating scenery imaginable. Plus of course a crowd of animals and plants found nowhere else on the planet.

Given the near absence of other traffic Royle could afford to take in some of these delights for himself as he drove. So, for the second successive morning it was Charlie who took a call for him, this time on the satellite phone.

It was Paula. "Charlie, I need to speak with Phil."

Charlie explained he was driving, so could she help?

"Doug's in hospital with a rattlesnake bite. Are you sure he's too busy?"

"Whitland's been bitten by a snake," she explained, covering the phone with her hand. "Paula's in a state."

Without a word he pulled the vehicle over to the edge of the track and took the phone. "What's Doug been up to?"

"You need to be careful, Phil. He checked Dan's apartment – someone put a snake in the mailbox."

"He say anything?"

"He said it was too much of a coincidence. That whoever they were, they had to be after you."

Royle was trying to imagine all possible implications arising from this latest development. "Give me the emergency number for Warren Garcia in Washington."

Paula read out the number while Royle scribbled on his hand.

"I'll make sure Winnings is not sent to cover for Whitland," he explained, beginning to realise he had been wrong not mentioning the suspected Winnings connection in Washington.

Paula sounded better already. "Be careful. Both of you."

Royle made the all-important Washington call and then rang Paula back, confirming that a temporary department head would be arriving. But not Gus Winnings.

"Just another day at the office?" Charlie asked as he switched off the phone.

Royle checked his watch and started the engine. "What do we make of Whitland's predicament?"

"What we should ask ourselves is not just where Winnings fits into this, but why? Is he protecting some personal interest?"

He did not respond immediately, staring instead at the distant horizon. "There's probably no easy explanation. But if I'm right about Winnings being involved, then why not assume he did this snake thing to take charge of the Department. And, therefore, of this whole investigation."

What really concerned him, though, was that despite all their running around, they still had no firm idea who might be responsible for Dan's death. Or the subsequent threats to their own safety. Equally frustrating was the growing feeling, tucked away at the back of his mind, that all along they were failing to spot something crucially important.

Royle pushed on now and they soon reached the Strzelecki junction, where he turned south as he had said they would.

Charlie continued to voice her doubts of them finding one reclusive bird trapper in all this uninhabited desert. Her partner, though, seemed full of confidence as he passed her the map.

"See for yourself. There just aren't any side tracks, or none going anywhere far. Most go to water boreholes and that's where the main concentrations of birds will be, around any standing water."

Charlie seemed unconvinced still.

"Mickey's difficulty is that the boreholes are mostly close enough to the main track for his trapping activities to be seen."

"So why doesn't he get caught?"

"Even if someone does catch him at it, what can they do? The nearest police are several hundred kilometres away."

He pulled the vehicle over and stopped.

"Some years back I was driving through here and stopped at that borehole," he indicated a point on the map some twenty kilometres further south. "The place was heaving with cockatoos and parked there was a vehicle matching the description of Mickey Bird's. I knew immediately what he was up to, but he roared off up the main track."

He paused for a sip from his water bottle.

"On the ground was a cockatoo with a broken wing, fresh blood on its snowy-white feathers. Mickey had somehow been using it to trap others. I had no satellite phone on that occasion."

Ten minutes further south they reached one of several side tracks shown on the map and could see fresh tyre marks disappearing along it! The map also showed an abandoned building two hundred or so metres further in.

"We need to see what's going on," he suggested, reversing the vehicle out of sight into the track-side scrub.

Reaching beneath the seat he extracted a pair of hand radios, passing one to Charlie and slipping the other into his shirt pocket. They then headed in the direction of the mystery building, Royle tucking the Browning into his belt and pulling on his rucksack. It took just minutes to top a large sand dune and get their first view of the dilapidated building, now only metres away. Even from there they could hear what they both recognised as the sound of parrots, coming from the direction of the building.

It very much looked like they had found their man. The problem now, though, was that they couldn't tell from there whether Mickey's vehicle was parked behind the building, or if he was away somewhere.

"I need you to stay here and keep watch," he explained. "Call me if he turns off the main track up towards here."

"What are you going to do?"

"I'm going to try making some of those birds identifiable."

He had already decided on an approach from the rear, mainly because there were no windows overlooking that direction. Reaching the building he cautiously moved around to the front, confirming there was no parked vehicle. Rusty old wire netting had been stretched across the two downstairs window openings, and glancing through each in turn he could see mostly the commoner white cockatoos, with fewer of the larger and more valuable pink ones, the latter easily identifiable by their flashy pink and yellow crests.

He checked with Charlie there was nothing moving out on the main track, before producing a small box containing a tube of superglue and what looked a lot like medicinal tablets. They were in fact a mixture of transponders and satellite micro-cards – the first normally injected under the skin of birds or other animals to identify them if lost or stolen, the second recording wherever in the world the creature had been.

Quickly he caught twenty pink cockatoos, gluing each of the two devices out of sight beneath each bird's feathers. Then, still moving quickly, he checked upstairs where it was obvious their man was staying, taking some photographs.

The timing of Royle's activities seemed perfect, for no sooner had he returned downstairs than he heard Charlie warn of an approaching vehicle.

"Where?"

Her response was equally brief. "Up the side track towards you, now."

Quickly he exited the building, moving around to the rear. He heard the approaching engine stop, followed by the distinctive sound of stairs being climbed. Cautiously he sneaked around the end of the building and photographed the vehicle – the same he had seen a couple of years back. He also reached behind the adapted water tank, seeking somewhere to attach the magnetic tracking device.

Their mission now accomplished, the pair retraced their steps to the hidden Land Cruiser, where Charlie noticed the attention Royle's hands had received from the cockatoos, though only some of the bites had drawn blood.

"We need to get away from here," he urged. "Which direction did our man appear from?"

"From the south, presumably where you disturbed him last time."

Royle needed to update his notebook with details of the tracking devices he had applied to the birds. He settled back to attend to this, leaving Charlie to start heading the vehicle in the direction of first the Corner Country and then Sydney. He also made two satellite calls, the first to his Australian assistant, Madge Broome, who was already up in Queensland in his other vehicle.

"I reached Cairns mid-morning," she explained. "I've not had time yet to look at Alynski's place, though I talked to his wife. She told me where to find a young Aboriginal lad who until recently did most of Alynski's trapping."

"Did she mention him collecting eggs?"

"She did, mate, yeah. Mostly parrot eggs."

His second call was to Miami, and he was relieved to hear Whitland's snake bite had not been as serious as expected. He'd still had on his leather driving gloves and so only received part of the poison. Royle also knew it would take an extremely determined doctor to keep Whitland in hospital once he felt able to return to work.

THIRTEEN

MID-AFTERNOON, THE DAY FOLLOWING THEIR CLOSE ENCOUNTER WITH Mickey Bird out on the Strzelecki Track, the pair buckled up in preparation for landing. Although no stranger to Cairns, Royle never tired of the spectacular views as the aircraft made its final approach, with wall-to-wall rainforest dominating the landward aspect, and breathtaking sea views from the other window. Also noticeable were the number of international airlines using the airport, from seemingly all corners of the world. It occurred to him that any airport handling that diversity of international traffic must surely qualify as a target for smugglers. Of one kind or another.

Madge Broome met them in the arrivals hall and Royle introduced the two women, interested to see how they got along together. Typically, Charlie had travelled up from Sydney in something 'cool and comfortable', whereas with Madge you pretty much got what you saw. And away from the office what you normally saw was Madge dressed for outback Australia; she would be the first to admit she was not strong on 'dressing up'.

Their immediate objective was to get themselves away from the airport complex, Madge grasping Charlie's holdall and throwing it over her shoulder before coming to a halt next to Royle's *other* Land Cruiser. Unlike the newer model he and Charlie had used earlier in the week, Royle reserved this one for the really long trips that seemed to come around quite often in Australia.

Madge opened the rear door, shuffling things around to make room for their luggage.

Charlie indicated the vehicle's contents. "What's all that?"

Royle looked at Madge, who shrugged her shoulders in response.

"This and that. Tents, water, fuel, tucker. Start charging around the outback and you never know what you might need, until you discover it's not in the bloody vehicle."

"Which reminds me," interrupted Royle, "there should be a rifle in there somewhere." They could see Madge nodding.

"Want to see where we're staying?" Madge queried.

Royle motioned Charlie towards the front passenger seat and, taking her cue, Madge fired up the engine, negotiated the exit road and turned south onto the Captain Cook Highway, before immediately turning left along Cairns Esplanade. As she did so Royle leaned forward, tapping Madge on the shoulder and asking her to pull over. His office mobile was ringing so he took a walk under the palm trees.

Watching him return a few minutes later, both women could see he was troubled.

"Whitland's not good. The snake bite aggravated a heart condition he failed to tell anyone about."

Charlie gave his hand a squeeze as he climbed back into the vehicle, and they continued along the esplanade, Madge drawing their attention to the tourist boats returning from a day out on the Barrier Reef.

At the motel they left Madge to sort out the luggage, whilst the pair of them drove along to a police meeting Angie Watts had arranged. Briefly they explained how they were pursuing the possibility of wildlife being smuggled out of Queensland. It was obvious their hosts were not taken with the idea of American federal agents putting themselves about on their patch without any police involvement.

"With any luck," Royle suggested, "you'll never know we're here."

★ ★ ★

Madge had reserved a table for eight o'clock and, after they were settled and had ordered, Royle asked what she had been up to since she'd arrived in Cairns.

"I went to see the young native guy who did most of Alynski's trapping and nest finding. The one his wife mentioned."

"Did he say why he no longer works for Alynski?"

"Seemed a bit vague on that. Lives with a woman on the edge of town here."

"Did you get a look at Alynski's place?"

"I gave it a quick go. Hour and a half north of here, old sheep station beside the Central Highway. It needs care but we can probably see what's going on from a nearby hill."

"Where do you suggest we start?"

"I'd try Alynski's place first. Get an idea of the layout before you speak with his wife and the Aboriginal fella. His name's Mandu, by the way, Mandu Green."

This time it was Charlie's turn to take a call so, excusing herself, she disappeared from the table. Royle watched her, phone to her ear, pacing up and down outside the restaurant, until Madge interrupted his thoughts.

"She's a good-looking woman. You kept that quiet, mate."

He directed his attention back to Madge, surprised by her frankness. "It all happened rather quickly; it's not something we planned." Then he followed that with a question, aware Madge was inclined to speak her mind. "What do you think, from the little you've seen?"

She considered for a moment. "Let's face it, Phillip, any woman who works with you all day but still wants to spend her nights with you, she can't be all bad."

148

He decided not to respond and was about to enquire further regarding the Mandu character when Charlie reappeared.

"Mindy Goldsmith, updating us on California," she explained. "She's got the paperwork from Cordero's place, thinks it's powerful stuff. She'll get back on that."

"Do they have Cordero and the other two locked up still?"

Charlie was frowning. "Good and bad news there. The two Columbians are being held still, but the DA let Cordero walk. He's probably already back in Mexico."

"We kind of guessed that might happen," he sighed. "Though if Mindy did as we asked then any birds not seized should have been fitted with tracking devices. Small satellite tags," he added, noticing Madge's questioning expression. "We'll look at that later."

At this point the discussion was curtailed by Charlie suggesting she and Royle take an evening walk along the esplanade, an offer he accepted without hesitation, leaving Madge to sort out the bill.

Madge navigated next morning as Royle coaxed the vehicle along rainforest tracks to a point overlooking the sheep station. The whole of Alynski's operation was now laid out below them, commencing where the entrance driveway left the main highway. The most notable features were a single-storey main building and five or six variously sized outbuildings, including two with tin roofs and no windows, plus two more looking a lot like wire-netted aviaries. Following two hours of patient observation there seemed to be just two people involved, with most activity centred around the outbuildings.

With the help of Royle's field glasses they could make out one heavily bearded male, presumably Alynski, plus a single Aboriginal male. Royle had imagined Alynski's set-up would be sited in open country, with little protection for any 'uninvited' approach. The reality, though, was far more encouraging, with dense forest crowding in on the complex at both the sides and the rear.

"I need to get up-close and personal with whatever's going on down there at some point soon," Royle suggested. "Meanwhile, though, I suggest we leave this and go catch a word with Mrs Alynski."

Madge commenced stowing their things back into the vehicle, until Charlie stopped her as she was about to close the door.

"Let's have a look at that rifle."

Madge moved the vehicle's contents around again before eventually coming up with a rifle case, Charlie laying it on the tailgate and extracting the weapon. Complete with laser sights, the Benelli semi-automatic was clearly designed for long-distance work. As previously out at the ranch, she first checked the gun was not loaded before running a hand over the weapon, raising it to her shoulder to test the fit.

"This feels pretty useful," she admitted to Royle. "What does it hold?"

"Four rounds, but that's usually enough to get the job done."

The disaffected Mrs Alynski now resided in popular and expensive Port Douglas, an hour north up the coast road from Cairns. Madge directed them to a corner bungalow on a newish development out on the edge of town, with views over the adjoining golf course. Mrs A opened the door wearing a skimpy pair of shorts and an equally revealing top. Madge attended to the introductions, and Royle was intrigued to see that the woman exactly fitted the picture he already had of her. Early forties and undoubtedly attractive, with an outgoing personality and a figure suggesting she worked out a lot; it seemed obvious to him why Madge and Mrs A got along so well.

"Just call me Dot," the woman said in response to his question, sticking her head in the tall fridge and emerging with four beers. Slamming the door closed with her foot she suggested they go outside, where a compact lawn was separated from the golf course by a water-filled ditch.

"I guess you want to talk about that bastard husband of mine?" she suggested, leaving no room for doubt what she thought of him.

They had agreed to let Madge kick off the questioning. "We're interested in what he's up to right now. Have you seen him since we last spoke?"

Dot shook her head. "I try staying away from the old wombat, but I can tell you what he's doing. Same as he does every year around this time, building up his stock of birds ready to ship them out and get his money. He'll be up in New Guinea making arrangements."

"Do all the birds go to the same place?" Royle enquired.

The woman appeared to study him. "Madge said you're the one to watch. Said you have the answers to questions before you ask them. Where do you think they go?"

He was beginning to appreciate what they were dealing with here. "Well, I think we're dealing with two separate issues. Live birds, and hatching eggs. Would you agree?"

"Go on."

"The birds perhaps go out at night, you say to New Guinea. Probably flown out; either that or by boat?"

"You're on the right track, mate. I suppose you want to know who gets the birds out of the country?"

He considered her question, sensing they might be near the limit of how much Dot was prepared to say. "That could be helpful, though perhaps not essential. But where they go from or better still when, would be really useful."

Then to take the woman's mind off any thoughts of how much she was prepared to say, he tried changing the subject. "I'm guessing the eggs go out concealed with other animals."

She smiled. "It's easy seeing why they sent you. Anyway, how come a pommy bugger's working for the American government?"

Charlie laughed. "Don't go there, it's a long story."

"You're spot on though," Dot continued. "The eggs go out in specially adapted crates. Direct to Europe or North America, any day now."

"This young Mandu, can we trust him?"

"Absolutely, mate. He's a ripper."

"Would it help if we made it worth his while?"

It occurred to Charlie her partner could be sticking his neck out here. But regardless of whether Royle was going farther than authorised, the possibility of financial reward had obviously grabbed Dot's attention.

"I can't say," she responded. "But it might make a difference to what I know. How much are we talking about?"

Royle was conscious of his partner's eyes boring into him from across the patio. "Tell you what let Charlie and me pop inside and talk it over."

Inside, his partner sought clarification on what payments Whitland had authorised, forcing Royle to admit there was no such understanding. He explained that up until when he had last worked for the Department there had always been a small fund to cover such eventualities. It was this he had relied upon during their meeting with Zip McGee. He nevertheless took the opportunity to give Angie Watts a call and was relieved to learn there might also be money available within her budget – though she urged discretion.

Back outside Royle let his partner handle the negotiations.

"The good news, Dot, is that we can offer you something. Though we may need to leave the amount to whatever the people in charge think is appropriate. How does that sound?"

Dot seemed happy with the arrangement, aware that she might need to balance her interest in any cash reward with an even greater desire to get back at her husband. Either way she felt motivated enough to fetch more beers.

"Guess I'll have to trust you on that. He has a place in New Guinea where he sends the birds; from there they cross into Papua on the west side of the island, in Indonesia. There'll be papers saying they were captive-bred."

Good as all this was, there were things Royle needed to know still, while Dot was feeling talkative. "Has your husband ever been in court?"

She slowly nodded her head. "Couple of times, once here in Queensland. He was bloody furious; it meant he had a criminal record and that affected his chances of being granted export permits."

This was precisely the direction in which Royle had been thinking.

"But it didn't stop him," she continued. "He just created a false identity and got another address to use on his licence applications."

Royle hesitated, deciding whether or not to ask. "Care to say what his alias is?"

"No worries on that. Toombs, calls himself Lincoln Toombs."

His eyes automatically met Charlie's, though he still had one other matter to try and resolve. "Knowing when any shipments might be going out would be useful. Any thoughts on how we crack that one?"

Dot took a long drink from her bottle, considering her response. "Couple of things. If the aviaries are empty, then the birds are either packed to go or they've already gone. He ships the eggs in crates used for exporting sheep."

Charlie was driving as they left Port Douglas.

"There's just one thing wrong with all that," she suggested as they re-joined the coast road. "If Alynski's up in New Guinea, then who were we watching out at the sheep station this morning?"

"I've been thinking the same thing," admitted Royle. "Perhaps we should try grabbing a word with this Mandu feller on our way back."

Mandu Green's house was situated in the river swamplands on the northern edge of Cairns, in stark contrast to Dot Alynski's smart new Port Douglas development.

Madge had warned them the yard seemed over-populated with small children and dogs, neither particularly enthusiastic about strange company. But they were quickly rescued by an attractive dark-skinned young woman who descended from the veranda and introduced herself as Mandu's partner

"I'm guessing you've come to see Mandu," she said, calling his name.

Moments later the door opened, and a tall young Aboriginal man emerged from the dark interior. Royle was immediately impressed, experience having taught him to anticipate a withdrawn, unenthusiastic individual, dragged down by social distrust. Mandu Green, though, could hardly have been more different. An alert, upright young man who, as they could see from his broad smile, enjoyed life to the full.

Mandu shook hands all round. "You guys fancy a beer?"

Inside in the cool they spread themselves on a collection of old but clean furniture and again Madge started the conversation. "You said your family are from southern Queensland, so what brought you up north?"

"Easy, I heard Alynski was looking for people to find birds' nests."

Mandu's partner handed around the beers before settling herself on the floor beside him.

"Dot says you and Alynski fell out. Any reason?"

"It wasn't like that. Alynski's been up in New Guinea for weeks. The new fella doesn't know what he's doing. When I suggested he was treating the trapped birds badly he told me where I could go."

"What made you think he doesn't know what he's doing?"

"Way he does things, mate. He obviously never cared for large numbers of birds; too many were dying."

"The other guy, the one who still works there. You two still mates?"

"Yeah, good mates. Why?"

"Just something that might help. Don't worry about it."

Madge had been waiting for one of the other two to ask the obvious question. "What's this new man's name?"

"Sylvester Reed. He works for the people who buy the birds."

"This Reed and your old workmate, they ever away at the same time?" Royle wondered.

"My mate's mostly only there during the day. But if you're asking is Reed ever away during the evening, then yes, sometimes."

"Then I could get a look around?"

"You could, yeah. Except for the dogs."

It occurred to all three that no one had mentioned dogs before.

"We didn't see any dogs," Madge volunteered.

"They only let the dogs out when no one's around."

Royle looked thoughtful. "How many dogs?"

"Just two, but bloody big ones."

Royle glanced at Charlie for confirmation as he addressed Mandu. "Could you come with us tomorrow, while we look the place over again? Tell us what goes on where?"

It was clear from the grin that Mandu was agreeable. "No worries."

However, as the evening was already closing in they decided to cut the visit short and head for their motel.

Charlie and Royle showered and changed before meeting up with Madge and walking the couple of blocks to the

155

restaurant. On the way he called the hospital holding Doug Whitland. Asking to be put through to the ward, he waited several minutes before a nurse informed him that Whitland was still not well. It did not surprise him; a snake bite and a heart problem did not sound like a good combination.

Charlie drove again the next morning, back up the rainforest track to yesterday's position overlooking the sheep station, this time with the addition of Mandu. Royle drew a rough plan of the various buildings stretched out below them, getting the young Aborigine to put names and uses to each in turn.

Apparently, the single-storey house-cum-office was quite basic and Reed was living in just one room. The two windowless tin-roofed buildings were used to hold smaller parrots in cages; that way these still 'wild' birds were less able to throw themselves about and risk injury. Even without Mandu's assistance they could see that the two wire-covered aviaries they had identified yesterday now held numerous large white birds. Presumably cockatoos. Neither Royle nor his two colleagues could recall seeing birds in there the previous day.

Parked in front of the house were two vehicles: a long-wheelbase four-by-four and a large white windowless van. Mandu also pointed out the location of a low perimeter fence along the forest edge, plus a small building housing the guard dogs.

"Is there a garage?" Royle wanted to know.

"There is, yeah. That's where they build the shipping crates."

"Does your mate drive?"

Mandu shook his head, his black curls fanning out in all directions. "Both vehicles belong to the station; my mate gets lifts to work from any passing traffic."

Next, Royle went to their own vehicle, before re-emerging with his laptop, his suspicions aroused by the presence of new birds in the aviaries. He started up the computer and a series of data files appeared on the screen.

"Something interesting?" Charlie queried.

"It's the satellite data from the tracker I put on Mickey Bird's truck back out on the Strzelecki Track."

Next, he studied the road map, running his finger across and then up the sheet, until it came to rest roughly at the point where they now stood. He explained to Mandu how satellites had been relaying the location of Mickey's truck ever since he attached the tracking device. From early morning two days ago the line of arrows on Royle's screen headed away from the Strzelecki Track, across the state border into Queensland, until they arrived late the previous evening below where they were standing.

Royle indicated the screen again. "You can see he's already on his way back home, doubtless with a huge bundle of cash in his pocket."

"You really think cash?"

"In this business it's cash up front, Charlie. No cheques, no receipts and certainly no questions."

Next, he opened a screen showing the locations of just one of the pink cockatoos he had attached a tracker to in Mickey's abandoned building. They saw that it followed an identical route to the truck, though unlike the truck it remained below them still. He closed the computer and stowed it away again, at the same time removing four cold beers from the esky. Then, after checking there were no ants, he sat himself down against a forest tree.

"Let's see if we agree where we're going with this," he suggested. "Any thoughts, Charlie?"

"If we believe Dot Alynski, then our man Reed down there is collecting wild-caught birds ready to ship them out to New Guinea. Which fits what we're seeing. We also know that the longer he keeps the birds the more likely it is that some will die, and that costs him money."

157

"So?" Royle prompted.

"You need to get in there and look around."

He looked across at Madge. "Anything we're missing here?"

Ever the practical one, Madge suggested that the sooner they stopped talking and got on with the job then so much the better.

"In which case we only have one option," he suggested. "We sit here until Reed disappears somewhere, and then I get myself in there."

He asked where Reed might normally go and Mandu pointed north up the highway.

"There's a gas station half an hour's drive that way. He might need fuel, plus they do food and booze. And he'll need cigarettes." Then he indicated the road south. "There are some shops about an hour that way."

Royle let out a sigh of resignation. "Well, I guess that settles it; we wait here patiently until Reed decides to go somewhere. We'll take it in turns; Charlie and me for the first hour while Madge and Mandu get some rest."

He then set about sorting through the various tracking devices and other communication gadgets they had brought with them all the way from Florida, putting into his rucksack everything he might need in the event that he managed to get inside the sheep station.

FOURTEEN

ROYLE WAS STRETCHED OUT IN THE SHADE OF THE VEHICLE, ONLY HALF awake and with Charlie's head on his stomach, when he felt a boot nudging his ribs. He looked up to see Madge standing over them.

"Reed came out a few minutes ago and put something into the four-by-four. Mandu's mate left a couple of hours ago."

As he got to his feet Royle noted the sun was already disappearing over the trees beyond the buildings. He crossed to where Mandu was watching through the field glasses, seeing the puff of diesel smoke as the vehicle began moving towards the road. The question now of course was which way would Reed turn – north up the highway for perhaps an hour, or south for hopefully longer? There was a moment's suspense as Reed stopped to attend to the rear doors, but he was soon moving again, and turning north.

"Okay, so we've got an hour," Royle confirmed. "Charlie will stay up here with a radio and keep a check on what's happening, while Mandu and I go in with the equipment. Madge will drop us off near the driveway entrance."

He next did a quick recheck of the rucksack's contents before handing a radio to each of the two women. Then finally he reached under the driver's seat, extracting the Browning and checking it was loaded.

"Let's go," he instructed. "After you drop us, Madge, back the vehicle into the scrub a kilometre or so to the north and give me a call when Reed comes past." He looked around at his small team. "Anyone see a fault in any of that?" Hearing no response, he placed a hand on Mandu's shoulder. "Time to see if the dogs remember you."

A single vehicle passed in the opposite direction as Madge drove north up the highway towards the sheep station entrance. In seconds Royle and Mandu were out of the vehicle, quickly disappearing into the trees surrounding the buildings. Royle's immediate concern was whether the dogs were free, and if so then how to handle that little problem. He had considered using a drugged bait, but realised Reed might guess something was wrong if he returned to find both dogs asleep. Or even dead. Clearly, though, he was not the only one giving this some consideration.

"It would be best, boss, if you let me deal with the dogs," Mandu suggested quietly. "They should know me, but they might not like you. I'll try getting them back into the shed."

Even here inside the forest in the fading light Royle could see the grinning teeth. He was also interested in his apparent elevation to 'boss' status.

"Give me a whistle once the problem's sorted," he instructed, though even as he spoke he had already spotted the plan's potential weakness: someone still had to let the dogs out again once they were done here.

As so often happens, all Royle's concerns came to nothing. Mandu disappeared for a couple of minutes while Royle stood motionless in the quiet of the trees, until he heard a low whistle up ahead. Moving forward he discovered Mandu grinning from ear-to-ear and pointing to a place in the perimeter fence where he could easily step over.

"Dogs shut away and enjoying early dinner, mate. Food's in a bin outside the door. I only gave them a little so they don't leave any evidence."

Royle realised the light was disappearing fast. He also knew they needed to work quickly and efficiently if they were to accomplish everything he had planned. Logically he had three, possibly four, tasks to perform. Firstly, he needed to check whether any cockatoos in the aviaries were the same ones he had marked down on the Strzelecki Track. Secondly, he needed to find and mark any birds trapped elsewhere; and thirdly get any transport containers fitted with tracking devices. His fourth objective, if time allowed, was to see whether there were any hatching eggs on the premises, and if so then hopefully also get them marked.

The first of these objectives was quickly achieved, as he went through the two aviaries in turn, catching a selection of cockatoos. The number of marked birds seemed to match his recollection of what had occurred a few days before. Next, Mandu led Royle to the two windowless tin-roofed sheds, and on the way heard something interesting. Sheep.

"Where are the sheep?"

Mandu indicated the far side of the house. "Sounds like they're in the garden. If he already has the sheep then he should move the eggs soon."

Unlike the cockatoos he had just checked, the parrots in the two sheds were smaller and in cages, making any handling simpler and quicker. Amongst them were some of the endangered golden-shouldered parrots he had shown Charlie the skins of back at the British Museum. Mandu handed Royle the tracking devices as he asked for them, and in what seemed no time they had marked what he thought were enough birds. Which just left the shipping containers to be found and dealt with.

The dogs barked momentarily as they passed the kennel, whereas inside the garage it had the feel of a professional workshop. In the centre stood a newly completed bird-shipping container, roughly three metres by two and about two metres high, designed to take five slide-in cage drawers. Royle did a quick calculation, deciding each drawer could take up to fifty cockatoos, meaning this one container could transport two hundred and fifty medium-sized birds. Two more identical containers at the rear of the workshop suggested a total smuggling capacity of seven hundred and fifty parrots, with a minimum European street value of around £375,000. However, once allowance was made for the rarity of birds like the golden-shouldered parrots, the possible value went off the scale.

Royle's next challenge was to fit at least one of these crates with a tracking device; and because the trackers communicate with satellites it was best they not be obscured. Ideally, they needed to go somewhere on top. But faced with three crates how could he know which would be on top, assuming they could be stacked? Logic then suggested attaching a device to each of the crates.

Fitting trackers to anything made of timber usually took seconds, but unfortunately these crates were aluminium. He allowed himself a moment to consider the matter, briefly inspecting the garage workbench, aware he and Charlie had come too far for them to fail now. Grabbing a convenient battery-operated drill and a box of self-tapping screws he attacked the crates, fitting a device to the underside of each of the three upper frames.

Even before he finished this Royle had noticed what looked like a fourth container, similar to the others but obviously designed to hold larger animals, like sheep. Examining the crate closely he saw that the base had been modified to take four portable egg incubator trays and their batteries, so this too he fitted with a transmitter.

It was now dark, so he felt confident of noticing the lights on any approaching vehicle. He shone his headtorch at Mandu.

"Where did Alynski put the parrot eggs you collected?"

The lad pointed over Royle's shoulder. "Inside the house, in large..." he paused, struggling for the word he needed.

"Incubators?"

"Yeah, mate, incubators. Lots of them."

"Will the house be locked?"

"Not sure there is a lock."

Royle hesitated, aware that entering the house substantially increased the risk factor. The driveway came right past the only entrance door. If Reed came up the adjacent main highway while Royle was still inside, he'd have just seconds to get out of the door and over the fence into the forest. Plus the dogs would remain locked away. Yes, it was a risk, but hopefully one they could manage.

Taking out his radio he called the two women. "Time to concentrate. I'm going inside the house. I need as much warning as possible of Reed's approach, well before he turns down the driveway."

Both women acknowledged his message, though he had not forgotten the dog problem.

"I want you to stay by the kennel," he instructed Mandu. "If I get a call from the girls I'll be straight out and into the forest. I'll give you a shout to release the dogs, then you get yourself back in there," he pointed to the trees, "and find me."

Inside, the place was a mess. Clothes were strewn around, and it smelt of stale food, cigarette ends and neglect. Royle made his way through to what was clearly the incubator room, aware that this was the furthest point from the only exit door. The good news was that the six large incubators were crammed full of eggs, which as expected were white and round, which he knew meant parrot eggs. But because the incubators were working, he also knew the biological clock must be ticking. These eggs were going to hatch in no more than twenty-five to thirty days. However, not all eggs would have been laid at the same time, so he might reasonably expect some to start hatching sooner. Whichever way you looked at it, any arrangements to transport these eggs to the other side of the world must surely already be in place.

Quickly he used a security pen to invisibly mark egg after egg with his initials and the date. Methodically working his way through the incubators, he had marked over a hundred eggs when he heard Madge on the radio.

"Shit. Royle, you there?"

He extracted the phone. "What's up?"

"Sorry, dropped my phone under the driver's seat. Our man just passed me, going like hell."

He realised Madge may have just put him under pressure, though having taken the precaution of wearing his rucksack as he worked, all he needed to do was turn off his headlamp, close the door behind him and step over the fence into the trees, giving Mandu a shout as he did so. Literally as he lifted his remaining leg over the wire and into the forest the vehicle's lights swung in an arc, away from the road and up the driveway where he had just been standing. He stepped back into the protective darkness of the trees as he listened for Mandu's approach.

Royle slipped away from the breakfast table the next morning while he arranged for reception to post an urgent small package for him. The day's priorities included him and Charlie catching up with any text, telephone or email messages. He twice tried ringing Paula Howath and had been forced to leave a message. He was pouring himself another coffee when she finally called back. With the phone to his ear and the mug in his other hand he walked across the road to the water's edge, where he talked for some time.

"Whitland's still not good," he announced, re-joining his companions.

Charlie looked at him, questioningly. "Is that it?"

"That's it," he responded.

Then his phone rang again, and he spent several minutes sitting next to Charlie and chatting to Angie Watts. She heard him discussing the likely timing of events in Cairns, also pointing out to Angie that whilst they still had no firm idea when the birds might leave Australia, the eggs would soon be accompanying a consignment of sheep out of Cairns – in a single crate. She understood Angie would check with Cairns Airport regarding livestock movements.

Phone calls completed, Royle opened his computer and went into the satellite tracking programme. He seemed pleased with what he found there, angling the screen so the two women could see.

"Mickey Bird's well on his way back down to Sydney, though none of our crates from last night have gone anywhere yet." Then his phone rang again, and it was Angie Watts returning his call.

"You picked a winner, Phil. There's a crate of pedigree sheep leaving Cairns mid-morning tomorrow, in the name of Reed, direct to Los Angeles."

Although not unexpected, it was still good to get confirmation. "Excellent," he responded. "My guess is the birds and the eggs will both leave here around the same time."

But he sensed Angie was still not wildly enthusiastic.

"I know what's bugging you. You'd still like to nail these guys in possession of the birds. Suppose we were able to find out who's doing the transporting but still let the shipment go, so you could round them up later?"

He could tell he might just have hit upon an agreeable compromise, though the problem was making it happen. What he needed now was time to work through all possibilities and firm up on their plans for the next few days. They now knew when and from where the eggs were leaving and could identify them at their destination. As for the birds, although they could both identify them as individuals and track the containers, they had only a rough idea when they might leave Australia and, more importantly, no idea where from. They could go by air or boat, in either case from one of numerous potential departure points.

Therefore, the single most important factor, Royle decided, was that if they intended following Reed to some airstrip or river mouth, they needed to know where he was. All the time. They needed to get a vehicle tracking device fitted. Two, in fact, because it was unclear whether Reed might use the four-by-four or the white van to transport the birds. Importantly, though, they knew that one of those two vehicles would be used to transport the crate with the sheep and its hidden eggs to Cairns Airport tomorrow morning, leaving the second vehicle back at the sheep station.

In which case the immediate plan seemed unexpectedly simple: discover the airport's requirements for daily livestock deliveries – presumably there were set times – and have someone on hand to attach a device to whichever vehicle turned up with the sheep. While someone else attended to the second vehicle back at the sheep station. It seemed worryingly simple, though Royle could think of no obvious reason why it might not work, except perhaps if both vehicles left for different destinations at the same time. But that required a second driver, which argued against what they believed to be the situation.

It was approaching midday by the time Royle felt confident he had a workable plan. following which he made another call to Angie Watts, asking her to check Cairns Airport's earliest and latest livestock delivery times.

Dinner over, it was Royle's turn to suggest he and Charlie get some evening air. As before, they walked along the waterfront, and ten minutes into their stroll spotted what he described as a 'serious birder'. Asked how he arrived at such a conclusion, he drew her attention to what even she could see was an expensive looking telescope and tripod.

"Only serious birders invest that sort of money in their equipment," he suggested, gently steering her in the man's direction. "Anything interesting about?" he enquired.

Recognising a fellow birder from Royle's question the man mentioned a few species he had identified, most of the conversation meaning little to Charlie. The evening was warm and several other couples were out walking, so sensing her lack of interest Royle promised to catch her up shortly.

In less than five minutes he was by her side again.

"Feel any better for that?" she wondered.

"I do actually; it's good catching up on the local bird information."

"If I'm honest," she admitted, leaning her head on his shoulder, "I have difficulty understanding what people get out of just looking at birds. Does he live in Australia?"

"Who, that birder? No, he's from the States."

* * *

The agreed plan next morning was for Charlie and Royle to deal with whichever vehicle arrived with the sheep at Cairns Airport, while Madge and Mandu returned to the sheep station in a rental car, intent on attaching a similar device to whichever vehicle remained behind.

The two agents arrived early at that part of the airport where livestock shipments were checking in. They parked in the nearby staff car park, the white van from the station arriving thirty minutes later. Royle made his way across to the cargo shed, leaving Charlie where she could both see everything and direct him.

The van came to rest nose-in to the loading bay and Reed entered the building, quickly re-emerging and opening the rear doors as a yellow forklift appeared. Expertly it approached the van and just as quickly reversed away, carrying what looked to Charlie suspiciously like Royle's description of the garage containers, Reed following it back inside.

"Are you seeing this?" she asked.

"Got it, Charlie, give me a call if anyone comes out."

She watched as he approached the vehicle, smacking the magnetic device onto the back of the partially obscured fuel tank and carrying on walking.

FIFTEEN

UP AT THE RAINFOREST LOOKOUT LATER, WITH BOTH REED'S VEHICLES now fitted with tracking devices, there were obvious signs of activity down below. There were no longer any white cockatoos visible in the outside aviaries, plus the four-by-four was backed up to one of the tin-roofed sheds.

Madge and Royle were busy checking their own vehicle, ensuring they knew where everything was stowed. With no idea where the next twenty-four hours might take them, they had decided it made sense having Mandu along again; although Royle had the utmost confidence in Madge's ability to cope with anything the outback might throw at them, they perhaps still needed a backup. Throughout the afternoon they took turns watching the buildings below, until Charlie reported a flurry of activity as the light was fading. All the four-by-four's doors were now open and they watched bags and other items being loaded onto the rear seats, presumably because the cargo compartment now held the three bird crates. The driver, presumably Reed, was accompanied by the sole remaining Aboriginal worker.

The vehicle's lights came on in the dusk as Royle watched it move slowly towards the main highway, aware that its next move represented a defining moment. Assuming Reed's intention was to rendezvous with either a plane or a boat, then a left turn here suggested they were heading north up the rugged Cape York Peninsula, with all the challenging

169

possibilities that presented. Whereas a right turn indicated a probable destination somewhere south along the relatively close Pacific Coast. Or just possibly a long overnight drive, first south and then west all the way to the Gulf coast. With some relief he saw Reed turn south down the highway as they all climbed aboard the Toyota. Charlie drove, maintaining a three-kilometre gap on the tarmac road, with its near total lack of other traffic at that time of day.

Royle studied his computer screen, aware that if Reed failed to take any of the next three left turns down onto the coast road, then he only had one logical alternative: to turn right ninety kilometres farther on and head west in the direction of Normanton, way over on the Gulf.

Fifty minutes later Royle saw the moving arrow on his screen falter at the junction up ahead, before turning west and heading for the Gulf. Realising it looked like being a long night Charlie suggested that, as she and Madge were already in the front seats, they should continue with the first leg, leaving Mandu and Royle to try to get some sleep.

Royle handed Madge the computer. "At the risk of stating the obvious, if he stops moving then we should do likewise. The last thing we need is to bump into him." He glanced at his watch; it was almost eight o'clock. "He'll probably re-fuel at Georgetown."

Madge too had some advice for Charlie. "There'll be kangaroos all over the place, plus cattle, wild horses, camels and dingoes. It gets pretty busy out here after dark."

Shortly before dawn, with Royle driving, Mandu announced that the arrow on the computer screen showed Reed turning north, towards Normanton. A brief discussion followed on whether he might be heading for Normanton itself, at the inland end of a long river inlet, or even out towards the coast, perhaps intent on meeting a boat. But Reed then surprised them all by doing neither and instead passing straight through Normanton, apparently heading for the track up Cape York's west coast and into some pretty rough country, which made little sense. They were making good time chasing Reed down, when Mandu announced the man had changed direction again.

"There's a disused old sheep station with its own airstrip off to the right here somewhere," Madge suggested. "Perhaps that's where he's heading."

Royle stopped the Toyota, reaching under his seat for the map, which when he found it confirmed the existence of Madge's sheep station. But could they be sure it was still deserted?

"How long since you were here?"

"Year or so. It was pretty run-down; I just pulled in overnight. The approach road divides, left to the airstrip, right to the buildings. Or was it the other way around?"

Royle's concern had to do with the fact that they were expecting an aircraft to be landing or taking off close by – right now they were a bit obvious from the air. If there were any buildings, then perhaps there was a chance of concealing their vehicle from the pilot's eyes. Their immediate problem was that although the road map supported Madge's recollection of a divided station track, were the buildings to the right or to the left? In the end it was Charlie who made the decision, rationalising that from where they were now stopped the land to the left, or what little they could see of it in the dawn half-light, looked flatter and therefore more suitable for landing an aircraft. In which case they should turn right at the junction and hope to soon find the buildings, which indeed happened.

Royle immediately pointed out what remained of a three-sided barn, urging they get the vehicle under cover. That done, their obvious next priority was obtaining a view of the nearby airstrip, which involved making their way through low sand dunes in search of an observation point.

Young Mandu was the first to the top of the dune, turning to encourage his three companions, who like him went down on their knees before peering over the top. Stretched out in front of them, left and right in the cool dawn light, lay the abandoned landing strip, whilst off to their right was Reed's now dust-covered vehicle. Of greater interest, though, were the three people carrying a large crate from the four-by-four towards a twin-engine, short-takeoff de Havilland Otter – a crate containing what could only be white cockatoos.

Royle extracted his camera, realising that even in this bad light his pictures would still show the aircraft's markings. It also occurred to him that this was a well-planned operation, with the aircraft running to a tight schedule and Reed doing his bit to keep things on course. He got the impression this was not the first time these people had carried out this particular operation.

It also crossed his mind that there could be more than one way of viewing their own position. To his certain knowledge there was a great deal of money involved in the business of wildlife smuggling, so they might reasonably expect these people to do all they thought necessary to protect their considerable investment. Potentially, then, this was an extremely dangerous game his team was playing.

They continued watching while the remaining two crates were transferred from vehicle to aircraft, and with the help of Royle's field glasses Charlie confirmed that the last container held mostly the smaller parrots. That done, the Otter's engines roared into life, before the brakes were released and the aircraft rushed past them, lifting easily into the still morning air and setting a course for the top end of Cape York and New Guinea.

They continued watching until the aircraft disappeared from sight, lying where they were in the eerie silence that followed, waiting for Reed's vehicle to clear the area.

"Well, that was fun," Royle finally announced. "We came a very long way just to witness that. The question now, though, is can we get ourselves breakfast in Normanton?"

In response to this, Charlie offered a cautionary word amidst the general feeling of self-congratulation. "We need to watch Reed doesn't have the same idea about breakfast."

★ ★ ★

Somewhere on their return journey back east to Cairns, Mandu was up front, with Madge driving. She half watched the young Aborigine open Royle's Australian bird guide, flicking through the pages.

"I don't mean to offend, Mandu, but can you read that?"

He did not seem in the least offended. Indeed, she was treated to a full version of the big wide grin. "Not good but it's mostly pictures."

Madge tried to concentrate on the track ahead, noticing he had the book open at one of several pages showing the Australian parrots. He held it up for her to see.

"This one," he said, pointing a finger at the page; "that's the one Alynski wants us to get."

She saw he was indicating the golden-shouldered parrot. "Phillip says they sell for hundreds of dollars."

"How much for this feller, then?"

He was now pointing to another small parrot on the same page: a paradise parrot. "You got it wrong, mate, that one's extinct." Then, wondering whether 'extinct' translated for him, added, "None left anywhere."

Glancing across to gauge his reaction, she was surprised to see the young man smiling. "Not if you know where to look."

"You know where we can see that one?" Madge queried, again checking which illustration he was pointing to.

"Bloody hard, though. Long way in bush."

Madge suggested that Mandu reach behind and give her boss a poke. Royle sat up, gently lifting Charlie's head off his lap.

"Time to take over?"

"You're right for a while, Phillip. Thought you might like to hear what young Mandu's got to say about some parrots he knows of."

The lad twisted in his seat, holding up the page showing the paradise and golden-shouldered parrots, both of similar size and appearance.

"We just watched some being put aboard the plane," Royle responded.

"You got it wrong, mate. Would you believe he's pointing to the paradise parrot?"

Then Madge addressed herself to the young Aborigine. "Question is, Mandu, do you trust us enough to say where these birds are?"

There was a long pause, before they were treated to the now familiar grin. "I trust you guys, but big problem if Alynski or Reed find out."

Royle was clearly interested, as well he might be. If Mandu was to be believed, then this was of world significance. The young Aborigine was also right about the level of risk involved – it would be disastrous if word got out.

"I'm guessing southern Queensland, over towards the Northern Territory somewhere?" he suggested. "We should check it out once this job's done. Meanwhile, though, Charlie and I are going to try getting back to sleep."

Following this he was as good as his word, until the satellite phone rang some fifteen minutes later.

"Phil. How are you doing?"

"We're good, Paula. How are you managing without us?"

"I was wondering how you're getting along."

"We were going to update you later," Royle apologised, guessing the reason for her call. "The birds are already in New

Guinea, if my laptop is to be believed. And the sheep crate with the eggs is somewhere in LA airport."

"Whitland will be pleased."

"How is he?"

"Not bad, but not good either. They're keeping him in for a few more days, his heart's still not behaving. Oh, and I got the lab to examine that sample you sent. It's exactly as you suspected."

Somewhere near the end of their long return journey to Cairns they passed a vehicle parked beside a small billabong back from the road. Down by the water's edge was a lone birdwatcher.

"Isn't that the man you were talking to the other evening?" Charlie observed.

Royle agreed that it was. "Hang on here while I have a quick word."

The three of them watched him speaking with the man for several minutes, even looking through the telescope, before the two shook hands and Royle returned.

Charlie swung the door open for him. "Anything worth knowing?"

"Not really. He seems a nice guy, though."

Back at their motel Royle seemed particularly pumped up, though not without justification. Between them they had achieved the undeniably difficult objective of not only making the four crates traceable, but also a goodly proportion of their contents, birds and eggs. Consequently, they now knew precisely where all these items were in the world. The crate containing the sheep, plus several hundred parrot eggs, cleared LA customs mid-morning Australian time and was now en route down Interstate 5, presumably heading for the Big Experience desert site. Similarly, the three parrot containers they had photographed being loaded aboard the

175

aircraft had already crossed from New Guinea into adjoining Papua, on the Indonesian side of the island, doubtless in readiness for shipping to Belgium. In addition, Royle had transferred his photographs of the smuggler's aircraft across to his laptop and emailed them to Angie Watts, who seemed suitably impressed when she replied.

He was aware that any group of individuals this committed and with so much at stake, both financially and in terms of penalties if caught, must always be considered potentially dangerous. Extremely so, in fact, and Royle reminded Charlie that only a fool would assume total success. But what could possibly go wrong? Tomorrow morning they would tidy up any Queensland loose ends in preparation for their flight down to Sydney, before heading back home to America, while Madge made the long drive down to Sydney.

There was not a lot to say about their evening back in Cairns. The three of them had lost a great deal of sleep over the past twenty-four hours, so it came as no surprise to find them all heading for bed soon after nine.

Somewhere around dawn Royle's personal mobile announced there was a text message waiting to be read. Seeing that it was still early he pulled up the covers and tried ignoring the phone, reaching out and running his hand along the smooth curve of Charlie's back. In the end, though, curiosity got the better of him, so quietly slipping out of bed he took the phone to the window, more than a little sleepy.

He pressed the button and the screen lit up. 'Be at my place by 11.00' was all it said.

He read it through again, then a third time, not recognising the number. Who on earth was it from? And where was *my place*?

He considered the message some more, sitting quietly in the dawn light. There was only one logical explanation. It had to be someone up here in Queensland, and so it had to be connected to their parrot enquiry. Quietly he pulled on a pair of shorts and let himself out, walking across to the waterfront and applying his mind to this unexpected development. Where was my place? Who had sent the message? And more importantly, what did they want from him?

A key feature of the message was that it came to his personal phone. Although a lot of people had that number, few of them knew he was in Australia and even fewer that he was up here in Queensland. Whichever way he viewed this there had to be a connection with parrot smuggling. And if so, then it was difficult not linking the text message to the sheep station. Plus, there was one additional matter convincing him of a connection, something he had not so far revealed to either Charlie or Madge. Now this had happened he was not about to, though both seemed likely to find out before the day was through.

Feeling happier about things, Royle headed for a shower, before pouring two coffees and stretching himself out beside Charlie. Carefully he explained his receipt of the message, plus his conclusion that the place he was expected to be by eleven o'clock was the sheep station, further concluding that the most likely sender of the message must be the mysterious Sylvester Reed.

Clearly this was a lot of information for someone still only half awake. "You intend just going in there as Reed demands?" Charlie queried. "He presumably knows we followed him, but what can he possibly hope to gain?"

"I really don't know. But we won't find out unless I turn up there at eleven o'clock; we're a bit short on options."

"How did Reed get your number?"

He was slow in responding. "I'm not sure but I guess we'll find out in due course."

Royle then outlined his plan to his partner, the finer details of which could be worked out on their way to the site. Both agreed it would be a good idea to take Madge and Mandu along, plus a second vehicle that Charlie would drive.

As Charlie was going to be keeping watch from the forest track, Royle suggested she move any items she might need across to the rental car while he signed the contract in the office. Shortly after nine all three headed for the sheep station in the two vehicles, collecting Mandu en route. While Charlie remained up on the hill and watched there was no one else around, Madge and Mandu would be down at the forest edge next to the house, in case Royle shouted for help.

He handed each woman a radio. "Talk to each other while I'm in there and if you need to take action then do it."

He sensed Charlie was uptight still.

"Remind me what it is you're hoping to achieve down there."

He removed the Browning from his waistband, doing the usual checks. "I'm going to have to play it by ear. We need to find out what this is about, but we won't do that unless I get down there and talk to Reed."

Royle eased the Toyota along the driveway in the direction of the buildings, turning it around at the far end so it faced the exit if he needed to leave in a hurry. He had seen no sign of movement, but he did notice the unexpected rear end of a car projecting slightly beyond the wall of the house. He allowed himself a brief glance up the hill, partly to check the hire vehicle was not visible but also to ensure the sun was not reflecting off anything. There did not appear to be a problem.

As Royle closed his driver's door, a scruffy, bearded individual emerged from the house, right hand in his jacket pocket, not saying a word, just watching Royle.

Royle took a step in the man's direction. "What are you up to this time, Dan?"

As Charlie had pointed out three or so weeks ago, their discovery of Dan's mutilated body in the Florida tiger pen presented as many questions as answers. And as Royle had explained to her, once your brain becomes occupied with an enquiry of this complexity there is no switching it off. Somehow, over the past few days he had subconsciously worked out the identity of the man they had been watching.

The turning point probably came with Mandu's revelation that Reed smoked. It seemed logical, then, that whilst he was inside the house marking the parrot eggs, he should also collect a sample cigarette end from the many on offer. He had then mailed that to Paula back in Miami, suggesting that the lab perform DNA checks on:

(i) the Queensland sample he was now providing;

(ii) the body parts they still held labelled 'Daniel Morgan'; and

(iii) something from either Dan's apartment or his office desk that they were certain contained his DNA.

Paula's telephone call to the car on their way back to Cairns the previous afternoon had confirmed his suspicions. The unkempt individual now confronting him was none other than his one-time Marine and federal partner, Daniel Morgan, the same as was supposedly torn to pieces by the tiger.

"That's far enough," Dan growled, withdrawing the hand from his pocket and pointing what looked to Royle like a standard Department-issue 38 calibre revolver in his direction. "And we'll have that Browning on the ground where I can see it."

Royle stopped obediently, raising both hands in a mock show of submission before dropping them and reaching behind, extracting the automatic and placing it at his feet.

Dan waved the 38 in a beckoning motion. "Kick it over here, and I'll have the phone."

Again, Royle did as requested, using his toe to gently nudge the Browning and his personal mobile in his former partner's direction. He could see that the man's eyes were all over the place.

"And the other one."

"Other one what, Dan?"

"Don't try being clever. The other phone. Whitland will have issued new phones after you found the body."

Extracting his office phone, Royle placed that too on the ground, again toeing it in Dan's direction, and wondering where the Aboriginal employee might be. He decided Dan would have given him the morning off.

"Looks like you got yourself into a bit of trouble, one way or another."

Dan was slow in responding. "You just had to go poking your fucking nose in."

"That's not how it happened, Dan. Whitland dragged me in to help find you, and for a while there we thought we had."

"Who's we? Bloody Charlie Lacey?"

"How did you find working with her?"

"She's a looker right enough but I cut her out."

"Seems like you cut everyone out, including Whitland." Then Royle changed the subject, taking a sideways step towards what was beginning to look like a police car. "You had another visitor?"

Dan became even more threatening, waving the gun above his head as if reminding Royle he still had it. "I said stay there."

However, what Royle could now see of the other vehicle filled him with concern. The driver's door was open and a limp hand hung down, brushing the grass.

"Damned police. I phoned them to report you for messing around in our business, and that bastard started questioning me. Wanted to see my passport, wanted to look around the buildings."

"This is not some lawful operation, Dan. And I'm guessing you're not officially in Australia, so you decided to shoot him. Sounds like a dumb move."

He could almost hear the wheels grinding away in Dan's head, plus he was beginning to think Dan was probably the worse for a drink or two. He realised this might work to his own advantage.

Dan pointed the gun towards the police car and its silent occupant. "They say that once you've killed one then it doesn't matter. Besides, neither of us is any stranger to killing; we did it for a living."

Royle was beginning to realise that alcohol might be just part of the answer and that Dan could truly be losing it, exactly as Sharon and Charlie had suggested. Either way, he decided to try and steer the conversation away from the dead officer.

"One thing I would like to know is who owned the body in the tiger enclosure. I'm guessing Alynski? He seems to be the only one unaccounted for in all of this."

Dan reached left-handed into his pocket, extracting a cigarette packet and removing one with his lips before producing a gold cigarette lighter. "The idiot had it coming from all directions. If I hadn't killed him there were plenty more volunteers."

"I heard he was a bit of an animal; his wife's certainly gone off him. By the way," Royle added, "it was the absence of that fancy cigarette lighter of yours that first set me wondering if the body we found might not be you."

★ ★ ★

Up in the forest clearing Charlie was having difficulty interpreting what was happening down below her. She had seen her partner get out of the Toyota and had seen Reed simultaneously emerge from the house. What puzzled her was the rear end of another vehicle protruding from behind the building. Try as she might she could not see any third person.

However, she had seen Reed produce a gun from his pocket, in which case there seemed to be nothing preventing him from using it on her partner. But there also appeared to be a great deal of talking going on, and she recalled what Royle had said about the importance of obtaining information. If they were still talking then presumably Royle must be listening.

★ ★ ★

Still facing Dan's revolver, Royle recalled what Sharon Morgan had told him about her estranged husband needing to offload his troubles from time to time.

"Heard a rumour you and Gus Winnings' wife Pat might be an item," he suggested. "That would have caused problems."

He seemed to have hit a nerve, if the reaction of his former partner was anything to go by.

"Typical Winnings. Because he hadn't the balls to do anything about it himself, he persuaded Alynski to fly to Florida to take me out. It had nothing to do with Pat; Alynski and Winnings were worried about the possible loss of income, now I was onto their parrot licensing racket."

"If you shot Alynski, then who dumped the body after you switched clothes and personal items? Quigly?"

"My, you've been busy," Dan sneered. "What else do you think you know?"

Royle was finding this all very useful, although the trick, rather obviously, was to not get so far up Dan's nose that he felt forced into doing something silly. Royle tried moving a little closer.

"I'll not bother telling you again, Phil. Just stay put."

He backed off, returning to Dan's query about how much he knew. "I've thought about this. My guess is you discovered there was serious money to be made in bird smuggling, so you wanted a piece of the action. You also discovered Winnings was issuing the dodgy import permits."

Dan just smiled at him.

"Your shooting Alynski must have created a bit of a deadlock," Royle continued. "Winnings knew you'd killed his partner from the Asian end, whereas you knew enough to make him feel threatened."

"So you say."

"I'm also guessing Quigly upset Winnings, who decided to get rid of him. Probably because Quigly was exchanging smuggled parrot eggs with other collectors but also, unfortunately for Winnings, complete with details of who collected the eggs and where."

"We couldn't trust Quigly."

Royle grinned. "Involving Quigly was where it started to unravel. I'm guessing he was paid to drive up from Miami and swap your clothes and personal items with the dead Alynski's. And risk his own neck getting the body into the tiger compound using a map someone drew for him."

Again, Dan said nothing.

"What you don't know is that Quigly was not up to the job. He was supposed to clean out your vehicle where he parked it by the motel. But he left your bag in the trunk."

Royle could see Dan shifting his weight from leg to leg, obviously becoming bored with the confrontation. There were a few matters that still needed tidying up, however.

"I presume Winnings thought up the snake in the mailbox. Did you know Whitland has a bad heart?"

Dan flashed him the briefest of smiles. "Winnings had some crazy idea that with Whitland out of the way he could regain control of the Department, stop you nosing around and persuade you to back off."

"I'll not back off, Dan, you know me better than that." But then he changed direction entirely. "What do you know about drugs?"

Dan stared back at him. "You already know what I think about drugs."

Royle realised he probably did know Dan well enough after all these years to decide whether he was lying or telling the truth. And this sounded like the truth.

"You're not smuggling drugs along with the birds?"

Dan was clearly annoyed now. "I'm not going to bother discussing this. It's not happening. Go home and spend some time with that daughter of yours."

Royle was about to pursue the point when from somewhere close behind him there was an explosion. He immediately knew the cause; this was not the first time he had been close to an exploding grenade. It seemed to come from the area of the boundary fence, between the forest and the buildings. Royle was immediately aware of someone screaming in pain, and without thinking he turned to help, only half aware of Dan shouting for him to remain where he was.

Briefly he returned his attention to Dan, realising his ex-partner had set lethal traps to intercept anyone attempting a surprise entry via the rear of the property.

"Crazy bastard, you put trip-wired grenades around the fence! I'm going to help, so you'd better use that gun if you're going to."

Even as Royle turned away he saw Dan raise the 38 in his direction. Amidst the confusion of the continued screaming, his ears still ringing from the explosion, he felt the blast from Dan's gun, accompanied by a burning pain in his left shoulder.

Returning his attentions to his former partner, Royle watched an ominous red laser spot appear in the centre of Dan's chest, followed instantly by the crack of a rifle from up on the hill. Dan sank to his knees, one hand clutching his chest, the other still holding the 38. Then, with some supreme effort, powered probably by anger, he raised his arm and the gun was again pointing in Royle's direction. He held his breath, watching Dan's finger tighten on the trigger, just as a second bullet struck the side of the man's head, exactly where another small laser dot had just appeared.

SIXTEEN

Royle felt quite unmoved at seeing his long-time working partner stretched face down in the parking area. Retrieving the Browning and his two phones he kicked Dan's revolver away from the man, who even in death appeared to be reaching for the weapon. He next headed in the direction of the explosion, carefully seeking out any additional tripwires as he went. It was soon obvious he would have had no chance of saving Mandu's life, even if he had arrived immediately.

Unlike Dan's death, this did upset him. It also crossed his mind that, apart from the obvious, there were two other important issues arising from the young man's tragic and unexpected death. Firstly, there were several small children and their mother to consider; and secondly, if Mandu really did know the whereabouts of the supposedly extinct paradise parrot, then he had just taken the secret with him. Wherever it was he had gone.

Returning to the parking area Royle confirmed the police officer was indeed dead – from three separate bullet wounds. Then, using the satellite phone, he called his police contact, suggesting someone come and deal with three violent deaths, one of them a police officer. He could tell the news was not well received. Whilst he was attending to this he noticed Charlie approaching along the driveway, still clutching his rifle.

He watched her examining the body, lying face down where she had shot him, aware that to the best of his knowledge she had never previously killed anyone.

"There's something you need to know," he explained. "That I couldn't tell you beforehand, so I apologise." He knelt down and turned Dan over.

She looked for quite some time, a tear in the corner of her eye. Watching her drag her eyes away from the body, he sensed she was about to take him to task for not revealing Reed's true identity.

"I only found out for sure a few days ago. I thought it would be easier this way. I knew Dan; there was no way he was going to be cooperative. This solves a lot of problems."

She made no response.

"Anyhow, who's coming up with the surprises now? You took my rifle."

He guessed she was about to respond, but then her face switched from anger to one of concern. "He shot you. Take off that shirt."

He did as she asked, realising he was ignoring the pain of his own injury amidst all the commotion. The round from Dan's gun had gone through his left arm, from front to back, missing the bone and exiting below the shoulder. Charlie sat him down on the back of the Toyota, plugging the wound as best she could before removing the other shirt sleeve and using it as a bandage.

"You took my rifle from the Toyota while I signed the hire car agreement?"

She managed a brief smile. "It's what comes of keeping doubtful company. Madge says it's bad with Mandu?"

"It's very bad so I suggest you don't go there."

"When did you think it might be Dan?"

"I thought it was strange when we failed to find his cigarette lighter in the tiger pen. Then when Mandu said Reed was a smoker I started wondering, so I sent Paula a DNA sample and she confirmed it yesterday. The phone call in the car."

Royle tried focusing his mind, aware time was slipping by. "What we must do now is leave the police in no doubt we have urgent business back home. They're not going to be at all impressed by this little mess. I'll give Angie Watts a call."

Royle suggested using a dust sheet from the garage to cover Mandu's shattered body, taking care to seek out any remaining tripwires and disarm the grenades. They next searched the main building, confirming the incubators were now empty. By the telephone were two folders of correspondence relating to bird transactions, plus an address book. They also found a bag of Dan's clothes, from amongst which they recovered his passport and American driver's licence. They then went through the bag a second time, ensuring they had removed all evidence of 'Reed's' true identity.

Turning their attention next to the bed, beneath it they found a rucksack, all three expressing their surprise as Charlie undid the zip. It was crammed full of a mixture of Australian and US dollars, mostly in bundles, a quick count suggesting the equivalent of around US$200,000. Surprisingly, Royle seemed unhappy with the find. As far as he was concerned it was a problem they could do without, though he could just possibly see an upside.

They had no knowledge of whose money this was or where it came from, though logic suggested a connection with bird smuggling. With Alynski and Dan now both dead, Winnings would doubtless be denying any involvement in these activities. It therefore seemed likely this money would end up in the hands of the Australian government. Although, still considering their options, it occurred to Royle that if there were any justice in this world then some of this cash would go towards taking care of Mandu's family.

They took the money and any other items of interest outside, hiding them in the Toyota. Next, Royle returned to Dan's body, removing his cell phone before quickly checking for any other personal items. At that point Charlie took them back inside, pointing to the telephone answering machine.

Unlike more up-to-date machines this one saved any incoming messages to a removable cassette. There were three recent messages, two concerning deliveries of bird food, but it was the third that grabbed their attention.

'Dan, it's Gus Winnings. The eggs are already at the California site and the birds are heading for Europe. I've issued the American import permits.'

The partners exchanged broad grins as Charlie pressed first the 'Stop' button and then the one marked 'Eject'.

"My bet is Dan also failed to erase any earlier messages," she suggested, slipping the cassette into her pocket.

As anticipated the police officer who attended was far from happy. Expecting some tense discussion Royle commenced by reminding the officer that he and Charlie were officially there as American federal agents, also explaining how they were working in conjunction with Australian customs. He made clear too that whatever the officer might be contemplating to the contrary, he and his partner were about to leave for first Sydney and then America.

The one question the pair were waiting for the officer to ask was the one they knew least how to answer, namely the identity of the person lying dead at their feet. Somewhere at the back of his mind Royle understood the embarrassment likely to follow revelations that an American federal agent – now wanted for murder back home – had entered Australia illegally, killed a police officer and then died at the hands of fellow US agents. He decided the only way forward was for them to deny all knowledge of the dead man, leaving that for the diplomats to sort out. Anyway, wasn't it true that this place belonged to Carl Alynski, so why not assume that that was him lying there? Either him or the mysterious Sylvester Reed.

All things considered that was about as far as Royle wished to take the matter. It was now for the police to deal with; he and his partner had pressing issues elsewhere. Royle next took the officer to Mandu's body, pointing out the need for extreme care still around the perimeter fence, unless he wished to end the day in a similar state of anatomical disorder.

Charlie drove back to Cairns with Royle as a wounded passenger, leaving Madge to return the rental vehicle. He thought through Dan's likely reasons for forcing him to hand over both cell phones. Dan surely knew about the general lack of any outback cell phone signal. Which of course was why Royle had his turned off at the time; they were still turned off on the dashboard in front of him. So what was the point in Dan's removing his phone, or even both of them?

Reaching into the glove compartment, he extracted the satellite phone and spent time explaining the three deaths and the money to Angie Watts.

Angie did not seem overly impressed. "Your present partner just shot dead your former partner? Bloody hell, what's the body count now, three in Australia and four in America?"

"You can add two more," he suggested. "For reasons best known to himself Dan shot the guard dogs."

"What's your next move, then?"

"As far as Charlie and I are concerned we're done here. We're heading for Sydney briefly, then off back to the US tomorrow."

He next made various calls to America, including updating Whitland, who had finally been released from hospital, though with strict instructions to take it easy. He seemed to accept the news of Dan's second passing better than expected.

Charlie then took over the phone, Royle hearing her check with Mindy Goldsmith that things were still on track in California, before squeezing in a quick call to her parents. He noticed she made no mention of shooting Dan. Lastly, he heard her calling Dot Alynski.

"A man's been shot out at the sheep station. We're afraid it could be your husband."

"Best bit of news I've had for a long time – good riddance to the bastard."

Charlie ended the call by informing the woman that before she and Royle left Queensland they would be handing over $1,000 Australian for her cooperation.

Back in Cairns, plans for their departure south to Sydney included a visit to A&E, where it was decided that like it or not Royle's wounded arm should be in a support. The pair then spent a tense hour making police statements regarding the three deaths at the sheep station. That done, they prepared for Madge getting the Toyota back to Sydney once she had handed the money over to Dot Alynski. She was also to open an account in the name of Mandu's partner, with a deposit of $50,000 Australian from what they were now calling the 'parrot money', the balance being paid into Royle's Australian account by Madge in smaller amounts as she moved south. It was dark by the time they had dealt with various remaining issues, amongst which explaining Mandu's death had been the most difficult.

Getting on for midnight Madge drove the pair around to Cairns Airport, Royle surprising Charlie by explaining how he had chartered a private jet to get them back to Sydney.

"You heard me ask Whitland what the budget was. He said 'it costs whatever it takes'. At this moment a charter jet is what it takes, plus we have the parrot money to cover it."

Because the aircraft was not quite ready the pair went for something to eat, Charlie's mobile ringing as they sat down. It was Angie Watts.

"I'm trying to contact your partner. Both his phones seem to be off."

Charlie passed Royle her phone.

"What's the problem?" he enquired, taking the phone and realising he had still not switched on his mobiles.

"It's Angie, she seems a bit stressed over something."

"Angie, what's up?" He waited for her response, but nothing came. "What's going on, Angie?"

"I don't know how to tell you this."

"Try, Angie."

"Your daughter arrived here in Sydney after you two left for Cairns. She wanted to surprise you, and see your sister, Chris."

Now it was Royle's turn to go quiet. "Why didn't someone tell me Sam was there?"

"Chris and I discussed it. We decided you might not be too happy, and anyway you had a lot going on. We agreed she could use my garden house until you got back here."

"And?"

Again, there was a brief silence before Angie responded. "Sam didn't come home this evening. Normally she calls if she's late."

Royle had a cold, empty feeling in his stomach and he was fighting back the panic.

"Look on the bedside table," he suggested. "See if her watch is there."

"There's no watch; I just checked her room."

Surprisingly he almost sounded relieved. "It's not just a watch."

There was a minor explosion at the other end. "You put a tracking device on your daughter?!"

Royle explained how a couple of years back Sam had gone down into Mexico with some girlfriends. As a kind of backup he had presented her with a fancy watch, complete with compass, except that it also contained a tracking device the Special Techniques section made for him. Just in case. She had still been wearing it on their recent ride out into the swamp.

"There's probably a simple explanation. Give me time to get at my computer and we'll at least know where she is."

191

"What if it's more serious? There are some weird things going on in your investigation."

He was slow in responding. "Charlie and I both thought we had this kind of possibility covered. Someone's really starting to piss me off."

Thanking Angie and ending the call, he and his partner went back to the hangar and extracted his laptop. He turned it on and opened the tracking programme, relieved to see Sam's watch was still active. According to the computer screen she was now over the Blue Mountains well to the west of Sydney. It occurred to him that it was just a few days since he and Charlie had travelled that same route, on their way out to the Strzelecki Track. Then, opening the screen, following Mickey Bird's truck, they both saw that it mirrored the location of his daughter's watch. There could only be one explanation: Mickey Bird had taken his daughter, and they both had an idea where he was heading.

He felt Charlie's hand stroking his back.

"Sam can look after herself," she encouraged. "Do we think Dan put him up to this?"

He shook his head. "Dan had no idea Sam was in Australia."

"Who, then?"

He thought about that. "There's no way Mickey Bird would know about Sam, so someone back in the States has to be pulling his strings. My money's on Winnings still."

Clearly a change of plan was in order; they were no longer going to Sydney, but instead needed to get themselves back out into the desert country. They could also forget any thoughts of driving out to the Strzelecki Track; this called for a far more immediate response. Logging onto the internet Royle went in search of an airfield in Broken Hill, the nearest town of any size to the Strzelecki Track.

★ ★ ★

Settling into her seat in preparation for leaving Cairns, Charlie thought through the events of the past few days. Again, he had failed to keep her updated on developments in their supposedly joint inquiry, particularly not mentioning he knew it was Dan Morgan they were dealing with at the sheep station. She was still coming to terms with him placing a tracking device on his daughter, though she was beginning to appreciate the difficult situation Royle must have found himself in. Take her shooting of Dan; had he told her beforehand who they were really dealing with, she might just have hesitated before squeezing the trigger. Realising Royle must be worried for the safety of his daughter, she was nevertheless unclear on a couple of matters leading up to this morning's confrontation.

"I can understand how Dan might change sides and try hiding himself away on this side of the world." She watched him seeking a comfortable position for his shoulder. "What concerns me is how easily we assumed the body in the tiger pen was his."

He sat up again, his face momentarily distorting in pain. "You can see how it could happen. We were looking for a body and we found one. Better still, we found Dan's badge and phone."

"You agree it was our fault, then?"

"We're all to blame, Charlie, but mostly the people in the lab. We were seeing what we expected to see, based on what we were being made to believe. The lab, though, works on the principle of accept nothing, check everything. Or it should do."

He leaned back in his seat, obviously thinking the discussion was over. But she just sat there, looking at him, making clear she was troubled still.

"Get it off your chest," he suggested, searching his pockets for the pain tablets.

She selected her words carefully. "I can't help noticing how unmoved you seemed to be by Dan's death, on both occasions.

Considering how close you two were, I expected far more of a reaction."

"I could pad this out, be diplomatic, as I'm sure Whitland would."

"But it's not that simple?"

"Dan was not very nice. If he'd had his way all of us on that rescue would probably be lying in unmarked graves in Central America."

"What did he do?"

"The mission was going wrong and our best chance of survival was to get ourselves out of there, quickly. Dan panicked when the firing started and two of the rescued men got shot climbing aboard. He wanted us to put our hands up."

"What happened?"

"A couple of the guys held him down until I got the chopper out of range."

"Is that why you never mentioned the medals while you both worked in the Department?"

"Partly."

She assumed Royle realised she was giving him the psychiatrist's treatment. "Was that the only reason you two never got along afterwards?"

"Dan was a serious threat to any woman he went near. I learned to keep my mouth closed, but knowing how well Paula's radar works I'll be surprised if she didn't know. And if *she* knew, then Whitland did too."

Charlie realised they should be trying to sleep, but he was in a talkative mood and she needed to make the most of it. "Is that it, then? Nothing else?"

"About what?"

"About anything, but Dan in particular."

She saw him hesitate. "There is more, but it's hardly bedtime reading. You'll think I'm making it up."

"Try me."

"Our orders included bringing back one of the rebels, to help obtain intelligence. In the dash back to the helicopter the marines grabbed a guy carrying a Kalashnikov, dragging him in through the door. That's when we discovered he was just a kid, around fifteen years old."

"Sounds like something out of a cheap movie."

"More like a nightmare. Once we were out of range of the gunfire we turned our attention to our captive. The kid was terrified and obviously knew nothing. I suggested putting the helicopter down somewhere and releasing him."

He paused, clearly unsure whether to continue.

"You can't stop there."

"Dan lost it again. Started on about not risking our lives over some kid. Next thing we know he pulls the lad over to the open door and pushes him out, *at one thousand feet*. I can still see the look of terror on the kid's face as he disappeared."

She lightly placed a hand on his wounded shoulder. "You two worked together all these years, with those kinds of memories lurking away in the background?"

"It's surprising what the brain can cope with, especially when you're young. You're right, though, you don't forget, and once you've lost that relationship you never regain it."

They both finally settled and were quiet for a while, before he sat up again.

She watched him searching his pockets. "Pain tablets?"

"Forgot to turn my mobiles on again."

His personal phone reacted to the start-up command, but the office phone failed to respond. She watched him checking the battery, which had probably become dislodged during the business with Dan. Having fixed the problem, he turned his attention to Charlie.

"You think I'm weird putting a trace on Sam, but I'm not alone."

She looked at him questioningly.

"Ever look inside your office phone?"

"Are you saying it contains a tracking device?" she queried, rummaging through her bag before extracting the phone and removing the cover.

"Behind the battery."

She immediately located the device. "It's true what they say, then. Trust nobody in this business but especially those closest to you."

"Present company excepted," Royle suggested. "And anyway, Whitland does it for all the right reasons."

She was shaking her head. "So why did we have trouble tracking down Dan's phone?"

"Dan objected to anyone knowing where he was, probably because of all his extramarital activities. He repeatedly removed the device; it really annoyed Whitland." But then he paused.

"Something else I don't know about?" she wondered.

"It just came to me why Dan wanted both my mobiles back at the sheep station. He realised Whitland would have bugged our replacement phones."

SEVENTEEN

D<small>ESPITE ALL</small> R<small>OYLE'S EARLIER ORGANISING, THINGS WERE NOT GOING TO</small>
plan. Certainly, when he and Charlie landed at Broken Hill at
first light the Gazelle helicopter was out on the tarmac and
ready to go. The pilot, though, had not appeared. According to
Light Airfreight's harassed boss, Walt Campbell, his pilot had
the unfortunate habit of needing to sleep off the occasional
'bugger of a hangover'. Furthermore, Campbell's suggestion
that the two get themselves into town and chill out while he
located his man did not go down at all well.

"Perhaps I didn't properly explain things," Royle began,
standing in front of the packing case masquerading as
Campbell's office desk. "When I hired you to get us out to the
Strzelecki Track first thing this morning, I meant first thing.
Not whenever you can get your pilot off his arse and into the
bloody helicopter."

Campbell appeared unmoved as he lit his next cigarette.
"What you bloody tourists don't understand is that here in the
outback we need to be sure we've got all the equipment we're
likely to require. Plus, to get to where you want to go we'll be
near our fuel limit."

Royle indicated the walking stick hooked over the corner
of the desk, plus Campbell's leg sticking straight out.

"Seeing your stiff leg, I'm guessing you couldn't fly the
helicopter even if I suggested it." He glanced in his partner's
direction. "It's a while since I flew a chopper of any kind, but

it seems to me we're faced with two options: either you fly the bloody thing, or I do."

"Don't think we can go that route, young feller, my insurance doesn't cover you. But never mind my leg, what about that thing?" He indicated the sling supporting Royle's arm.

Royle's response was predictable. Removing the support, he threw it onto the desk. "What thing might that be?"

You did not need to be a mind reader to see what Campbell thought of that. "You've got to be fucking joking."

Royle leaned forward, hands palm down on the make-do desk. "We're obviously not having the same conversation here. Charlie and I need to get out there now and you have the only helicopter capable of doing the job. Like it or not your machine's elected."

He could see the man shaking his head, but he also felt Charlie's hand slide across his back and pull the Browning from his waistband. He heard the click of the safety catch as the weapon appeared past his face, coming to rest against Campbell's left ear.

She sounded like she should be listened to. "One of us needs to make a decision, so I just did. Phil's going to fly your precious helicopter, while you tell him what he's doing wrong. I need to see the three of us in the air and on our way towards rescuing a very frightened young girl."

Campbell looked justifiably surprised.

"Oh, and we're not 'bloody tourists'," Charlie added. "We're American federal agents. So, if your precious flying machine gets scratched the American government will pay for any repairs."

For one reason or another there was a distinct change in the man's attitude.

"Hell, I had no idea you felt that strongly," Campbell said, turning his attention back to Royle. "You *really* flown one of these things, I mean a Gazelle?"

"I've put them down in the most difficult situations imaginable and got them out again without any damage. Ask the British or American forces."

Charlie smiled to herself, recalling Paula's description of Royle's helicopter at the end of their Central American mission.

"She's got none of them fancy military gimmicks. No heads-up display and all that rubbish," Campbell explained. "And we'll be near our fuel limit, though some sheep stations keep a supply. Let's see you put your money where your mouth is, then."

Royle surprised even himself with how quickly he got the hang of things. In no time at all he had the Gazelle heading in a straight line, northwest across the desert country at near the machine's maximum 260 kilometres per hour. Unlike sitting in a commercial aircraft, at twenty-something thousand feet, seeing the ground streaking past a couple of hundred feet away brought all manner of memories flashing through his already busy mind.

Charlie realised he was unusually quiet. "How does it feel?" she enquired, seeing the flicker of a smile in the corners of his eyes.

"To be honest I wasn't sure I could do this, but if we keep this up we should be there in a couple of hours."

"Anything I can do?"

He pointed over his shoulder in the direction of his rucksack. "You could get the laptop out and see what's going on with the tracking devices."

She did as he requested, confirming that Mickey Bird's truck appeared to be stationary out near the building where she and Royle had found the cockatoos, though the data from Sam's watch appeared to be playing up.

Sitting in the co-pilot's seat, Campbell seemed more relaxed now it looked like he could trust his precious helicopter to Royle's tender care. "You know where these people are from that computer?"

Charlie rotated the screen so he could watch what was happening down on the ground, at the same time opening the rifle case and reassembling the weapon, before inserting the magazine, loading a shell into the breach and applying the safety catch.

Campbell watched her before turning to Royle. "What's the story with this feller? How come he's holding your daughter?"

It was Charlie who responded. "He thinks he can obstruct our enquiries, but he doesn't know the game's already up."

Campbell glanced around at her again, sitting quietly, knees together, loaded rifle on her lap in the middle of the rear seats – looking like one scary Sheila.

Coming up to two hours out from Broken Hill, Charlie rechecked the computer. "Mickey Bird's truck's now on its way north up the main Strzelecki Track, presumably heading back to the Corner, but Sam seems to have gone walkabout."

Royle thought this development through, aware the satellite information updated every few minutes. It seemed likely Mickey would be driving the vehicle, though that failed to explain his daughter's movements. Interestingly, it did not worry him unduly that Sam might be out there on her own, though if she was now free it was difficult understanding why she had not headed for the nearby Strzelecki Track, given the possibility of an occasional passing truck.

"We only have one sensible course of action," he decided. "First, we check the building, then we see if we can overtake Sam and find out why she's out there. Then we head Mickey Bird off somewhere up the track."

Arriving over the Strzelecki Track, Royle and Campbell discussed landing the helicopter. Royle's suggestion of setting the Gazelle down on the track itself did not gain favour with Campbell, who was quick to point out the damage any passing road train might do. They eventually agreed on a patch of desert several hundred metres to the south.

Campbell offered to stay and take care of their only means of transport out, whilst Royle and Charlie prepared to approach the building. Royle realised they might be taking a risk in agreeing to this – if Campbell decided to leave in the helicopter then he and Charlie were in big trouble. But he was counting on the fact that the man had not yet been paid, besides which Campbell might be pushing his luck flying around out here on his own with a now limited fuel load.

Despite what the computer was telling them, the pair realised they could not be certain about Mickey's whereabouts; there was an outside chance some third person could be driving the truck. One thing that did seem clear, though, as they approached the building was the absence of any parrot noise. After a brief discussion they decided to approach the shack from opposite sides. Neither, though, was prepared for what confronted them as they met opposite the entrance doorway, the experience being not dissimilar to their supposed earlier discovery of Dan's body in the tiger pen. They were acutely aware of the sound of flies, lots of flies.

Placing one hand over his mouth and holding the faithful Browning in front of him, Royle leapt through the doorway, all but disappearing in a black cloud of insects. Charlie, though, decided on a more sensible approach, pulling the neck of her tee-shirt up to cover her mouth before charging through. Both were momentarily lost for words, for attached to the inside of the door, upright by some as yet mysterious means, hung what they guessed must be Mickey Bird. A very dead Mickey Bird. Quickly, Royle checked the building for any additional occupants.

"Someone's been tied to the bed upstairs but there's no one there now."

Mikey had obviously been speared through the chest. They could see where the spear's shaft had been broken off, leaving him impaled on the door. Although no closer to locating his daughter, Royle's relief was nevertheless obvious.

"Any thoughts on what happened here?" Charlie wondered, aware a further change of plan must be due.

"How Mickey died is obvious; we'll hopefully know by whom and why once we catch up with Sam. Though if it is her driving the truck, what's her watch doing way out there?" he queried, pointing to the far horizon.

The route from the old building back towards Sydney by vehicle involved a forty-kilometre drive north as far as the turn-off, followed by a further hundred and fifty kilometres east to the Corner. Through remote country all the way. The good news, though, was that in the helicopter they could take the shortcut and probably intercept Mickey's truck in less than twenty minutes.

* * *

During yesterday's long drive out from Sydney, Sam Royle had been kept shut inside the same converted water tank Mickey Bird used to transport trapped parrots. Mickey had previously cut rough ventilation holes in the tank, so she had a limited view of what was happening outside and had tried making a mental note of their route. Nevertheless, it had been hot and dirty, and she was close to collapse when they finally arrived at the derelict building. But regardless of her already helpless state, Mickey kept her tied to the bed.

The two Aboriginal boys appeared yesterday evening while Mickey was fetching water from a borehole. Hearing whispered voices downstairs she had feared the worst and was even more concerned when one of the boys appeared in the bedroom doorway. But she need not have worried; he was obviously concerned at her predicament and immediately set about untying her. Unfortunately, that was when her captor chose to return.

Hearing the vehicle, the young man descended the stairs in a rush and appeared to have been hit by a bullet from Mickey's battered old rifle. Seeing his friend in a heap at the foot of the stairs, the second lad appeared, throwing his spear at Mickey and impaling him on the entrance door. Still tethered upstairs, Sam heard first the shot and then Mickey's shout as the spear hit him. She was still struggling with the rope when the second young Aborigine appeared, quickly coming to her aid and cutting her free.

He smiled at her. An obviously friendly smile. "Bad fella's dead," he said, motioning for her to follow.

Descending the stairs, Sam was unsure what she felt. There was no doubting Mickey must be dead; his head was slumped forwards and blood flowed from the wound in his chest. The other young Aborigine, the one who first tried to help her, now lay in the hallway, clearly in pain.

"Him hurt bad."

She looked at the speaker. "You understand what I'm saying?"

"Good enough, Mrs, him hurt bad."

Reared on a working ranch, Sam was no stranger to the occasional serious injury. The boy pointed to his foot which was already badly swollen, though it seemed the gunshot had missed him.

"I think he's hurt his ankle," she suggested, seeing the other young Aborigine smiling at her. "Are you sure you understand?"

The lad nodded his head enthusiastically. "Him hurt bad."

It occurred to her there should be fresh water in the truck, so the least she could do was provide the patient with a cold bandage to try and relieve the pain. Throughout the night she took care of him, changing the bandage and inspecting the swelling, which did seem to be going down. Most of that time his young companion sat silently watching, apparently unmoved by events, or so Sam thought. Though she quickly changed her mind when this morning he produced a crutch he'd made from a piece of wood he'd found around the building.

"We go home now," he said, before pointing to the truck. "You can go longaway in that."

Sam saw that the key was still in the ignition. It seemed more than a little bizarre, but there was no denying that she and the two young men had very different agendas. She needed to get herself back to what she considered civilisation, whereas they were clearly headed for the dry country. Even so, she felt the need to somehow show her gratitude. Going over to the injured young man she removed her watch and strapped it to his wrist, his face breaking into a broad grin as he reached out and touched her.

She stood watching them for a long while, heading out into the broad expanse of apparently endless desert. Then, having started driving her captor's vehicle back up the track the way they had come the previous day, she saw the helicopter landing on the track up ahead. Whoever it was, they were more than welcome.

★ ★ ★

"So, this is the young lady you were threatening to blow my brains out for," Campbell said.

Charlie wiped away her tears. "We'll never know if I would really have done it."

Sam briefly outlined the details of her capture, including the death of Mickey Bird and the injury to one of the two Aborigine boys.

"Sounds like a couple of lads out hunting kangaroos," Campbell suggested. "We'll probably never hear any more about it; some of these Aboriginal guys never come near the white communities."

They were now only an hour's drive away from The Corner Roadhouse, and since only Royle could fly the helicopter Charlie and Sam agreed to take the vehicle and meet the two men there. Back in the air, Royle got Campbell to connect him with the police in Broken Hill, asking for a senior officer and spending some time explaining what had occurred, concluding with the death of Mickey Bird.

Although obviously interested, the officer seemed at pains to point out what Royle already knew, that Broken Hill was in New South Wales, whereas the building containing Mickey Bird's body was well inside South Australia – in a different police area. But Royle also knew that, given the remoteness of much of the outback, this kind of situation must often occur, so there surely had to be established procedures. And anyway, it was not his problem.

"I'll tell you one thing, though," he suggested, perhaps a touch irritably. "If someone doesn't quickly collect Mickey's body it will soon be able to crawl out of there on its own. You realise how many flies there are out here?"

That difficult matter dealt with, or at least for the moment, he next got Campbell to connect him to someone at the airport who might be able to fly the three of them back to Sydney that same afternoon.

★ ★ ★

With Royle, Sam, Walt Campbell and her all now reunited at The Corner Roadhouse, Charlie organised a couple of cabins so they could shower. She also attended to Sam's swollen wrists. Arrangements were then made to leave the truck for the police to collect, whoever agreed to assume responsibility. Following this, Royle used the roadhouse's phone to make calls, letting Whitland and Angie Watts know Sam was safe, before they were all four in the air and heading for Broken Hill.

Back at the airport Royle sorted out the finances with Campbell, even negotiating a small reduction on account of him flying the helicopter. He thanked Campbell for his help and Charlie apologised again for pulling Royle's gun on him.

The man appeared to take it all in his stride. "You two buggers certainly livened things up. We don't get too much excitement out this way."

He gave Royle a pat on the back. "You ever get tired of dashing about the world killing folks I could always use a good bush pilot. Don't know what the US government's paying you pair but it's not enough."

Next, Campbell turned his attention to Sam, giving her a hug. "Been a real pleasure, young lady. Come and see us again sometime."

The police officer Royle had earlier spoken to then arrived as arranged, and the four of them spent time going through the usual formalities. Then late afternoon they boarded another charter jet and were soon safely back in Royle's house overlooking Sydney's inner harbour. Bearing in mind the combined mental and physical demands of the past few days, after an early meal in one of the harbour restaurants all three were in bed; it was also true that the girls were booked on early flights back across the Pacific the next morning, Sam through to Miami, Charlie only as far as LA.

Next morning saw Royle seated in Angie Watts' office in Sydney Airport.

"Sounds like you had a busy time in Queensland, and not without its problems?"

He pretended to concentrate on stirring his coffee. "I might as well tell you, the body count's up to ten now."

"You're kidding?"

"Shows there's big money in wildlife crime."

"So, where are we at with this business?"

"We're on a roll. Charlie's on her way to California to help Mindy recover the eggs and any hatched young from the desert bird site."

"And you're off back to Florida this evening?"

"Overnight flight. We need to organise a raid on the birds in quarantine in Miami, find out what drugs are involved, if any, and bring in Gus Winnings."

"What about the Indonesian bit, where the birds went to after New Guinea?"

"We need to hold back on that until we recover the birds and the eggs, or word will get back and the evidence will start disappearing."

"I understand all that but are you happy with me handling the Australian and Indonesian ends?"

"If I'm honest I rather hoped you might."

She grinned at him across the desk. "Tell Charlie she has my sympathy. Who else would let his colleague shoot her former partner, without saying who she was killing?"

"Charlie thinks I need treatment for putting a trace on Sam."

"You're weird, Phil, but there's no denying your methods work."

Keen to change the subject, he explained what they had done with the money from the sheep station. "Once you and Whitland agree who gets what, I'll transfer the money accordingly."

EIGHTEEN

CHARLIE UNDERSTOOD THE PURPOSE OF ROYLE'S PRE-ARRANGED MEETING between her and Mindy, though she had been puzzled by his mention of a possible third participant, which he only informed her of as she was checking in for the Los Angeles flight.

"Want to tell me more?"

"Her name's Roxie, and she does occasional work for me. She knows all about the Big Experience set-up," he had briefly explained, before turning to attend to his daughter, who was also checking in.

★ ★ ★

At the LA Federal Building, Charlie was introduced to Roxie Meadows, an attractive girl in her early twenties with an obvious liking for fashionable, if somewhat risqué, clothes. Although not 'revealing' in the accepted sense, her tight top left very little to the imagination.

There was something vaguely familiar about Roxie. "Have we met?" Charlie asked.

She smiled. "I'm the receptionist at Big Experience, where you came with Phil."

"What's going on?"

"Why don't we let Roxie explain," Mindy suggested, nodding her head in the girl's direction.

"I'm studying drama. Phil and my dad worked on a big investigation; he's my godfather."

Roxie paused, anticipating a question.

"Go on," Mindy urged.

"Phil rang a few weeks back. He wanted me to apply for the vacancy of receptionist at Big Experience."

Charlie had already identified what to her was the main point in all of this. "You mean when Phil and I came to Big Experience with Deming Akroyd, you were already working for us, but he never told me?"

"Perhaps he was worried staff might get suspicious if we risked talking."

Roxie, though, had missed the point, and anyway Charlie was not buying that. "I don't mean he should have told me while we were there. I mean in our office in Florida, or on the plane coming across."

"I can see why he might want to do that," Mindy intervened. "But we need to hear what Roxie says."

"Three days ago," the girl continued, "a shipment of eggs arrived hidden in a sheep crate. I think from Australia. They were transferred into our incubators, but then yesterday there was a big panic. All the incubators and any hatched birds were loaded into a truck and taken away."

"What do we make of that, Charlie?" Mindy asked.

"There is only one explanation – they somehow got word we're onto them. Which raises two questions. How did they know and, more importantly, where are the eggs now?"

Roxie seemed unconcerned. "I can probably answer that. One of the reasons Phil wanted me there was to record all telephone numbers called or received."

"And you have that list with you?"

The girl nodded. "I also recorded the licence plates of any vehicles."

Charlie found herself momentarily speechless, desperately trying to imagine what gave Royle this ability to anticipate the future, at the same time realising that she and Mindy had urgent work to do checking the phone and vehicle numbers on Roxie's list. It looked like being a long night.

However, it was at this point that the girl dropped her bombshell.

"There's something else. That California state man, Deming Akroyd, he's in it with them. He knows everything that goes on there."

This time it was Mindy who responded. "From the top, Roxie. Everything."

Removing the gum from her mouth and attaching it to the underside of the desk, the girl explained how that same afternoon after Charlie and Royle had been out at the breeding facility, she had put through a call from Akroyd. And how Akroyd had later driven back out to the site and spent an hour shut away with O'Reilly in his office. As an apparent consequence of that meeting Roxie had handled a large volume of calls, mostly to or from numbers she'd had no previous contact with, including several in the Florida and New York areas. Details of those calls were on the list she had provided, along with dates and times.

Charlie waited until Roxie had finished. "How much of this does Phil know?"

"He knows all about it. I've spoken with him several times."

* * *

Royle was in the office soon after nine, first checking in with Paula, who confirmed Charlie was expected back from LA after lunch. The secretary was keen to hear how things had gone in Australia and for the second time offered her condolences for the loss of Dan Morgan.

"No doubt Whitland will cover the point in a minute," he suggested, "but has he been to see Sharon Morgan again? She must be wondering what's going on."

Paula was quick to reassure him. "Doug's been to see her and she's fine. You shouldn't go beating yourself up over this; you had no reason to think the body might not have been Dan's. If anyone messed up it was the lab."

He briefly outlined how he came to identify Dan as the mystery bird dealer, unsure exactly how much information might have filtered back to Paula. More importantly, though, he explained how Charlie had ended up shooting Dan.

"I'd not heard some of that," she admitted. "Presumably it was easier to cope with this time, you two thinking he was already dead?"

"Perhaps, but there's going to be fireworks when she gets back."

"What have you done to upset the poor girl this time?"

Briefly Royle outlined Roxie's part in the investigation, including how he had chosen not to confide in either Charlie or Mindy.

"Mindy will be okay with it, but Charlie's going to be spitting fire."

Paula looked at him. "Seeing as you've touched on it, what about you two? Rumour has it things are serious."

"There's no denying we're seeing a lot of each other, which hasn't been difficult in the circumstances. Anyway, who was it forgot to mention Charlie's father's a federal judge?"

Paula knew he had a point. "I can't speak for Doug, but I was under Charlie's instructions not to tell."

"And you didn't seem too surprised when I mentioned Roxie."

Paula laughed. "Charlie and Mindy were on the phone last night calling you all sorts of names, though they think they've tracked down the missing eggs."

Then the secretary glanced at her watch before pointing to Whitland's door. "Charlie won't be the only one displeased if you don't get yourself in there."

As he turned to leave, she called to him, "Don't forget who sees all the invoices, including how many rooms get booked each night."

Royle could see no visible sign of Whitland's encounter with either the rattlesnake or the previously undisclosed heart problem, though he noted various boxes of pills in the 'Out' tray. The department head listened intently as Royle outlined events in Australia, particularly Charlie's shooting of Dan and their recovery of the American and Australian dollars.

Whitland seemed pleased. "There'll be the odd problem still but the question now, Phillip, is what we do about Gus Winnings?"

"Depends how ready they are over in California," Royle suggested. "I'm hoping Charlie found time to play the tape from Alynski's answering machine. What's on there might affect what Gus is charged with."

Royle enquired after Sharon Morgan, and Whitland's body language suggested he was uncomfortable.

"Problem?"

"For Sharon, perhaps. It looked like someone had been knocking her around."

"Then we may be doing her a favour by locking up Greg, though I'm still unclear what we have on him."

Whitland was about to continue when something more important occurred to him. "Never mind all that, how's my goddaughter?"

"She's fine, Doug, really."

Whitland rephrased his question. "I still don't understand how you knew where to find her?"

Now it was Royle's turn to look uncomfortable. "Bit of a problem there. The women are ganging up on me, though in my defence we tracked Sam down and rescued her."

212

"What problem?"

Briefly, Royle explained how come his daughter was wearing a watch with a tracking device fitted.

Both of Whitland's chins wobbled as he laughed. "I can see they might think your methods unusual, though they're missing the point. It worked, didn't it?"

"Exactly. Where would we be if I'd not done it? But there's something else Charlie's going to be mad as hell about."

Whitland's face suggested a slight smile. "I thought you two were getting along quite well?"

Quickly, Royle outlined how he had gone into Big Experience's website after they found the body in the tiger enclosure. And how he had persuaded Roxie to apply for the vacant job of receptionist at their California site.

"Like the tracking device on your daughter," Whitland suggested. "Bit of a long shot but well worth the effort if it worked."

"Thing is, I never told Charlie. She will know by now that when we went to the desert site with Akroyd, the receptionist, i.e. Roxie, was already working for us."

Whitland was giving this the appropriate amount of thought. "Won't she understand if you explain it like that?" he asked, and then was quiet for a moment. "Who will Charlie speak to first once she gets back?"

"Paula, of course, they're bound to want to discuss all this."

"All you need do, then, is convince Paula you were acting in good faith and she's bound to pour cold water on Charlie's hot coals." He saw Royle hesitate. "There's more than you're saying, still?"

Royle felt a huge weight lifting from his shoulders. "Actually, Doug, there is a bit more. The DEA has a long interest in the people we're dealing with, commencing way before you first called me on the plane. It's been all I can do getting them to hold off."

"That might explain a few things," was all Whitland said.

Relieved by his boss's apparent controlled reaction, Royle seized the moment. "I took the liberty of asking the DEA's man in charge to come along here today. We've known each other for years; anyone else and I might not have been able to control the situation."

* * *

Contrary to her partner's expectations Charlie was feeling good following her stopover in California. She had been upset at discovering Royle's secret arrangement with Roxie, but then, having proved a location for the missing Big Experience eggs, it had been Mindy's suggestion they went for a meal. Both women had been secretly pleased to hear Roxie announce she needed to be elsewhere, and it was Mindy who opened the conversation.

"This thing of yours with Royle, is it better or worse?"

Charlie pretended not to understand.

"You're obviously in love with him," Mindy continued. "And equally obviously you're seriously annoyed with him."

"I guess that sums it up. I just wish he'd stop doing things without telling me."

"Like what?"

Charlie briefly outlined Royle's failure to mention his suspicions regarding Dan's continued existence, plus of course there was Roxie.

"What is it, though, that upsets you?"

Charlie was quiet for a moment. "Actually, that's a good question."

"Could you have had some input into his decision-making?"

"If I'm honest probably not, or none that might have significantly altered his decisions."

"But you sometimes feel he's cutting you out of the partnership?"

"I guess so. By not including me he's threatening our relationship, or am I overreacting?"

"I suspect you may be. His not mentioning Roxie seems sensible. It was early days still, and wasn't he convinced someone in the Department couldn't be trusted? He was right, of course."

"What about Dan? By the time Phil worked out who we were dealing with in Australia we were already sharing a bed. I'd like to think he could trust me by then."

Mindy was ahead of her. "Let's not damage our brains working out how, but we know he can anticipate situations. By the time he knew it was Dan in Australia he had still not seen you use a weapon in anger. I'm assuming he realised that when he went in there you might have to shoot your former colleague to save his life. So, it was probably best you didn't have to choose between him and Dan before squeezing the trigger. In his place I'd do the same."

Charlie thought she could see the fault in that. "But he didn't ask me to cover him with the rifle; that was my idea. He knew nothing about it until I fired the first shot."

Mindy grinned at her.

"You're not suggesting he knew what I would do?" Charlie exclaimed. "Take the rifle and shoot this supposed Sylvester Reed if I had to?"

"Why would we accept he can anticipate all these other things, but not work out something as obvious as that. My guess is he checked to see if the rifle was missing from the Toyota, and why would you take it if not to cover his back?"

Mindy stopped a passing waitress for the wine list before continuing. "How does it feel being on the psychiatrist's couch yourself for a change?"

"I'm still not convinced, though I hadn't thought of some of that. Let's see how it goes."

Mindy was smiling again. "Just out of interest, what makes you so eager to put up with all this pain he obviously causes you?"

"You really want to know?"

"No, Charlie. I want to see if *you* know!"

"I've never actually had that conversation, though I've been close to it with Paula."

"So?"

"Well, there's all the usual stuff. Good-looking, well-read, well-travelled, not short of money, houses in Florida, London and Sydney. But he's also good fun to be with."

"Put like that I wonder why we're bothering with this conversation."

"But there's more," Charlie continued, "that you only see if you work alongside him. He's passionate about what he does, plus he's as comfortable in a meeting across from the White House as in a shack in the forest."

"Talking of the White House," Mindy interrupted, "word is he may get the new international job."

"I'm not sure that's common knowledge."

"Oh, it's common knowledge, sweetie. But will he take it?"

"He's not mentioned it."

"Did he ever discuss Dan with you?"

"You mean when they were in the Marines together?"

"I mean what kind of person Dan was."

Something about the way Mindy asked the question suggested she already knew of Dan's darker side. "You know there was more to Dan than Phil lets on?"

Mindy leaned forward, wine glass in hand. "Your partner and I were involved in a nasty job – a man was killed while we were chasing someone else. Phil took it badly and he came back to my place for the night. We ended up drinking the best part of a bottle of whisky before we got onto the subject of Dan. There was always something about the man I couldn't take to. But throwing some kid out of a helicopter?!"

★ ★ ★

216

Royle checked his phone messages, including one from Steve McGill regarding Jimmy Quigly's missing cell phone.

"Mac, it's Phillip. Sorry, been away."

"I heard, bit busy, hey?"

"You found the missing phone?"

He heard Mac laughing at the other end. "It was in the apartment all along, under the bed with a flat battery, along with the dust and the porn magazines. There are a few calls to or from Sharon's man Greg Saunders."

"I still think we need to have Greg in, along with all the others," Royle suggested, realising Mac knew nothing yet about their finding Dan in Australia.

"Bloody hell," he exclaimed, having listened to a brief account of the Australian trip.

"If you think that's bad imagine how Whitland feels, having to explain Dan's second death to the various other authorities involved. And another thing, does Dan get a full Departmental burial? Or do we tell everyone what a shit he was?"

Royle next spent time online, checking aerial views of the two Big Experience sites and the area around the Winnings' home, following which he called Mindy Goldsmith and discussed plans for dealing with the California searches.

"I had an idea all along it might be Gus you were after," Mindy admitted. "Anyhow, I guess you did it again."

He hesitated. "Introducing Roxie into the investigation, or the important information she obtained?"

"Both. You never told Charlie or me, and yes, your blasted foresight saved the day again. Dammit, you can be annoying. I hope you appreciate how much work Charlie and I put in last night, checking all those phone numbers and addresses."

He tried sounding suitably humbled, freely admitting that Roxie had come up with far more information than might be expected from such a last-minute arrangement.

NINETEEN

ROYLE INTRODUCED TODD SHEPHERD TO WHITLAND, CHARLIE AND Paula, aware he and Charlie had already met, firstly during their walk along Cairns Esplanade, and then on the return drive after watching the parrots being loaded aboard the plane. Around Royle's age and of a similar temperament, it was obvious why the two of them got along so well. The introductions over, Shepherd explained the DEA's involvement in what others in the room had until now considered the Department's exclusive investigation. He commenced by explaining that for the past six months they had been following up suggestions of substantial imports of drugs entering the US through southern Florida.

"Allegedly connected with the import of live animals," he emphasised. "We're also told a senior manager in either a State or Federal Wildlife office is involved, and I don't need to tell you the problem we've had with that one."

Whitland was nodding understandingly. "If that's true then you wouldn't know where to make your initial approach to those departments?"

"That's our problem, or it was," Shepherd corrected.

"Todd and I met up months back at a conference in Europe," Royle interrupted. "He knew I'd worked for the Department, so he told me what the DEA believed was going on. In the strictest confidence."

"No one could have been more surprised when Phil called me recently saying he'd been co-opted back into the

Department," Shepherd continued. "Obviously, we started leaning on him to get his cooperation."

"To do what?" Whitland wanted to know.

Shepherd looked a touch uneasy. "We wanted him to continue with Federal Wildlife's investigation into Dan's disappearance, though at the same time seeing if drugs were involved."

"You should explain how our arrangement included the DEA not interfering with Federal Wildlife's enquiries, or not until the drugs connection was proved," Royle prompted.

"Okay, so is there a drugs connection with our case?" Charlie interrupted.

Shepherd started to answer but Royle stopped him. "Not until Cairns, when I went to mark the birds and eggs in what turned out to be Dan's hiding place. All four crates used the same design, but only the bottom of the sheep crate was adapted to hold eggs, which set me wondering what could be concealed in the false bottoms of the other three crates."

"And that was when things began to make sense," added Shepherd.

Charlie, though, had another question, this time for Shepherd, briefly and to the point. "Why did you need to be up in Cairns if you already had Phil looking after your interests?"

"That was going to be my question," added Whitland.

"Phil's interests began and ended with the birds. When he texted me about a spare compartment in the crates I immediately flew out. My job was to see if any drugs were delivered to the station, though we realised they could be added in Asia or Europe."

They could see Charlie was unimpressed.

"Then whilst we were watching what went on at the sheep station, so were you?"

"More or less. Though I was just watching the station, while you guys were all over the place."

Royle guessed what might be troubling his partner. "If you're wondering was Todd still watching when I went back to confront Dan, then he was not. Once the crates left there was no need for Todd to be there."

"Good, because I'd hate to think my shooting Dan might have been unnecessary."

★ ★ ★

Whitland realised the meeting was getting a bit out of hand so he decided to restore order. He also had a couple of questions of his own that needed answering.

"Sounds like the birds and the drugs might all end up in the same place eventually, so can I assume we'll be coordinating this?"

Shepherd was clearly in agreement. "It's your show. The DEA will fit in with whatever you arrange."

Next, Whitland turned to Charlie. "You and Phillip searched Dan's hiding place. Any suggestion he might have been involved with drugs?"

Charlie's response was instant. "No, none."

"Phillip?"

"Like Charlie says, none whatsoever."

Whitland's relief was obvious. "I'm glad about that, then."

"It's all coming together nicely," Royle suggested. "The three bird crates went from Guinea via Java to Holland's Schiphol Airport, from where they crossed the border to Big Experience's Belgian set-up."

"When did they leave there?" Whitland asked.

"Big Experience has three bird containers checked in to leave Schiphol around now, arriving Miami tomorrow morning. And Charlie tracked down their quarantine centre, by the way." Royle pointed to Shepherd.

"I got our European people to check the crates after they were booked in."

"And they tested positive for drugs," Whitland guessed.

"Cocaine, all three. It's just a matter of making sure the crates arrive, then in we go."

"Listen up, then," Whitland instructed, "this is how it's going to be. Todd's people will deal with the Everglades quarantine site, while my team simultaneously raids the upstate hunting ranch, just in case they have drugs or birds. Your state man Ed Kimberley can assist us there, Charlie."

Whitland made some notes on his pad.

"Meanwhile, Mindy and her team get to work wherever the birds came to roost over in California." He smiled at his own joke. "Anyone got issues with that?"

"Don't forget Akroyd," reminded Royle. "Mindy has that in hand."

Whitland made another note. "Anything else?"

No one said anything so Whitland looked towards Royle. "I presume Steve McGill's sorting out Sharon's man, Greg Saunders?"

"All under control."

"Right," Whitland continued, "while all that's going down Charlie and Phillip will be taking Gus Winnings into custody up there in Tallahassee."

Whitland excused himself for a second whilst he extracted some pills from the 'Out' tray and poured himself a glass of water. He knew he should be taking it easy, but to hell with it. As he understood things, Gus Winnings was about to become history, and not before time it had to be said. He had also witnessed Charlie Lacey transforming into an increasingly experienced and dependable agent, precisely as he had promised her father she would. He had even been entertaining thoughts of trying to regain Royle's services on a permanent basis, perhaps seeing him take charge of the Department following his own retirement, though informed sources suggested Royle may have received an even better offer from Washington. Nevertheless, if everything he understood about the Charlie–Royle relationship was true, then he might still be seeing a great deal more of his favourite agent. Regardless.

★ ★ ★

The pair's return from Australia called for a change of accommodation on Royle's part; with uncertainty still surrounding the security of Dan's former apartment it seemed unwise to continue to stay there. The alternative, though, required little discussion and that evening they collected his belongings on the way over to Charlie's place.

Later, in bed, he propped himself on one elbow. "I owe you an apology," he whispered.

"Why, what have you done now?"

"I kept you in the dark about what was going on, especially me knowing it was Dan we were dealing with."

She lightly brushed the back of her hand across his chest. "It's me who should be apologising. I was upset with you not sharing information, when all the time you were struggling with a much bigger problem."

"It's not worth discussing."

She pressed a finger to his lips "Well, I think it is. I had no idea of the pressure you were under. Not only have you been keeping track of the bird smuggling activities, dealing with Dan's supposed death, his subsequent resurrection and then his actual death. Plus all the worry of the shootings here in town and what was happening to Sam. Unbeknown to any of us, you were also balancing the demands of two federal departments in a world-scale inquiry."

"That's what they pay me for."

He drew her towards him, but she gently pushed herself away again.

"There's still something I don't understand."

"Which is?"

"How did you and Shepherd know where and when to meet in Queensland?"

He smiled. "You're forgetting the phones. Todd has access to my tracker."

★ ★ ★

Charlie and Royle took an early flight up to Tallahassee the next morning. There they collected a hire car and drove across town to the Department's Licensing office, picking up two uniformed police officers on the way. At reception Charlie asked to speak with Abbie Wise, who came down in the lift to meet them. Charlie explained they had come to see Winnings.

Abbie was shaking her head. "He took yesterday off, and he's already an hour late. Normally he's boringly punctual."

Upstairs in Abbie's office Charlie closed the door, explaining to the secretary how they had come to take Winnings into custody.

"It's to do with what Phillip was asking over dinner," Abbie exclaimed.

"Here's what we'll do," Charlie continued, ignoring the secretary's speculation. "I need you to start pulling out all files referring to any Asian bird-licensing decisions Winnings dealt with. Say, over the last three years."

Abbie was clearly less than keen on what was being asked of her. "That's an awful lot of work, Charlie."

"If you need help then take whoever you want from the other staff."

Next, Charlie took a moment to consider their options, realising that being seen making too much of a commotion before they had Winnings in handcuffs could work to their disadvantage. Someone might ring him and then who knows what he might do?

"We'll wait a few minutes before we go over to his house. But I'll leave one of the police officers here, just in case."

Like Royle, Charlie had done her homework. She had studied various pictures of the Winnings' house, plus she knew he and Pat each had their own car. She also knew Pat did not work, though she did spend a great deal of time assisting various charities, particularly organisations tackling child poverty.

The Winnings' house turned out to be surprisingly large and situated on a prime corner plot. As soon as they arrived it was obvious something must be wrong; the main entrance door was wide open and both garage doors were up. Someone had also been busy with a paint spray – several in fact, judging from the various colours involved. Particularly obvious were two large mauve arrows, one pointing towards the entrance door, accompanied by the word 'UPSTAIRS', the other directing attention towards the 'GARAGE'. Tapping the remaining police officer on the shoulder, Charlie pointed him at the garage while she and Royle entered the house, uncertain what they might find.

Inside they were greeted by another arrow at the top of the stairs, this time suggesting they enter what looked like the main bedroom. Here the paint sprayers had been busy again, most obvious being the words 'WASTED YEARS' over the bed. Suddenly this had the feel of a domestic dispute, though admittedly one of considerable intensity. Confirmation of this was to be found on the bed itself, in the form of Gus Winnings, minus any clothing and with hands and feet tied to all four corners.

It seemed Pat had finally decided to end her marriage, and in quite a spectacular fashion. And the walls were not the only paint target, Winnings himself having received his fair share of attention. His face was now an attractive shade of violet, whilst his genitals had been much favoured by the red can. Since arriving, Charlie had noticed her partner taking various evidential photographs, seeming particularly keen on pictures of Winnings tied to the bed. It occurred to her she could expect to see one or two pinned up in the office in due course.

The man had also been effectively gagged using what looked a lot like a dressing gown cord tied behind his head. Charlie was about to relieve him of his discomfort when the police officer reappeared, taking in the scene with the barest suggestion of surprise.

"I don't know who you've been upsetting, friend," the officer observed, directing his remarks at the bed's occupant, "but your Ferrari's going to need a new paint job."

They watched Winnings roll his eyes, clearly unhappy.

"Where's this other arrow directing us to?" the officer enquired, pointing along the landing. Charlie temporarily rearranged the bedding to cover Winnings' embarrassment, realising that for the moment the licensing boss was probably safest where he was. The three of them then headed across the landing to a door adorned with the intriguing statement 'IT'S HERE' in a vibrant flame-orange.

They were now in some sort of office, though what particularly grabbed their attention was the open wall safe, plus what must have recently been its contents. Stacked in several neat piles on the desk was a considerable sum of money. Having recently experienced what $200,000 looked like, Charlie tentatively suggested they were dealing with twice that amount. She did a quick mental reappraisal, realising the situation had progressed well beyond the mere arrest of Winnings. She decided to leave the police officer to attend to the soon-to-be-ex Licensing boss while she and Royle focused on what evidence needed removing. Turning to enquire whether he had any thoughts on the subject, she found Royle had disappeared. She also heard her phone ringing.

She could tell straight off that Whitland was unhappy. Apparently, the airport lorry had arrived at the quarantine facility as anticipated, the three crates still carrying the birds and tracking devices Royle had fitted in Australia. They could also prove that the birds involved had been forensically marked by Royle. What they could not find were any drugs hidden in the bottom of the crates, though tests proved they had recently been present.

In a bid to ensure the operation's success, Todd Shepherd had opted to not have the vehicle followed from the airport. In hindsight that was a mistake, the drugs having disappeared somewhere between the airport and the quarantine centre. Whitland was now in the process of getting various security and other cameras checked along the route; meanwhile, though, the drugs element of the investigation was on hold.

Charlie enquired about developments elsewhere. Nothing new had turned up at Big Experience's upstate Florida facility, unlike over in California where Mindy and her crew recovered almost all the missing eggs and young birds. Unfortunately, though, Greg Saunders and Sharon Morgan were not at home when Steve McGill's police officers arrived to arrest him.

Charlie tracked Royle down to the Winnings' garage, where he was admiring Pat's artwork. The police officer had been right, there was no alternative to a full repaint for the Ferrari. From there they went in search of the officer, finding him out front of the house with Winnings now dressed and handcuffed. The Licensing boss seemed understandably subdued.

"There's no point us discussing it now, Gus," Charlie advised. "But we found several things we'll need to talk to you about later. Including a considerable amount of cash – about half a million dollars."

Winnings' head shot up. "There should be more than that," he responded, before realising the mistake he was making.

"Are you suggesting there's more cash somewhere?"

Despite the obviously difficult situation he was in, Winnings could not resist a response. "You've nothing on me, it's my wife you should be looking for."

"There are a couple of things you should know," Royle explained to his former department head. "Then we'll wait for the formal interview."

Winnings just stared back at him, now saying nothing.

"We can prove birds involved in this inquiry came into America last night, from Australia via Asia and Europe, and that you signed licenses authorising that. We also have evidence you were speaking with Dan Morgan in Australia regarding illegal bird movements, just before he died."

"So you say," Winnings responded, though now with noticeably less conviction. Then curiosity got the better of him. "Dan's dead?"

Royle paused, making sure he had the man's attention. "You remember the 'lovely Charlie Lacey'? Well, she shot Dan, so if you take my advice you'll do as she says."

TWENTY

THE THREE OF THEM WATCHED THE WOMAN THROUGH THE ONE-WAY GLASS.

"We've questioned her for over an hour and we're getting nowhere," Steve McGill explained. "She hasn't the ghost of a chance but still she's denying any involvement. Claims they just happened to be there."

"Does she know he's dead?" asked Charlie.

"Not yet. Once we tell her then she's bound to blame it all on him. And if she doesn't think of it then her lawyer in there certainly will."

Royle recognised the defence counsellor; Walter Jackson had been around longer than most Florida enforcement officers could remember. He and Royle had locked horns on numerous occasions, and not without good reason was he known as 'Stonewall' Jackson: he was hard and tenacious, but also as honest and as fair as they come.

"Any other evidence?" Charlie wanted to know.

"The swab tests proved cocaine traces all over them, plus they were in the goddamn vehicle with the stuff."

"Charlie and I might just get her to talk," Royle suggested. "But we won't get anything clever past old Stonewall."

★ ★ ★

Royle opened the interview room door, two paper coffee cups balanced on his clipboard.

He acknowledged the aging defence counsellor. "Charlie Lacey," he explained, pulling out a chair and nodding towards his partner. "Been a long time, Walt."

The old lawyer briefly grasped Royle's hand. "And we're none of us getting any younger, Phillip."

Royle positioned the clipboard and pen on the interview table in front of him, pushing one of the cups in the woman's direction. "Well, Sharon."

Sharon Morgan stared back at him, saying nothing, her eyes red and tired but loaded with defiance nevertheless. Also obvious was the facial bruising Whitland had previously mentioned. Royle wondered what the woman must be thinking. She surely realised his involvement changed things; he knew her background and he knew how she thought. Or did he?

★ ★ ★

Royle's mobile had gone off at some silly hour that same morning.

"Phillip, it's Steve McGill. Something going on here I guess involves you two."

Royle listened as Mac explained how one of his specialist drugs teams had just encountered six people in a Miami parking lot. Four of the five men involved were known drug dealers, and firearms had been discharged on both sides. The fifth male had been confirmed dead on arrival at the hospital.

The woman and the dead man arrived in a top-of-the-range Mercedes four-by-four, with darkened windows and all the trimmings – plus several hundred thousand dollars' worth of cocaine in the trunk. She had refused to reveal either her identity or that of her shot partner, though a quick check of the vehicle's registration came up with the name Gregory Saunders. This was quickly confirmed from the dead man's fingerprints, along with the revelation that the female answered to the name of Sharon Morgan.

Mac had explained how his drugs team had been following the movements of the four dealers for several days, knowing they were anticipating a delivery from an unknown supplier. Mac also knew that when the DEA searched the three bird import crates yesterday, there was no cocaine, the assumption being that it had been removed after leaving the airport; though by using Royle's tracking data they had now identified where the switch was made.

All they could do last evening was ensure Steve McGill knew there was a large amount of cocaine out on the streets somewhere, the probability being that someone was expecting it. With luck, that information might match something his officers already knew, as obviously seemed to have happened.

* * *

"You realise, Sharon, this is about as serious as it gets," Royle commenced, purposely not looking at her lawyer. "We're talking a probable long prison sentence and there's little we can do about that. We could perhaps try reducing the sentence, though that rather relies upon you cooperating."

Sharon said nothing.

"You should listen to Phil," Charlie suggested. "We can't get you off this, but we might get you a deal."

Sharon still did not respond.

Royle tried approaching the interview from a different direction, his eyes briefly meeting Charlie's.

"This is all getting a bit complicated, Sharon. Why don't we start from the beginning?"

Although the woman's expression indicated disinterest, logic suggested otherwise.

"We know the Big Experience people were smuggling parrots and eggs into their site in California, either directly or via Miami. That's a fact. We also know that Winnings, plus Deming Akroyd over in California, has been supplying them with false permits. That too is a fact."

"I've no idea what you're talking about," Dan's estranged wife offered, glancing around at her lawyer.

Royle smiled. "We now think no one involved with the bird smuggling, including Winnings, knew anything about the drugs. How do you think that works, then?"

Sharon shook her head. "Like I said, I've no idea what you're on about."

"Let's examine another bit of the puzzle, then," Royle persevered. "Quigly was doing various jobs for Winnings, running errands, taking my picture at the airport, getting rid of bodies. Know anything about that?"

"Like I keep telling you, I know nothing."

Royle glanced around at Charlie again, briefly raising his eyebrows.

"Dan told me he shot Alynski, before Quigly put Dan's clothes on the body and got it into the tiger compound, presumably after Winnings obtained the gate key. What do you think?"

Both agents detected a change in Sharon's expression. The defiance was now gone, as they watched her trying to read Royle's face. She presumably realised that by the time he had reappeared on the scene, from Mexico City via Houston six weeks ago, the Department had already been looking for her former husband. In which case how could he possibly have spoken with Dan?

Charlie too had a feeling she no longer knew all the answers, though at this point she responded to a knock on the door, taking the three sheets of paper Mac handed her. Briefly she examined these before passing them on to her partner, who glanced at them equally briefly.

231

Royle knew they had Sharon wondering.

"Truth is you're all in this bird smuggling thing together. You, Greg and Winnings, along with Deming Akroyd and Shaun O'Reilly in California and Mick White in London. Oh, and of course Dan. Except that you and Greg were running an extremely profitable drugs operation on the side that all the others knew nothing about."

They could see from her face that she was rattled.

"Clearly the game's up now and you're in big trouble."

"I can't speak for what Greg and the others do."

Royle laughed. "That's kids' stuff, Sharon, we're not discussing Greg. We're talking about you, dealing in millions of dollars' worth of drugs on the streets of Miami."

The defiance was back in her eyes. "You don't know a thing. You're guessing."

"I know Greg or Winnings killed Quigly. You appearing all upset over Dan's death was an act; you knew he wasn't dead. You probably also knew Dan killed Alynski."

"So you say."

"I'll tell you what else I say," he continued. "It was a mistake you cooking up some clever story about Dan fearing he might be killed by Toombs, who doesn't exist by the way. Though if I hadn't discovered the name in Quigly's egg collection we would probably never have made the Australia connection."

Withdrawing one of the three pieces of paper from beneath his clipboard, Royle slid it in Sharon's direction.

"The police gave Greg's Merc the full treatment. Alynski's body was in the trunk at some stage, presumably when Greg took it to Quigly."

Charlie did not know Sharon anywhere near as well as Royle, but she noticed the woman's cheek muscles twitching nervously.

"I'm not accountable for what Greg does."

Both federal agents realised this signalled something of a change in Sharon's response. She was no longer questioning what they said, but instead was trying to distance herself from what was happening. Both also noted the woman's failure to ask how come he had been speaking to Dan. However, although Royle knew he had accurately outlined to Sharon what she, Greg, Winnings and her former husband, Dan, were up to, he was less clear still on the extent of any continuing relationship between Dan and Sharon.

Again, his eyes met Charlie's. "Did I mention Dan's dead?"

This time he could see he had Sharon. The colour literally drained from her face as it lost all expression.

"Are you saying Winnings killed him?" she responded, tears now evident.

It seemed she had just answered his question; there had still been something between Dan and her, though in proving it he had created a further difficulty. There was no knowing how the woman might react were she to learn that the person responsible for Dan's death was sitting opposite her.

He turned the second slip of paper over so that she could see it.

"There's another thing you should know," he continued, studying Sharon's face. "A street camera picked out you two moving the drugs from the bottom of the crates into Greg's Mercedes."

The woman was clearly worried now and was looking to her lawyer for guidance.

Royle pushed the paper towards her. "There's no denying that's you and Greg in the picture, even though we can't see the vehicle's registration plate."

Sharon looked around at the lawyer again.

Royle extracted the third piece of paper, an aerial photograph of the parking lot with three crosses marked on it.

"This is the really interesting bit. There's a cross showing where Greg's Mercedes was parked, and another where the dealers' car was."

She just stared at him.

"It's the cross in the middle that's interesting," he continued, deliberately hesitating. "It shows where Greg was lying when the police arrived. We're having trouble understanding how he came to be shot in the back."

Sharon had found her voice again. "The shooting started almost as soon as we arrived; one of the dealers shot him."

Royle shook his head. "It doesn't stack up, Sharon. Why would Greg turn his back on four pissed-off and armed drug dealers? Anyway, the police checked the bullets from Greg's wounds against the dealers' guns. They don't match."

Sharon turned to her lawyer yet again and Old Stonewall raised a hand, reassuringly.

"I wonder if I might be allowed a minute or two with my client?"

Seeing Royle's slight nod of approval, Charlie opened the door to a small side room. They could hear muffled conversation for perhaps five minutes, before the door opened again and Sharon Morgan and her lawyer reappeared and sat down.

"We're grateful for your forbearance," said Stonewall. "My client has a question of her own, if you wouldn't mind indulging her."

Sharon seemed to have regained her composure. "We've talked a lot about me and what you say I've done, but can I ask how Greg is?"

Royle had seen this one coming, even before they had commenced the interview. He was surprised it had taken this long. Clearly, they had no alternative to telling Sharon the truth; anything less at this point and the prosecution's case was heading for trouble. He was also pretty sure the question would have come from old Walter Jackson, not his client.

Royle looked around at Charlie seated next to him. It seemed to him that this was woman-to-woman time and Charlie accepted the challenge without hesitation.

"There's no easy way of telling you this, Sharon. As you know, Greg was shot before the police arrived. Unfortunately, he was dead by the time the ambulance reached the hospital."

Sharon buried her head in her hands. During the last thirty minutes she had learned first that her former husband and now her new partner were both dead, on top of which she was being accused of major involvement in the international movement of drugs. And as Royle had already suggested, it did not get much more serious than that and her lawyer knew it.

"I think, Phillip," Stonewall intervened, "my client needs time to compose herself, assuming you intend continuing with this."

Royle could see no obvious grounds for refusal, though he did look to Charlie for confirmation.

"I'm obliged to inform you," Jackson continued, "that Mrs Morgan will be denying any willing involvement in the activities to which you refer. It's a matter of record Greg Saunders was a violent man, and as such she was obliged to cooperate. But that's not to say she did so willingly."

★ ★ ★

A police officer took Sharon Morgan back down to the cells while Charlie escorted the defence lawyer as far as the front desk, before re-joining the other two in Mac's office.

"Well, we tried, but Jackson's no fool," Royle suggested. "He guessed Greg was dead, and he knew we'd be in trouble once she asked after him."

Mac seemed uncharacteristically philosophical for a police officer. "We did what we could. But you're right, if you'd continued the interview without telling her about Greg then the DA would surely have thrown the case out at some stage."

Royle was nodding his head. "The whole thing was a disaster waiting to happen. Quigly was trading in any smuggled eggs that failed to hatch, Winnings was having Alynski shot and my daughter kidnapped without telling the others, while Sharon Morgan and her fella were using all of that to import seriously large amounts of drugs. Add the odd idiot like Mickey Bird and it had to all blow up at some point."

Charlie screwed up her nose. "What's the position with Greg? Are we seriously suggesting she shot him?"

"Who knows. Logic suggests she did, and from what we've heard she probably had good cause. Greg did have a record of violence. Problem is we can find no proof of her ever owning a gun, and no evidence of another gun at the scene," Mac explained.

Royle was smiling. "If she is lying then she's doing it very well. Almost the perfect murder. Get rid of the violent boyfriend and take over an extremely lucrative drugs business, all in one go, except that it came unstuck at several points. There's no way any jury's going to believe her."

★ ★ ★

Sam Royle found her father in his favourite place, stretched out on the rear decking. Seeing her he held a finger to his lips, pointing to where his laptop was tracking the midday television news. It was Saturday, almost six weeks to the day since Whitland had introduced Royle and Charlie Lacey as temporary partners in the hunt for Daniel Morgan.

The news presenter was concluding a report on how a mystery woman had that morning left packages of around half a million dollars each at the reception desks of two Florida-based charities tackling child poverty.

The presenter shuffled his papers, pressing his earpiece with one finger in receipt of further information.

"Next," he announced, "federal sources say they have successfully closed down a multi-million-dollar international smuggling racket threatening some of the world's most endangered birds, combined with a drug smuggling operation of global proportions. In a fast-moving operation, Federal Wildlife agents tracked smuggled wild parrots from Australia and Mexico to both Florida and California."

The presenter re-shuffled his papers. "One worrying revelation concerned the issue of government permits falsely stating the birds involved were bred in captivity. Hundreds of parrot eggs were also smuggled into California to be hatched. Federal Wildlife agents searched properties in Tallahassee, the Everglades and California, with similar searches in Mexico, Australia, Asia and Europe."

"Refusing to name names at this stage," the announcer continued, "Federal Wildlife Head, Doug Whitland, confirmed that ten people were in custody in Florida and California, and over four hundred live parrots and a similar number of hatching eggs have been seized. Twelve people are also in custody in the New York area and in Europe. DEA agents and police recovered drugs with a street value running into millions of dollars."

"The same sources declined to comment on a report that Federal Wildlife's Florida Licensing Head Gus Winnings is among those who in court on Monday will answer accusations regarding the murder of at least four people, and why half a million dollars in cash was recovered from the Winnings' home. Federal prosecutors will be seeking maximum sentences for all involved."

The presenter was obviously now winding up the news item. "When asked how they uncovered the smugglers, Special Agent Charlie Lacey told our reporter, 'It was all a consequence of finding agent Daniel Morgan's body in a tiger enclosure.' She also said that the considerable sum of money recovered will go towards ensuring as many of the birds as possible will be returned to the wild in Australia."

★ ★ ★

Some months following the arrests, Doug Whitland settled himself behind his desk as Paula entered with the morning's mail. On the top of the pile was a handwritten envelope addressed to him personally. Opening it, he read it through, a broad smile spreading across his face:

The Honourable Vernon and Mrs Barbara Lacey
request the presence of
Mr and Mrs Douglas Whitland
at the marriage of their daughter
Charlotte Elizabeth
to
Phillip Edward Royle
4pm, Saturday October 15th
Field of Dreams
Upper Woodland Meadows
Tallahassee
RSVP

In with the card was a handwritten note on the judge's personal letterhead.

'Looking forward to catching up with you in October, Doug, and I hope the heart's behaving itself. The honeymoon destination's outback Australia, something about a lost parrot.'